STRIKE VOTE

Judie Freeland

Judie Freeland

Copyright 2018
Judie Freeland

Cover & book design by R. Gary Raham

All rights reserved. No part of this book may be reproduced, stored in a retrieval system, or transmitted in any form or by any means, electronic, mechanical, photocopying, recording, or otherwise, without the prior written permission of the publisher.

Library of Congress Control Number: 2018951302
ISBN-13: 978-0-9904826-7-3
ISBN-10: 0-9904826-7-7

Wellington, CO 80549
970.568.3557
www.penstemonpublications.com

STRIKE VOTE

My profound thanks to

The members of my writing group for listening carefully and criticizing constructively: Nancy Burns, Beverly Hadden, Libby James, Mim Neal, Susan Quinlan, Gary Raham, and Clare Rutherford;

Gary Raham, for getting the manuscript of *Strike Vote* ready for publication;

Audrey Haferman, for pointing out problems of timing, logic, tone, and police protocols, not to mention a few overlooked typos. Audrey is a criminal justice major and a wizard copy editor. Her husband Jason, a Ft. Collins, Colorado, police officer, recommended Audrey as the ideal person to edit the manuscript.

And finally, Miss Reynolds, my ninth grade English teacher, who encouraged me to keep writing.

Judie Freeland

STRIKE VOTE

1

July, 2002

Stanley Turner assumed his office manager was competent enough to run the travel agency for a day, and Stan had looked forward to a day's fishing. He asked himself again why the hell he had agreed to let Teddy, Clarence's 23-year-old nephew, join the party. Who in blue blazes brings a rifle on a fishing trip? The kid just shrugged at that question and said, "maybe I can pop a couple squirrels."

Last year when Turner first met the guy, he concluded he was a jerk. And maybe the boy's twitchiness was, as he claimed, the early sign of a serious medical issue, but Stan had seen druggies with similar problems. And Clarence had told him he thought Teddy was stealing drugs from the pharmacy.

Furthermore, the kid might know how to aim a rifle, but he had no concept of woods lore. Even Clarence had begun to lose patience by the time they reached the bank of the stream. "For chrissake, boy, whyn't you just get a bullhorn and tell 'em you're coming?"

"Huh?"

"Look where you're putting your feet. Every time you step on a loose twig and it breaks, any self-respecting squirrel can hear the snap from a mile away. You go stompin' through this here forest, even the fish will hide."

Stan suggested they rest a bit. He unscrewed the top of the coffee thermos while Clarence pulled a flask from his orange jacket. The kid reached into a pocket and removed a pack of cigarettes.

His uncle growled. "Hey! No smoking, stupid. These woods are tinder dry. You don't want to start a forest fire."

"I just thought a little weed would help you two mellow out."

Clarence muttered, "You thought? Trouble with you is, you don't think. Remember what I said this morning."

The coffee, the exercise, and the cold air produced a predictable reaction. Stan finished his coffee and watched as Clarence got to his feet and ambled over to a nearby tree to unzip.

The sound of the shot shattered the silence. Stan looked up just as Teddy lowered his rifle and turned away. Stan watched as Clarence sank soundlessly, almost in slow motion, to the leaves carpeting the forest floor.

Teddy had started running back toward the road. "I gotta catch that kid."

"What kid?

"One of them Indian kids saw me."

"Oh, crap!" Stan thought for a minute. "You need to find a cop before the kid does and report this tragic accident. Then it's your word – and mine – against theirs."

"Okay. I'll be back when I can."

"No. Do not come back. Go home. Go back to Ohio. No one here knows who you are. Let's keep it that way."

STRIKE VOTE

2

Polly Ann Passarelli was searching for morel mushrooms at the edge of the woods marking the boundary of the camp. She raised her head at the unmistakable sound of a gunshot. Idiots! They shouldn't be allowed within miles of a wilderness camp for underprivileged kids.

Minutes later, a small body crashed into her. Instinctively, Polly Ann wrapped her arms around it and made soothing noises. Finally the head came up revealing wild eyes and a nose badly in need of wiping.

"Please, please! Let me go! He'll shoot me, too!"

Polly Ann would have asked at least one question, but she heard the undergrowth rustle and snap and a voice that called out, "Come back, kid. I won't hurt you. It was an accident."

The slim body in her arms frantically reared back and tried to tear free. Polly Ann caught the child's arm. "Let's go this way. The counselors' cabin is close by. We can hide there."

Her words evidently penetrated the panic. A small hand wove its fingers through hers and together they ran the fifty yards to safety.

Once inside, Polly Ann locked the door, pulled the red and white gingham curtains across the kitchen windows, and lowered the shade over the cabin's only other window. Her guest cowered in a kitchen chair.

Polly Ann handed the child the box of face tissues before getting a washcloth from the cupboard. She ran it under the hot water tap. "Blow your nose, dear. After you wash your face, we'll talk. Maybe we could start with your name?"

"I'm Kat." The voice steadied. "I know you – you're the counselor for cabin 11. Polly Ann. Not the make believe goody two shoes named Pollyanna in that kids' book. She believed everything would be okay. You're always afraid things will go wrong. So am I."

"Why don't you tell me what's going on?"

"Have you got any cocoa? I think better with cocoa."

Polly Ann was relieved to see that the kitchen cupboard came equipped with a can of cocoa powder, sitting right next to the never opened box of Cocoa Puffs.

The drink was soon ready. "No marshmallows, I'm afraid. They'd probably be stale anyway.

"Okay, so why aren't you at your cabin packing up for the bus trip back to school?" Polly Ann asked.

"My backpack's all ready. Everybody else was messing around and I just had to get out of there. So I walked out the door and into the woods. After a few minutes, I was going uphill. When I got to the top, there was a little clearing, where three guys in jeans and t-shirts were standing around drinking from thermos cups. I recognized Mr. Hunter and Mr. Turner, but not the shooter. He's younger than them, about your age."

Kat drank the last of her cocoa and got up from the table. "Mr. Hunter set his cup down and walked over to the edge of the trees and unzipped his pants. Before I could turn around so's not to look, I saw the young guy raise his rifle, and then I heard a blast and when I looked again, Mr. Hunter was lying on the ground with blood all over his back."

Polly Ann tried to talk. What came out was a squeak. She tried again. "What did you do? I mean, I'd have passed out or something. And probably screamed."

The little face almost cracked a smile. "I might have whimpered. I didn't want him to see me, but of course he did, and that's when I started running. I was too scared to wet my pants."

Polly Ann forced her thoughts to line up instead of dashing all over the place. The child could not leave the cabin until they knew the danger was over. So as the brave adult in the room, she would have to go outside, look businesslike and casual and inconspicuous, and wait. Wait until it looked safe for her and her charge to make a last minute run for the buses that would take them back to the Tecumseh School – the boarding school for Native American orphan girls.

For once, luck was on her side. Just as she opened the cabin door, sirens announced a parade of police cars and an ambulance, all speeding up the track into the woods. Polly Ann ducked back into the cabin. "I'll grab my gear, Kat. Put on that hoodie that's hanging on the back of the door. We'll stop by your cabin to get your stuff and then get in line for a bus."

Kat backed away in a panic. "I can't go back to school! That's the first place he'd look."

Polly Ann had to agree. She needed a Plan B. There'd be time on the bus to think of something. Right now, she had to persuade this child that for once, Pollyanna could be right; they would be okay.

"You won't stay at the school. We'll get you checked in and then figure out a way for you to disappear. Trust me, Kat. I won't let him get to you."

Hoping that the concept of safety in numbers was more than a myth, she kept her arm around the child's shoulder as they wormed their way into the middle of the pack edging its way toward the open door of the bus.

Two state patrol officers stood near the camp director, who was checking off the names on her list as kids and counselors climbed the bus steps. As Polly Ann moved closer, she heard one of the men ask, "Did the shooter show up at the site?"

The other trooper responded, "No. Apparently he reported the shooting and kept going. The only witness we have swears it was an accident and says the man was a friend of the victim."

"No name?"

"Nope." The trooper scratched his head. "Wouldn't you want to know the name of a guy you're spending a day with?"

That information bothered Polly Ann – how would they find a man with no name? – but she was also relieved. The killer was evidently on the run, which meant he would not be at the school any time soon looking for the young witness.

The director checked Polly Ann's name off the list and looked at the next person in line. Kat said softly, "Katherine Tolliver, ma'am. Katherine with a 'k'."

The bus rolled smoothly along the east coast of Michigan, putting several passengers to sleep, including Katherine with a 'k.' Polly Ann tried to distract her overly active mind with ideas for dealing with the problem of how to help a child who could be the next target of a killer.

However, her thoughts kept returning to the visitors who had shattered her dreams for the future and to the man who had shared those dreams.

The first week of classes at the beginning of her junior year, Polly Ann rushed out of the university library keeping her eyes on the tall stack of books in her arms lest they lose their precarious balance. She should have been looking where she was going. The young man she ran into was also in a hurry to get somewhere. By the time her books were safely piled back in her arms, coffee, conversation, and further acquaintance held more appeal than previous plans.

Polly Ann and Trevor Passarelli dated all through that year, got engaged the Christmas of the following year, and were married the week after graduation.

With Trevor, juggling graduate classes, a job, and the upkeep of their tiny apartment was a joy. A year later, both completed the requirements for their master's degrees and accepted teaching fellowships in their respective disciplines. Three years later, Trevor finished his doctorate as the U.S. was getting more deeply embroiled in Afghanistan. The country had paid for Trevor's undergraduate years through an ROTC scholarship. He was still on active reserve. His unit was deployed.

Two months before Polly Ann was to receive her Ph.D., a man and a woman in uniform appeared at the door of the apartment. The woman introduced herself as a chaplain. Trevor was missing in action. "Before we lost contact, he was flying over rugged terrain where even native goats don't go," one of them said. Polly Ann never did remember their names. A week later, Polly Ann bought a pregnancy test. Two weeks later, she miscarried.

Polly Ann defended her dissertation in a fog. She interviewed for faculty positions at three universities and later remembered none of the questions. The campus, the apartment that had been home, became unbearable. She applied for out of town summer jobs and soon found herself in the Michigan woods, taking care of orphans, girls about to hit their teens, who looked upon their counselors as the mothers they didn't have.

Polly Ann looked down at the head resting on her shoulder. She felt a sudden fierce resolve to help this kid have a meaningful life. She put an arm around the slim body, laid her own head back, and finally slept.

A few hours later, Polly Ann walked Kat into the administrative offices and asked to speak with the principal. After a brief phone call, the receptionist said that would be okay, but that Katherine would have to wait outside Dr. Allen's office.

Polly Anne introduced herself. "Dr. Allen, I'm Dr. Passarelli, one of the counsellors from the university."

"I remember meeting you when we interviewed you," the woman said with a warm smile. "You'd just received your diploma and wanted to spend a little time deciding what the next move in your life was going to be. What can I do for you?"

Polly Ann quickly told the woman what Kat had witnessed, exaggerated the trauma a bit, and received permission to take Kat home with her for the night and maybe do a bit of shopping for school clothes the next day.

Back in the reception area, Polly Ann leaned over to whisper in Kat's ear. "Don't look too happy – you're supposed to be in shock – but you're coming home with me for now."

Given a choice between having the guest room all to herself or sharing Polly Ann's bed, Kat debated. To Polly Ann's relief, she chose privacy, after announcing that she was really tired and asking if it was okay if she went to bed right after her bath.

As soon as Polly Ann was sure that Kat was asleep, she went to her study, took her address book out of a drawer, and picked up the phone. *Be home, Liz. Please be home.*

"My Caller ID tells me it's a voice from the past. How did that camp counselor gig work out for you? And what else can I do for you?"

"Hi, Liz. The camp thing is sort of what I'm calling about. Mostly, it was good, and thanks for the referral, but there's a problem."

Polly Ann summarized the complications of the day for her friend and former roommate, Elizabeth Walker. "So, Liz, because you specialize in Native American law, especially as it concerns children, I need to find a safe, legal home for this kid."

"And you need it yesterday."

"Yeah, pretty much."

"I have a few ideas, Pol, and I'll put out some feelers. I agree with you that she's in danger, so let's keep her hidden. I'll get hold of Dr. Allen and see if I can persuade her to let the kid stay with you for at least the next week – and to tell no one where she is."

Half an hour later, Liz called back. "Dr. Allen says it's fine with her if you keep Katherine with you – and out of sight – for as long as necessary."

STRIKE VOTE

3

After sleeping for a week on a camp cot, Polly Ann looked forward to a night in her own soft bed. But her sleep was haunted by dreams of Trevor, lost and wounded in inhospitable terrain, calling her name and carrying a small child. She gave up the attempt to sleep at 5:30. Too early to wake up her overnight guest.

Polly Ann made a mental list of chores that needed doing. Load the washer with the contents of her backpack – but wait until Kat woke up to turn the machine on. Gather vinegar and newspaper to clean the windows sometime soon. She put the kettle on for tea, hoping that the lack of cocoa would not be a problem.

A smiling face framed by wisps of hair peaked around the guest room door. "I'm glad it's time to be up. I've slept enough. Can I help with anything?"

Polly Ann's phone began to ring. "You can indeed. While I take this call, will you put a tea bag and a bit of honey in those two mugs?"

Victor Passarelli, Trevor's father, was on the line. He had phoned once a week since Trevor's disappearance. Early on, he'd said that having lost his only child, it helped to talk to Polly Ann, the daughter he and his wife never had. Mrs. Passarelli never got on the phone. Polly Ann got the impression that she could not, would not talk to her about her son, or about anything else. Perhaps she blamed her son's wife for his disappearance.

"I hoped you'd be home this morning," Victor said. "How was the camping experience?" Polly Ann briefly told him that she'd enjoyed it without mentioning the excitement of the day before.

They rarely talked about the elephant in the room. It was as if not mentioning Trevor's disappearance would somehow bring him back. Today he ended their conversation by saying, "Even though the search is officially ended, they never stop looking, you know."

Polly Ann swallowed hard and thought to herself, *and I will never stop hoping*. "Bless you, Victor, and thank you for calling. Give my love to Louise." She hung up the phone and blew her nose.

She thought she'd successfully stifled her emotions, but Kat bluntly said, "Something's wrong. Is it about me? Can I help?"

"No, Katkin, no one can help. I've lost a friend and it doesn't look like he'll ever be found. But I do have some good news about you. You have Dr. Allen's permission to stay here at least a week.

"You can help me clean out my campus office; we'll shop for clothes for you – I could use a few things myself – and we have to get to a grocery store. Breakfast this morning is tea, toast, and peanut butter. Not even any jelly. And no cocoa."

STRIKE VOTE

4

Liz called back Thursday morning. "Grab a pen, Pol, I have news. A family named Tallfeather – close to Tolliver, right? Maybe a good omen. They live here in Ft. Collins. The parents, Hank and Estella, run a law office. They have eight kids ranging in age from seven to twenty and – drum roll, please – they'd be happy to foster your waif and, if everyone's happy with the arrangement later on, they'll file for adoption.

"Estella laughed when I asked if the neighbors wouldn't notice a new child. She said, 'Nope, kids come and go here all the time, our kids and all their friends. Who's counting?'"

Polly Ann caught her breath. "Oh my God, Liz, you're an angel, a genius. How soon can this happen?"

"They understand the danger she's in as long as she's in Michigan, so try to get her on a plane to Denver by this coming Sunday. The Tallfeathers will take care of all the legal stuff. Ask the kid what first name she'd like; too risky for her to keep the one she has."

"Hang on a minute, Liz, she's right here . . .

"You still there? Okay, she says she's always wanted to be Katrina. Is that too close to Katherine?"

"We'll work with it. If we can do something to make turning her life topsy turvy easier, we will. And once we accomplish this little miracle, you keep in touch, you hear? Maybe even come on out and join us."

Kat tugged at her arm. "Pol, what's going to happen? And do I have to change my name?"

As Polly Ann told her the details, Kat laughed and began to dance around in delight. Then her face fell. "But where will you be?"

"That's something I don't know yet. I've had a few interviews at colleges and universities that sound like they'd be a good fit for me, and I've heard back from half of them."

"Any in Colorado?"

11

"One. I'm still waiting to hear from them."

"Maybe you'll get a letter today and it'll be perfect."

"Maybe you should change your name to Pollyanna."

There was a letter. It was from Dr. Anne MacGregor, head of the English department at Ridge University in Ridgeview, Colorado. She was offering Polly Ann an assistant professorship, and she'd included a handwritten note: " One of your references, a dear friend of mine who had you in his final Old English course before he retired, told me if I didn't hire you, I would regret it forever. Please come. We need you."

Polly Ann grabbed Kat's hands and whirled her around in a circle. "Katkin, I think a double rainbow just appeared in our cloudy sky. I've been offered a job in Colorado!"

Three days later, Polly Ann picked up the copy of the *Ann Arbor News* from her driveway as she got in the car to drive Kat to the Detroit airport. She would miss the girl, but she was relieved to be sending her to a safer place. And they wouldn't be separated for long; Polly Ann planned to start her journey to Colorado in two short weeks.

Back home, she retrieved the newspaper from the back seat where she'd tossed it and took it into the apartment. She poured a stinger for herself, mostly in celebration of having the wrinkles in her life's path iron themselves out.

An inside page of the newspaper carried a report of the coroner's inquest into the death of Clarence Hunter. After Stanley Turner testified that he had witnessed the accidental shooting of his friend, the case was closed. One reporter asked if it was true that there'd been another witness, a young Indian girl from the camp, but Turner said that so far as he knew it was just a rumor. He himself had seen no one.

Polly Ann read that bit of news with dismay. He was lying. Might he do some snooping at the school? Thank goodness, Dr. Allen had told Kat's friends and the teachers that the girl had gone to live with a cousin in Minnesota.

STRIKE VOTE

5

August 2002 – February, 2008

Polly Ann bought a pleasant ranch house in a new development in Ridgeview, across the street from the old part of town. Many of the residents were also affiliated with the university, others worked in town. Her closest neighbors were the Ridgeview chief of police, Matt Brophy, his wife Patty, and their two children.

Kat soon became just one more of the many Tallfeather kids, changed her first name to Katrina, attended public school, and grew six inches. Only Polly Ann was surprised at the sudden growth spurt – all the Tallfeather kids were tall and they all played basketball.

Kat fussed at Polly Ann about living alone. "You could rent out your basement apartment to a student. Or, if you don't want a human housemate, get a dog."

"I'll think about it." Actually, she did. She even went as far as to visit the local humane society. The sight of cages of dogs and cats looking at her with soulful eyes, all saying, "Take me!" reduced her to tears. She couldn't take them all, and she couldn't choose one that needed her more than the others.

One cold November morning as she walked past the front of her little yellow car to get to the driver's side, she heard faint noise that seemed to come from under the wheel cover, as if some creature seeking shelter had snuggled in on top of the tire. Starting the engine might frighten it enough to leave its perch, but if it didn't, the result would be tragic.

Polly Ann bent down to peer under the wheel cover. Something moved. When she coaxed the filthy bundle of fur to leave its perch, she wasn't sure what it was, but she carried it into the house and wrapped a towel around it. "Food first and then a bath," she decided.

The food – slivers of leftover roast beef and bits of bread soaked in warm milk – was welcome. The creature started squirming and squeaking in protest as soon as she dunked it into the warm water of the kitchen sink. Polly Ann wrapped it into a warm, dry towel moments after seeing what she'd rescued: a Siamese kitten, not yet wearing the color points it would soon acquire. She cautiously sat down in her recliner, tucking the towel folds around the baby cat. It fell asleep almost immediately.

"What am I going to call you?" she asked. A tiny purr – or was it snoring? – was the only response.

When it woke up, it was hungry again. Tummy satisfied, the kitten began to prowl. Down the hall and into Polly Ann's bedroom. It emerged from under the bed batting a dust bunny.

"So within that itty bitty body of yours beats the heart of a mighty lion? Okay, Simba, you have a name."

Polly Ann soon learned it is impossible to watch the antics of a kitten and be depressed. She began looking forward to the weekly conversations with Trevor's dad. Shortly after Simba's arrival, she described his encounter with the almost empty corn flakes box, and for the first time since Trevor's disappearance, she heard Victor laugh. And she realized that she'd laughed more in the past few days than in the entire previous year.

STRIKE VOTE

6

2008-2013

On a blistering hot day in early August, Polly Ann picked up the newspaper from her driveway and glanced at the photograph under the fold. The face was vaguely familiar. She read the accompanying headline: "Ridge University alum to open travel agency."

Yes, she'd seen that face before. Stanley Turner, owner of a Michigan travel agency and witness to what he testified was an accidental fatal shooting. What was he doing in Ridgeview? Had he followed her here, or was his arrival mere coincidence? Perhaps some of each.

Days later, they met, surely by accident, at the grocery store. Turner smiled at her, then looked more closely. "Haven't I seen you before? I'm sure I remember meeting you. Was it in Michigan a few years ago?"

"Yes, it was, Mr. Turner. You helped me sort out a problem I had with some travel plans involving a group of us graduate students from the university."

They chatted for a minute and Polly Ann didn't feel any threat until his parting comment: "Have you been in touch with any of those Indian kids that were at the camp when you worked there?" She remembered stammering something and walking away.

When she heard via the campus grapevine that Turner had bought one of the lovely old homes across the street from her, she reluctantly told Kat that it was no longer safe for her to come over for lunch and/or dinner on weekends.

Kat moved into a dorm at CU Boulder a week later, ready to start her freshman year. From that day on, they avoided being seen together in public anywhere in Ridgeview and had to settle for a weekly lunch at one of the cafés in Longmont, halfway between Ridgeview and Boulder.

Kat didn't think Polly Ann's paranoia was justified. "Pol, even my own mother wouldn't recognize me as the little girl who spent part of a summer at a camp in Michigan. Look at me! I was a scrawny little

15

thing with hair cropped as short as a boy's, bruises all over my face, and a mouthful of crooked teeth."

Polly Ann saw a stunning woman, well over six feet tall, long black hair in a braid down her back, piercing brown-black eyes carefully made up with just the right amount of mascara and shadow, and flawless light bronze skin. Braces had taken care of the teeth. "He wouldn't recognize you if you were by yourself, but if he saw us together, his mind would start to wonder. And that's what we can't risk."

Kat spent two years at the Boulder campus before transferring to Ridge U for the 2011 fall semester. "I've got all the basics out of the way, Pol, and it's time to start concentrating on my major. And, be honest, Ridge has a better program."

Polly Ann had to agree with her. However, she insisted that they continue to meet infrequently and at cafes where Turner was not apt to show up.

By the time Kat received her undergraduate degree in 2013, Stanley Turner had become a minor power in Ridgeview and, as an alumnus of the university, was eventually picked to fill one of two vacancies on its board of regents. The second one went to a newcomer in town, Huntington Edwards III.

Following the sudden tragic death of the board chairman, Stanley Turner was the unanimous choice to replace him. When Polly Ann was elected president of the campus AAUP, the faculty collective bargaining agent, Turner sent her a note of congratulations that said, "May our paths cross often and our swords never."

"We'll see about that," Polly Ann muttered. "The regents seldom are on the side of the faculty."

STRIKE VOTE

7

Saturday, August 25, 2013

Polly Ann didn't exactly look for trouble; reviewing the latest Ridge University budget sheets posted on the internet was simply part of her weekly routine. Anyone could access the information, but few bothered. When she saw the figures for faculty salaries and for new buildings on the report dated August 25, she blinked. And looked again. And pulled up the report from the prior month.

Her unladylike expletive caused Simba to raise his head and focus his big blue eyes on her face. Polly Ann's first impulse was to use her authority as president of the campus AAUP, the faculty union, to call for a strike vote. "Pussy cat, if I call a full faculty meeting and show them this, they'll be up in arms and will readily support me."

A niggling voice from her conscience whispered, *Aren't you going off half-cocked? Sometimes when you leap into the fray, you later regret it.*

She realized that this crisis required careful thought, not impulsive action. She asked the computer to print the relevant pages, rose from her ergonomically correct office chair, and went to the kitchen.

She did look at the clock, noting that it was 9:30 a.m. "What the hell, this is serious. I must settle my stomach." To propitiate the health gods, she prepared a Bloody Mary rather than her preferred libation, a stinger.

Taking a hefty swig, Polly Ann returned to her study, drink in hand. The printer had, for once, done its job correctly. Fishing a yellow highlighter pen from a desk drawer, she illuminated the appropriate line items on the budget pages.

"Simba, we must do this right." He perked up his ears. He was the best listener Polly had ever known, never interrupting, always attentive. Well, almost always. That mouse in the pantry trying to get into the box of graham crackers had distracted him.

Simba waited for her to continue.

Polly scratched her head. "Maybe there's a better way to handle this.

A strike right before the start of fall term will hurt faculty and students far more than the administrators and regents. And to be fair, the regents should be allowed to respond before we go public."

Polly Ann took another sip of her drink, surprised to see that what was left in the glass was mostly melted ice. She padded to the kitchen for a refill to help her think.

"The regents need to see this. But if I send it to their office, the members won't see it right away and couldn't discuss it until their next meeting. Can't wait that long. This is urgent!

"Okay, I can't stand Stan Turner, but he knows how to get people to do what he wants, and he wants more than anything to get rid of President Limbach. So, I'll send this little packet of dynamite to him, anonymously of course, and wait for the fur to fly."

Simba looked questioningly at her. "Not your fur, sweetie. Figurative fur.

"Given my luck, this will get lost in the dregs of the post office, or he'll ignore it. So I need a Plan B. But maybe, for once, things will go as they should."

If the regents did the right thing and canned the current president, Horatio Limbach, *aka* Limburger, who – apart from unknown outsiders – might apply from within? Polly Ann ran the possibilities through her mind.

Her choice would be Anthony Angelocci, vice president for Academic Affairs. Tony was a genuinely nice man. Not necessarily a virtue when university politics were involved. He also had the right credentials and experience. Everyone liked him – students, faculty, administrators, and even those regents who didn't think he was tough enough. And he was fair.

Stanley Turner – she wondered if his ego really was that huge. Yes. Would he have a chance? Yes, again. If the regents didn't like the choices of other groups, they'd make their own decision. After all, they did elect him to chair their board.

She rejected other vice presidents and campus bigwigs, but hesitated a moment when she considered Wills Gladwin, vice president for University Outreach and director of the Ridge University Foundation. He met what others might consider to be the essential qualifications, but he was a pompous, cold fish.

Two days later, at the English department annual pre-fall meeting, held mostly to welcome new faculty members and discuss travel allocations, Anne McGregor, head of the department, frowned at Polly Ann. "Dr. Passarelli, you seem distracted. Is there a matter of department business you wish to raise?"

"Um, no ma'am. Sorry."

Anne asked. "Any other department business? If not, we are adjourned. Dr. Passarelli, may I see you in my office for a minute?"

Anne closed the office door and gestured Polly to a chair at the small conference table. "Spill it, Polly Ann. You look like you're ready to erupt."

"Promise not to tell anyone? Cross your heart and hope to die?"

"That bad?"

Polly Ann frowned, thought for a minute, and then grinned sheepishly. "Well, yes, bad, but maybe also good. Have you looked at the most recent budget revisions – not just the department ones? Here," she said, fumbling in her briefcase for four folded sheets of paper. "These two pages show last month's supposedly final figures for faculty salaries and buildings – that is, for the new presidential palace."

She laid the other two pages alongside the first two. "These are revised numbers, approved last week."

Anne studied the highlighted numbers on each pair of pages. "My God, Polly Ann, someone's approved cutting faculty salaries by over three million dollars and increasing the building fund by the same amount. This is a disaster! Have you called a faculty meeting?"

"I thought about it and decided a strike wouldn't be a good idea."

"But you've done something. I can tell by the look on your face."

"I sent the information to Regent Turner."

Anne howled with laughter. "Genius! Stan hates Limbach's guts. Stan wouldn't wait one moment longer than necessary to persuade his colleagues to fire the president. Only the regents have that power, and Stan must be rubbing his hands in glee. I doubt we'll have to wait long to see what happens."

8

Monday, August 27

Stanley Turner fished the mailbox key out of his pocket, muttering as always about the inconvenience of having to collect his mail from the communal array of boxes half a block from his home. Why couldn't they just continue putting letters and junk mail through the handy slot in front doors? He slammed the door of his Cadillac harder than usual and drove down the block and into his garage.

Once inside the house, he sorted through the assortment of envelopes and ad flyers, discarding most of it into the nearest waste basket. He frowned at the fat envelope still in his hands. No return address. He started to drop it in with the rest of the junk, but curiosity got the better of him.

He took it into the kitchen and slit it open with the serrated breadknife, unwashed since breakfast. He pulled out the contents and spread the pages on the table before sitting down to study them.

A rare smile lifted the corners of his thin lips. "Gotcha!" he whispered. He poured himself a stiff scotch and reached for the phone. As chairman of the Ridge University Board of Regents, he had the authority to call special meetings

Thursday, August 30

Tapping the gavel for silence, Turner announced, "The only item on our agenda for today is a budget report."

Rick Gregory looked puzzled. "Stan, what's up? We've already approved this year's budget."

Turner smiled condescendingly. "We approved the supposedly final one submitted in June. In case none of you has reviewed the latest version, I've made copies." He handed a sheaf of papers to Gregory to pass around and waited a few minutes before resuming.

"Look closely, first at the highlighted entry on the first page showing the revised numbers for capital improvements, specifically, the new presidential residence. If you'll recall, the original figure was $2.4 million. The updated budget shows $6 million.

"Now look at the second page: $87.6 million for faculty salaries."

Joanie Jameson blurted, "I don't understand." Hunter Edwards blanched. Glynda Gianetta scowled, opened her mouth, and simply said, "Oh, shit!" Burt Lincoln looked at the pages in front of him in disbelief.

William Brasseth sputtered, "The faculty budget was nearly $91 million. The minute Dr. Passarelli sees this, she'll call a faculty strike. And we have less than two weeks before the fall term starts. Who approved this?"

"Obviously, Bill, you didn't, nor did any of the rest of us. We may occasionally approve something we've not actually seen, but not budgets. The only other person with the authority to amend them is . . ."

"Limbach." Burt growled the name. "You all were so keen on hiring that slimeball, you pooh-poohed all the signs that I warned you about. So what're we gonna do about this? Fire the son of a bitch?"

Joanie raised her hand. "Can we do that?"

Turner nodded. "We hired him, we can fire him. Or at least we can give him a chance to resign before we contact the media. Our regular fall meeting to hear his pep talk for the year is scheduled for September 13. So there's time for us to think about this. But we need to decide by then. Consider the options carefully."

He tapped the gavel on the table. "I hereby adjourn this meeting. As I said, each of us needs to make a decision in the next few days."

If Glynda Gianetta had been alone on her way to the parking lot, she'd have skipped all the way to her car. She stifled a smile and resumed her habitual detached expression. She did, however, let the grin out as she entered her home and grabbed her husband's hands, twirling him around the hallway. "Wait until you hear!"

"Does this call for champagne?" Jorge asked.

"Maybe, but I can't wait for that. My usual margarita will do. I'll meet you in the living room."

She summarized the stunning news Turner had delivered. "Stan's right – it's up to us to get rid of Limbach. But you know, I have a disquieting feeling that there's something on Stan's agenda that he's not sharing. You've met him. What's your take?"

Jorge thought back to his first encounter with Regent Turner, whose greeting set his teeth on edge: "You been in this country long?"

What sort of response could he make? Tell the man that his grandparents were naturalized U.S. citizens? That his parents were born here? That he himself had lived here his entire life? He opted for keeping his cool. "Look it up. My vita is in the university files."

As he walked away, Turner called after him, "There's sure to be some dirt in your history. I'll find it."

Jorge wondered how deep the man would dig.

Now, he realized Glynda was waiting for his response. "I think you're right, Lyn. And I think we'll find out pretty soon what's hiding in that twisted mind of his. He's after something more than getting rid of Limbach. I'll bet he spends a lot of time digging up stuff on everyone he encounters to use whenever he needs their support."

"Blackmail?"

"I wouldn't put it past him. But it's a very dangerous game to play."

Joanie Jameson's best friend was her golden retriever, Ernest. He listened thoughtfully to every word she said and approved all her decisions. Rather like her deceased husband, who had listened to her, even if he didn't always agree.

"Ernest, I'm not stupid. I know Mr. Limbach shouldn't have diddled with the budgets, but he's always been really nice to me. When Robert died and there were all those questions about his drinking, Mr. Limbach made all the rumors go away.

"But Stan kept making nasty remarks. He even told me that he'd swear Robert hardly ever drank anything except beer – but I'd have to be nice to him. I know what he meant by 'nice.' He makes my skin crawl."

Ernest stood up when the phone rang and escorted Joanie to the kitchen. She reluctantly picked it up. "Hi, Joanie," a gravelly voice greeted her. "It's Burt. You okay?"

Joanie was relieved. There were a lot of people she didn't ever want to talk to, but Burt Lincoln wasn't one of them. "Hi, Burt. No, I'm not okay. I've always respected Mr. Limbach. What he did was wrong, but I don't want to say he should be fired."

"Yeah, it's hard. But, Joanie, how do you think the hundreds of faculty members will feel? What happens to the students when the faculty goes on strike? And believe me, they will strike. The president didn't simply break into a piggy bank; he stole three million dollars budgeted to pay for quality scholars to teach our kids."

"Stole it?" Joanie squeaked. "I thought he just borrowed it to pay for his house."

"Joanie! Borrowers pay back loans. They don't hide the fact they've taken something without asking. Limbach had no intention of repaying the money, or any way of doing so."

Joanie twisted a strand of hair around her fingers and rubbed one foot along the other leg. Finally she said, "I guess he has to go. But I'm sorry for him. What will he do?"

Burt's reply was a booming laugh that made Joanie smile. "Honey, Limbach will immediately apply to other colleges and universities and at least one of them will offer him a presidency. If they're smart, they'll watch their budget process very carefully."

Joanie sighed. "That makes me feel better. I guess the right thing for me to do is vote to dismiss him. Thanks for calling, Burt. You've really helped." She slowly returned the phone to its cradle and reached for a mug. She filled it with water and set it in the microwave. While the water heated, she took a Constant Comment teabag from a canister. "Ernest, I don't really like tea, but right now I need something soothing."

Rick Gregory poured three fingers of scotch – no ice – for the bank president in an attempt to soothe his ruffled feathers. Brasseth took a small sip, before draining the glass. "That's good stuff, Rick. I can feel my blood pressure dropping. But what is Stan really up to? Some morning that man is going to wake up and discover that his secrets have killed him. And what the hell is up with Hunter?"

Rick scratched his head and set down his drink, contents still intact. "Hunter looks up to Limbach, plays golf with him, attends the same church every Easter and Christmas. And he's never been comfortable around faculty members. He struggled to get an associate's degree from a community college and blamed his teachers for his struggles. He's said more than once that eggheads – his term, not mine – don't understand ordinary people, that they even expect our football players to attend classes. If he had his way, he'd fill all the faculty positions with temps."

Brasseth waved his empty glass. Rick took the hint and refilled it. Brasseth closed his eyes and waited a few moments. "So will Hunter refuse to make the vote unanimous? He postures a lot, but I can't remember any occasion when he went against the majority. Maybe Stan can pull him into line."

Stanley Turner bided his time for a few days. Knowing he could find Hunter most mornings having coffee at the Faculty Club, he timed his arrival carefully. "May I join you, Hunter?" he asked, sitting across the table from his prey without waiting for a response.

Sullenly, Hunter mumbled, "You expect me to turn on my friend?"

Stan leaned forward on his elbows and in a low voice asked, "Did your friend tell you what he'd done? Did you think that was okay? Can your friend sabotage the university by stealing millions for his new house and be excused? Will you have any friends when this goes public and you're the one regent who says it's okay? You stick with him and I'll make sure the investigation into your uncle's death is reopened."

Hunter blanched. "You wouldn't!"

"I would. Unless you make the vote unanimous. The Ridge University Board of Regents has always presented a united front and will do so now."

Hunter had to brace himself on the table before he could stand. Before he shuffled away, head bent, shoulders quivering, he murmured. "You win. May you wind up in Hell."

STRIKE VOTE

9

Tuesday, September 5

Classes began on schedule amid the normal first day chaos of lost students wandering the halls of the wrong building, snail-slow elevators jammed with people who had yet to realize that the stairs were often faster, and a few new faculty members suffering from stage fright.

The weather was perfect for playing hooky, although few did.

Thursday, September 13

Horatio Lancelot Limbach, MBA, eleventh president of Ridge University, strode into the room with the broad smile a reigning monarch might bestow on his worshipful subjects. As he looked at each of his regents, standing stiffly around the teak conference table, the smile faded.

Rick, almost never seen without his trademark smile, was scowling. William Brasseth, president of Ridgeview Bank and Trust, gave Limbach the steely-eyed stare he normally reserved for loan defaulters. Glynda Gianetta had never looked at the president with anything but disdain; she did that to almost everyone. This time, however, her normal elegant good looks were marred by an expression of pure hatred.

Hunter Edwards' hands were shaking. He didn't meet Limbach's eyes, focusing instead on the wall of portraits to his left, as if he'd never before seen the stern faces of the previous presidents of Ridge University. Burt Lincoln appeared ready to spit. Joanie stared at the floor, seemingly unaware that her hands were strangling a handkerchief.

Limbach acknowledged Turner as the person in charge. "What's all this about, Stan?"

"This, Horry, is about a little matter of budget tampering to the tune of three and a half million dollars, which leads to the unanimous decision of the Ridge University Board of Regents to fire you and inform the community why we so decided.

"However," Turner said after a moment of electric silence, "we're not vindictive – or at least not nearly as vindictive as the faculty will be if this becomes common knowledge – so if you choose to resign quietly for 'personal reasons,' that would be acceptable. Without, of course, a severance package. You've ripped off this institution for the last time."

Limbach blustered and stormed. And sweated. "You can't do this to me! I have a contract good for another three years. I'm calling my lawyer. If anyone's getting canned, it's you people." No one blinked.

The man was a crook, but he wasn't stupid. When he stopped blustering, he was silent, obviously thinking about the options. If he resigned and quietly left town, he could always find another college in need of a leader. His wife would be furious, but this was as much her fault as his. They'd gotten away with budget tampering before, maybe once too often.

"Do what you will," Limbach sighed. "You'll have my resignation later today. Don't bother informing the press; I'll do that myself." The heavy oak door of the regents' conference room slammed behind him.

Turner tried not to smile. "If he gets to the media first, he'll plead personal reasons. Shall we let him get away with that?"

Gregory nodded. "Yeah, I think so. The university's reputation would suffer as well as his. When we start getting requests for references, we can quietly get the word out. So, are we adjourned?"

Turner nodded. "We are for now. But we have work to do: a carefully worded ad for the *Chronicle of Higher Education* and suggestions for search committee membership. Our next regular meeting is in two weeks. Come with ideas."

Turner strolled the half mile to his home, an ivy-covered brick house built nearly 100 years earlier. Once inside he strode past the glass-fronted bookcase and curio cabinet, both older than the house, on his way to the kitchen. No antiques here, only the newest, shiniest appliances money could buy.

He poured a generous three fingers from the crystal decanter of Jim

STRIKE VOTE

Beam and set it down on the granite-topped table. A fresh yellow pad and three pens waited.

Turner sipped the bourbon and jotted down a few notes: admin, faculty, student, minority, gender mix, sexual preference, union. He left space after each category for names. Going back to the top of the list, he wrote three names, only to cross them out and nearly gouge a hole in the paper. In block letters, he printed the name of Freddie Ferrett. "That's one male. Well, sort of. Gay, but thinks no one knows. Except me. He's pretty low on the administrative totem pole, so we probably need someone higher up."

Turner thought for a moment and then smiled. A cat that ate the canary smile. He added Polly Ann Passarelli's name to the page. "Female and faculty. Perfect. It's time I reminded her that I suspect she has a dirty little secret."

Smiling to himself, he recalled running into Dr. Passarelli shortly after moving to Ridgeview. She stood at the deli counter of King Soopers, giving her order to the woman behind the counter. He moved up beside her, saying, "You look familiar. Have we met before?"

It took a few seconds before she nodded in recognition. "I lived in Ann Arbor for a few years. I did business with your travel agency there and I believe we met on one or two occasions."

"You fostered a little Indian girl, didn't you?" Stan hoped for a strong reaction, but she merely frowned and shook her head. "No, you must be confusing me with someone else. I was a camp counselor one summer for a bunch of Native American children, but that was my only contact."

Stan bowed slightly. "Oh, well that answers that question. It's good to see you. I'm sure our paths will cross again."

He was pleased with himself. He'd planted the seed and could watch it grow as he nurtured it with little innuendos whenever they met. If that Indian orphan had come with her to Colorado, they couldn't hide forever.

Turner picked up his empty glass. He got up to refill it, adding an ice cube this time. He returned to his list of potential search committee members.

Wills Gladwin, the vice president for University Outreach, CEO of the Ridge University Foundation, was, he thought, the obvious choice for an upper administration representative. How he hated that man! No matter; he could be controlled.

"Need another female. Ah, yes, the lovely Katrina Tallfeather. Minority lesbo female student. I can handle her.

"And last but not least, our campus cop union rep, Jorge Martin. He may be squeaky clean, but he's hiding something."

Turner looked over his list. "That's four solid votes for me, maybe five. A good start."

STRIKE VOTE

10

Thursday, September 27

At the next regents' meeting, Turner quieted the conversations among his colleagues. "Get yourselves more coffee and let's get started. We should put together an ad for *The Chronicle*. Take a look at some previous ads for presidencies and take notes on what they have in common. Last time we said doctorate or equivalent and we settled for an MBA. And look what that got us.

"Our next item of business is the makeup of the search committee. Hunter, your thoughts?"

"Well, we have to be politically correct, so roughly half men, half women. And solid minority representation."

Glynda waited for him to continue. Seeing that he had nothing to add, she raised an eyebrow. "We also need diversity of university affiliation: union, administration, faculty, and students."

Heads nodded. Turner waited for someone to start suggesting names. After an uncomfortable silence, Burt said, "The bigger the committee the more disagreement. Can we identify five or six people who combine all the factors?"

Glynda's suggestion surprised them all. "How about Jorge Martin? Hispanic, chief of campus police. Minority, male, and union all in one package."

Joanie whispered, "I thought you couldn't stand him."

"Well, I don't have to sleep with him, he does have a brain, and he knows how to get people to work together. Who knows a good female faculty member?"

Burt suggested, "I've always thought Polly Ann Passarelli had a good head on her shoulders, and she's a real nice lady."

Hunter frowned. "But she's also union. Wouldn't that pose a potential problem? Reps from two unions?"

Stan shook his head. "I don't think so. Cops and faculty don't have much contact and their contract issues – except money, of course – are different. Rick, you got any ideas?"

"Yeah. We could have a minority student female, and Katrina Tallfeather is a very impressive woman."

"Isn't she gay? I mean lesbian?" Joanie whispered.

"All the better," Stan said, laughing at Joanie's naivete. "Four qualifications in one.

"Okay, last but not least, an upper echelon administrator who understands fund raising." Several of the members groaned. "I know, Gladwin is not especially well liked, but who else have we got? I mean, take a look at the other vice presidents. They've all turned off potential donors without raising a dime that wasn't earmarked for one of their special interests: endowed faculty chairs, student scholarships, football scholarships, and the like."

Rick ticked off the names before asking, "Is four enough? Or is some group going to be offended because it's not included?"

Burt scratched his head. "Yup. We gotta have Human Resources."

"Not Freddie!" Several voices protested.

Turner tried not to smile. Burt had unwittingly done what Stan needed. "He's right. And an odd number is good – no tie votes. Five is a small enough bunch to get the job done fairly quickly."

Burt laughed. "As I said, big committees spend all their time arguing. Small ones get things done. We spend enough time disagreeing, and there's only seven of us."

"About to be six, unless you like odd numbers and decide to choose a successor. I'm resigning, effective immediately."

Turner's announcement was greeted with surprise, but not much regret. Hunter was the first to catch on. "You're going to apply for the presidency."

Turner smiled. "Right you are. I trust I have your support?" With that, he left the room without looking back.

STRIKE VOTE

11

Friday, September 28

The annual Ridge University all-campus reception celebrated new hires and recent retirees. It also served to let friends and casual acquaintances catch up on summer happenings, real or not. This year, the rumors, fanned by conflicting stories, focused on the sudden retirement of the university president, Horatio Limbach.

Polly Ann and her friend and neighbor, Patty Brophy, stopped at the women's restroom to see to their hair and makeup. Polly Ann checked that her deodorant was still working and blotted her face with a damp paper towel, hoping to set the face powder, not remove it. For this late in September, it was unseasonably – unreasonably – hot. The sun wouldn't set until close to 7:00. There would be no moon. In the ballroom, the air conditioners were working overtime.

Polly Ann compared her own freckled face and curly carrot-colored hair with Patty's porcelain smooth skin, raven-black hair, and deep blue eyes. Her friend was gorgeous; Polly Ann mentally shrugged her shoulders. One must do what one can with what one is given.

She saw Patty's husband, the Ridgeview Chief of Police, Matt Brophy, standing near the entrance to the ballroom, chatting with Jorge Martin, president of the small Ridge University campus police force. Both wore evening dress, since neither was on duty for this event.

Polly Ann had heard Martin's name pronounced as both "George" and "Horhay," She'd asked once which he preferred. "Doesn't matter. My grandparents and my father always used the Spanish pronunciation as my mom did at home, but around my friends, she Anglicized it, as they did. I answer to both."

People liked working with Jorge, who was quick to laugh and looked for the good in people, even crooks. It made him a good interviewer. However, he rarely revealed anything about his private life. Polly Ann didn't even know if he was married.

As the two men entered the ballroom, Matt waved and smiled at the two women. Polly Ann smiled back, comfortable that, for once, every hair was in place and her lipstick on straight. She kept smiling as Anne McGregor joined them. "You ladies look lovely. Shall we find the bar and the hors d'oeuvres?"

Momentarily, Stanley Turner blocked the way "Good evening, ladies. Lovely, as usual."

Polly Ann nodded and shouldered her way past him, Patty and Anne close behind. Moving toward the crowd gathered near the back of the room, they caught snippets of conversation. They passed a thin, youngish man wearing horn-rimmed glasses, a sport shirt, jeans, and Birkenstocks. "Why is it always our salary budget that gets whacked?" His companion, an attractive brunette in a black, knee-length cocktail dress, teetering awkwardly on four inch heels replied, "Polly Ann took care of that. She told them we'd strike."

The threesome stopped to allow passage for a young woman bearing a tray of champagne glasses past a small group deep in conversation.

"I heard that it was one of the regents that blew the whistle."

"I got the impression it was Turner."

"Jack said it was Rick Gregory. He's the only one that ever supports the faculty."

"Did Limbach really order a three million dollar cut?"

"I thought it was six million."

They eased by two groundskeepers who'd obviously come straight from work, still wearing jeans, denim jackets, and work boots. "So, the way I heard it, the original budget for a new presidential residence was two and a half million. Limbach signed work orders for another three and a half. He then ordered the Board of Regents to approve a revised budget taking three million from faculty salaries and putting it in buildings and grounds."

"That's how I understand it," the other man said, as Anne dawdled to hear a bit more. "That's when Regent Turner resigned and called the newspaper editor, who contacted all the other regents, who demanded the president's resignation."

As Patty and Polly Ann waited for Anne to catch up, they caught other bits of conversation. A whiny voice said, "The paper said Limbach retired for health reasons. So why didn't he get severance pay?"

Finally getting close to the food and drink, the women were joined by Marsha Reynolds, director of the campus library. "Good to see you all here. Ready for the new term? We are. I assume you've heard the latest scuttlebutt, that we're finally getting rid of Stan the Man. Look at him strutting around, glad-handing everyone who doesn't turn away fast enough. You'd think it was his farewell party. Oh, crap, he's coming this way. I'm out of here."

Marsha disappeared into the crowd. They watched the man in question elbow his way past several people, lifting a glass of champagne from the tray of a passing waiter, nodding left and right to acknowledge several wealthy alumni. Spotting Glynda Giannetta, who stood by herself a few feet away, he drained his glass, setting it on a nearby table, and sidled up to her. "Well, well, look who's here without her broom."

Polly Ann had calmed down since the earlier encounter and could observe him more clearly. *He looks worse than I do on a bad day.* The tuxedo on his portly body was obviously a rental – droopy across the shoulders, tight over the midsection, and too short in the sleeves. Overly large ruby cuff links completed the picture.

She and her two friends backed away, aware that Ms. Gianetta could handle the bully without their assistance.

Glynda raised an eyebrow as her eyes slowly scanned him from coiffed hair to glossy shoes. "Debonair as usual, Stan. And your rental tux almost fits."

Stan involuntarily raised an arm to check that his shirt cuffs extended the proper distance from the jacket sleeves. He flushed, but he quickly struck back. "Nice dress, but not really your color. And this isn't really your kind of party. Are you here to hit people up for scholarship funds again?"

"That's right," she replied. She turned to lift two champagne glasses from the tray a passing waiter held out and handed him one. "Unlike you, I don't come to these things for the liquor and hors d'oeuvres. And I did want a word with you."

"I'm flattered."

"Don't be. It's time you ended this charade. I doubt that there'll be even one regent or one search committee member willing to back your candidacy. What hold do you think you have on Freaky Freddie and Hunter that would force them into supporting you?"

Turner sputtered, "Are you accusing me of blackmail?"

Glynda shook her head. "It doesn't matter. You need to withdraw your application."

Stan took a large mouthful of the champagne. "Over my dead body," he said, before suddenly gasping for breath and sinking to the floor in a boneless sprawl. His eyes bulged. He gagged and choked as his mouth frothed. Seconds later, he was still.

Glynda's voice carried throughout the room as she ordered, "Someone call 911." Every head in the room swiveled to look at her. "Now!" she snapped. One man in evening dress pulled out a cell phone and barked into it. Polly Ann started forward. Patty grabbed her arm, "It's okay. Matt's here. He'll handle this."

Polly Ann watched as Matt Brophy knelt by Turner's body. For a moment, no one else moved.

The EMTs arrived within minutes; several more police officers and Walter Lewandowski, the medical examiner, followed almost on their heels. The ME stopped briefly to ask Brophy a question before he knelt beside the body. Matt beckoned to his officers, asking them to spread out and request all the notables, staff, and others to stay where they were. Three officers stationed themselves at the exits; others stood near the bar and table of hors d'oeuvres.

The onlookers, curious, alarmed, and annoyed, milled around. Conversation was muted, as if no one wished to be overheard.

"Did you see the look on his face?"

"He just sort of crumpled."

"Probably a heart attack."

"Who is he?"

"Stanley Turner. Used to be on the Board of Regents."

"Is he dead?"

The ME finished his brief exam and beckoned to the EMTs to remove the body. Stanley Turner was carefully transferred to a stretcher on wheels and rolled out the door, feet first. "A real change for Stan," an acid voice commented. "He usually leads with his mouth."

Most of those present were herded toward the exits, where the officers wrote down names, contact information, a description of where people were standing or sitting in the few minutes before Turner collapsed, and which other guests were close to him. A few wanted to linger after giving the requested information, but the officers sent them on their way.

Officer Dana Jonsgaard sent the waiters into the kitchen for a group interview. One by one, she interviewed Polly Ann and others who'd been standing near her. Polly Ann assumed they were all asked the same questions: "Did you know Mr. Turner well? Were you close enough to hear his conversation? To your knowledge, did he have any health problems? Did he have any enemies that you know of? Did he eat anything? Where did he get the champagne? Could anyone other than the waiter have touched that glass before it was given to Mr. Turner?"

Polly Ann also assumed that the answers were about the same as hers. She said that she'd known Regent Turner for about ten years. "As far as I know he was quite healthy. I don't know that I'd say he had enemies, but he was not well liked." When she was asked to elaborate, she ducked the question: "He could be autocratic and unsympathetic." *She can tell I hated him. If she's looking for a murder suspect, I'm not the only one.*

Jonsgaard didn't pursue that question, asking instead if Polly Ann knew where he got the champagne. "Yes, I saw Regent Giannetta give it to him. It wasn't me." *Isn't that exactly what a guilty party would say?* Taking a deep breath, Polly Ann explained, "She took two glasses of champagne off the tray of a passing waiter and handed him one of them. Yes, they both looked the same."

There was one surprise question: "Did the champagne taste all right to you?"

"I'm not much of a connoisseur, but I thought it had a hint of honey in it."

"Thank you." Jonsgaard scribbled an entry in her notebook before she turned away, gesturing for another witness to come forward.

Polly Ann had tried not to look at the EMTs lifting the stretcher bearing Turner's body. She could hear her own heart beating, feel it falter as her brain told her Stan Turner's heart would never beat again. She felt her eyes fill and forced her lower eyelids to hold back the flood of tears. What was wrong with her? She heartily despised the man. Why should his death cause any reaction but a mild relief?

Because he'd been alive and now he wasn't. He hadn't slipped gently away from life, hadn't lingered for weeks or months until even those who cared for him were ready for him to die. Stan Turner had died horribly, suddenly. But not suddenly enough to avoid the agony of trying desperately, unsuccessfully to breathe.

Stan Turner was dead. Did anyone care? Perhaps not, but looking at the faces near her, Polly Ann saw that, like her, others were appalled at the manner of his dying. She found herself gasping for breath. She had to get away.

12

Chief Brophy overheard Polly Ann's remark about honey and, unnoticed in the confusion, slipped through the door into the serving and kitchen area. Eric Devers, the officer inside the door said, "Sorry, sir, you can't . . . Sorry, chief, I didn't recognize you in the penguin suit."

Matt nodded. The waiters and kitchen staff barely looked until he spoke, not loudly, but commandingly. "Stop whatever you're doing and don't touch anything. I need every glass, clean or dirty; every bottle, full, partially full, or empty; and every plate on which food is or was placed. And we'll need your fingerprints." Responding to several looks of consternation, he added, "We know you handled the crockery and glassware. The question is, who else did? We need your prints to isolate the ones that don't belong."

He turned to a man in a chef's hat. "Hal, you have any gloves in here?"

"Good to see you, Matt. We do have gloves, those thin plastic things the staff use when assembling sandwiches and other items. Those work?"

"Perfect. I don't need everyone boxing up the dishes. Why don't you . . . Oh, hell, I don't need to tell you how to do your jobs. Just box everything up without getting any more fingerprints on anything. I'll send a few of the guys in to cart the stuff off to the crime lab."

One young man, new to the university food service, blurted, "Who are you and what's going on here?"

"I'm Matthew Brophy. In addition to being an invited guest, I'm Ridgeview's police chief. The answer to your other question is that one of the guests out there suddenly collapsed. We won't know why until they get him to the hospital but in case something he ate or drank caused a reaction, we need to check everything."

"Is he dead?"

This early in the investigation, Matt wasn't going to answer any questions, not even the most natural one. He replied, "I have no idea."

"Who is he?"

"I don't know that, either."

"So why all the hoopla?"

"Standard procedure. And that's all I have to say. Hal?"

The chef nodded. "Yeah. Let's get moving. Mario, Don, go get all the boxes we used to transport the stuff here. The rest of you, get gloved and team up – one pair for glasses and bottles, one for used plates, one for serving platters with food still on them."

Chief Brophy left the kitchen and began moving around the gradually emptying ballroom. He stopped to lift his cell phone from a pocket, frowning as he listened to the voice on the other end of the line. Putting the phone away, he watched as the last guests were ushered out.

His men gathered around. "Mr. Turner is dead," he told them, "as you all probably assumed. The ME's initial suspicion is anaphylactic shock."

"Like from peanuts?"

"Hal Bennetolli wouldn't use peanuts in any form for party food. There are other triggers. The lab will have all the plates, glasses, and bottles to analyze. If an allergen or poison is there, they'll find it.

"I want two officers to wait here until the evidence is ready for you to take to the lab. Devers, Johnsgaard, I'll meet you at the car; I need to make a phone call."

Brophy moved to a quiet corner and pulled out his cell phone. "Sorry to bother you at home, sir, but I may need a search warrant."

"Where and why?" was the response.

"A suspicious death at Ridge U."

"Not a student, I hope?"

"No. One of the regents, Stanley Turner, suddenly collapsed during a reception. Walt Lewandowski, the medical examiner, suspects foul play."

Judge Forbisher had a few more questions, and Brophy explained more fully what he wanted. "We need to do a thorough search of Turner's home in case a motive for murder surfaces."

"I'll have the warrant ready for you in ten minutes. You won't need it if no one's in the house, but it doesn't hurt to be prepared."

"Perfect. Thanks."

Brophy hurried out to the patrol car where officers Devers and Johnsgaard were waiting. "We'll swing by Judge Forbisher's for the warrant and head straight for Turner's place. I hope no one's beat us to it."

13

Polly Ann didn't remember pushing through the crowd, didn't remember running all the way home. She only remembered sitting on her front porch, curled up, shivering – although the September evening was warm – and staring into space. Without conscious awareness, her brain registered one shadowy shape enter a house across the street and minutes later furtively depart. Then another and another before full dark descended.

Polly Ann neither saw nor heard the Ridgeview PD patrol car glide past her house and park half a block away. Sometime later, she came out of her stupor when she heard a voice calling her name. "Yes, who is it?"

"Hi, Polly Ann. It's me. Matt. How long have you been sitting out here?"

Polly Ann shook her head to clear the cobwebs. *Matt. Matt Brophy. Friend. Neighbor. Ridgeview chief of police.* "Too long. My butt's numb. As is my brain. What time is it?"

"Nearly 8:00. The reception ended a while ago. You'd already left. Are you okay?"

The sick feeling returned, but much weaker. "Not really. It was awful. Turner's dead, isn't he? Am I a suspect?"

Matt shook his head and sat down on the porch steps next to her. "Have you seen anyone going into his house?"

She remembered shadows. "I thought it was just kind of a daytime nightmare. It was weird. About dusk, when it gets hard to see anything but shapes and shadows, I saw – or imagined I saw – several people going in. Not all at once. Each was sneaking in and a few minutes later sneaking out, apparently hoping they couldn't be seen."

"Recognize anyone?"

"No. Too far away, too dark, and my mind was elsewhere. I couldn't get Turner's bulging eyes and gasping mouth out of my head."

"Okay, if you remember anything else, let me know. For now, you need to get indoors and have some coffee – or something stronger. Do you want me to send Patty down to keep you company?"

"No thanks, Matt. I'll be all right. Your wife has enough to do without having to sit around holding my hand." She stood up on legs that felt wobbly after sitting on concrete for so long.

Matt gave her a quick hug before returning to his patrol car and driving off with a squeal of tires. Polly Ann wondered what she'd said to send him off in such a rush. She was inside her safe little home too quickly to observe Matt's car stopping briefly in front Stan Turner's house before speeding off.

Matt pulled up just long enough for his two officers to get into the patrol car. As he drove off, he asked, "Find anything more?"

Eric shook his head. "Not really. Someone was there before us. The file cabinet drawers were dumped on the floor. Three of them still had some files and papers inside, but one was totally empty.

"We dusted for fingerprints," Dana said, "and footprints. Looks like a whole platoon was in there. Recently. Judging by the rest of the house, a cleaning crew comes regularly, so the dust was pretty fresh. I got pictures of the footprints and fingerprint slides, but they may not help us much."

"Find out who, if anyone other than Turner, has been in that house in the last few days," Matt ordered.

14

Sunday, September 29

Polly Ann woke up slowly, her head pounding. When she opened her eyes, a pair of blue ones stared back at her. "Simba, don't bug me. I had an awful night."

It had been awful. She'd seen Regent Turner die in agony. She'd approached Turner's house and been forced to retreat, failing to get his secret file on her. She'd lied to Matt Brophy, a good neighbor and valued friend.

Katrina would phone before long. She had to be calm by then. Coffee first, then food. She swung her feet from under the covers and prepared to deal with the day.

When the phone rang, Polly Ann was ready with fresh coffee, her cigarettes, and an ashtray. "Good morning, Kat. How are you?"

"More to the point, how are you? You were right there when Regent Turner collapsed and then you disappeared."

"It was awful, Kat. I had to get out of there. I headed for home. As I got to Turner's house and was about to cross the street, I had this bright idea that if I got into his house, I could search for whatever information he might have about me. He must have had something or he wouldn't have kept dropping little hints all the time."

"Did you find it? Did he know about us?"

"Kat, I don't know. As I got close to his house, the front door opened and someone came out, carrying a briefcase. It seemed to be really heavy; he was listing to one side. I was standing behind a tree, so I don't think he saw me. And it was too dark for me to see his face. I waited until he drove away. But Kat, that briefcase – what if he had the file of supposed dirt Turner had on us?"

Polly Ann could hear the concern in Katrina's voice as she said, "I think he did. Don't be cross with me, but when I couldn't find you, I asked a friend to look for you and maybe try to get into Turner's house and look around. I know, it was dumb.

"Anyway, he did get into the house and found file cabinet drawers on a bedroom floor. He said the cabinet looked as if someone had taken a sledge hammer to it."

Polly Ann swore. "So now there's possibly another would-be blackmailer and we don't know who he is or what he has."

"Maybe we should skip our weekly lunches?"

Polly Ann thought about that for a minute. "No. We're not going to cower while some bully tries to control our lives. We'll just keep meeting in places where people we know are not apt to see us together. And we'll see what happens. Maybe nothing. Let's talk about something else. Who's your friend? Is he nice? Is this getting serious? I assume he's a student – what's his field?"

"You sound like a mom."

"I've been the closest thing you've had to a mom for quite a long time, so I've earned the right to be nosy."

15

Matt had been looking forward to a free Saturday, but the investigation into last night's murder couldn't wait. However, before leaving for the office, he took his morning coffee into the back yard. He needed time to gather his thoughts and meditate. So far, the sun and slight breeze held off creating what was going to be another scorching hot day. He sipped his coffee, set it down on the patio table, and picked up the clippers. Radiant red roses covered the huge bush in the corner of the fence. He spotted a few blooms about to shed their petals and snipped them off.

A grassy area, one lot wide, separated his house from Polly Ann's. From his back yard, over the roofs of houses and the sprawl of Ridge University buildings, he could see the Rocky Mountains rising behind the foothills.

"Morning, Matt." Polly Ann was out enjoying the same view, garbed in her fluffy white terry robe, one bare foot resting on a fence rail. Matt noticed that her toenail polish matched his rose bush.

"Morning, Polly Ann. Sleep well? Feeling better this morning?"

"I was afraid to sleep, afraid of nightmares, but I guess I was wrung out. I slept, but I don't feel rested. I feel guilty. Like maybe I could have done something."

"You look like you're dressed for work, Matt. It's Saturday, you know."

"Murder investigations don't stop for weekends. The sooner we pull some pieces together, the sooner we'll solve the puzzle. I may know more by this evening. Patty's planning a barbecue tonight. Will you come so we can compare notes? – sixish, as usual – and bring one of your fabulous salads?"

Polly Ann nodded and waved as he picked up his cup and headed inside. "I won't wish you a nice day, but I hope it's a productive one."

As Brophy entered the precinct, Captain Alice Larson, head of Administrative Services, greeted him. "Matt, Walt Lewandowski's on the line."

"I'll take it in my office, Alice. Thanks. One of these days we'll get approval to hire an official receptionist and you can relax at home on Saturday mornings." She snorted. Matt detoured to the break room to pour coffee into one of the mugs that bore the message, "Cops' veins run on coffee," before continuing into his office and picking up the phone.

"What've we got, Walt?"

"Preliminary tests of the samples reveal traces of mead in the champagne. I had the lab run tests on scrapings from the plates – nothing there – and on half of the open bottles as well as about ten percent of the used glasses. I didn't have them check unopened bottles. Do you want everything tested?"

Matt thought for a moment, frowning in disappointment. "No, I don't think that's necessary. I doubt you'd find anything."

"We already did – mead."

"I'm not following you."

"Oh, sorry. Everyone knows about peanuts, but hardly anyone's aware that honey can also cause anaphylactic shock. Infants are susceptible, but allergic reactions are rare in adults. Your victim was one of the rare ones. Someone spiked the champagne with a few drops of mead, which is a honey wine."

"Well, I'll be damned." Matt was so amazed that he almost forgot to ask his other question. "Any luck on fingerprints?"

"I didn't bother with the champagne glasses – every guest who imbibed, including our killer, would have left prints. Only the kitchen staff left prints on the bottles. Unless it was one of them, whoever added the mead probably wore gloves."

Matt groaned, remembering the neat box of thin plastic gloves sitting on Hal's counter. The killer didn't even have to bring his own.

Walt was still talking. "The sets of prints your men left with me last night from the victim's house are lovely, but useless without something to compare them with that identifies the people they belong to. Get me those, and we'll know more."

Matt ran his hands through his crew cut. "Thanks, Walt. No one ever said this job was easy. Identifying the poison is at least a start."

He stopped to get a coffee refill before going over to Officer Devers' desk. "We're going to have to get fingerprints to match everyone that was in that ballroom to have a hope of identifying whoever was in Turner's house last night."

Devers looked up and shook his head. "Nope. The personnel files include fingerprints for everyone who works at the university. To identify students, we could look at the most recent yearbook for pictures of all students except this year's freshmen."

"There is a god!" Matt smiled for a moment before he began to picture his people hunched over stacks of files for the next several days comparing the half dozen prints retrieved from Turner's house with those of nearly a thousand employees. He groaned. The federal government had software that could match a million prints in a couple hours, but Ridge U was not the federal government.

"We don't have much time, but it has to be done." His mind shook itself awake. "We don't need all the employees, only those who were at the reception. Does Human Resources have prints from the regents?"

"Dunno. I'll call Mr. Ferrett."

"Yeah, he can get the information quickly, and he knows how to keep confidences. Then get a couple of our guys over there to find matches for what we have from Turner's place. I need those names yesterday." Matt paused. "Oh, hell. It's Saturday. The odds of our getting hold of anyone before Monday are zilch."

He'd have to wait for fingerprint data, but he could make progress another way. Matt already had a mental list of those he'd seen standing near Turner. He never simply looked at his surroundings, he memorized them, could tell who was where, what they wore, and what their facial expressions revealed.

He jotted down names of those he'd seen near Turner: Regent Giannetta, Polly Ann, Anne McGregor, Katrina Tallfeather with two or three friends, Hunter Edwards talking with Bill Brasseth.

He also needed a list of people who left the reception early. Polly Ann escaped at close to 6:00. The shadows she might have seen could have left shortly before or after she did.

He took a sip of coffee. Cold. He walked back into the break room and put the mug in the microwave. As he waited for it to ding, he realized that the first person who broke into Turner's house must have been there for several minutes – long enough to locate the files he – or she – wanted. Those who came later would have stayed only long enough to see that what they sought was gone. The upcoming interviews would be interesting.

Monday, October 1

It took only three hours for matches to be found between the fingerprints from Turner's house and those from the personnel files of the Human Resources Department: Jorge Martin, a work study student named Chad Norris, Hunter Edwards, William Brasseth, others too smudged to identify and – Polly Ann Passarelli.

None of the names were on the lists his officers had collected of guests at the reception. Matt would have to ask if anyone saw them leave.

He took the list out and handed it to Alice. "Please set up interviews with each of these people for a chat sometime in the next couple weeks. I'd like to do them all as soon as possible, but I doubt that Ridgeview will remain crime-free while we investigate this. If anyone refuses, tell them I'll send an officer with a warrant.

"Oh, and before you do that, would you get Hal Bennetolli on the phone?"

Matt picked up the phone in his office. "Hi, Hal. Quick question: right after you heard someone yell 'Call 911,' did anyone come through the kitchen and out the back door?"

Hall asked him to hold on while he asked his people. "Yeah, Matt. Half a dozen people came through, in a hurry to get to the men's room. Not sure who they all were."

"Could your staff identify them from pictures?"

"We can try."

An emergency call came in shortly after lunch: a house had exploded and burned. Two of Matt's men were tracking down two or three people who were renters of record. "The evidence indicates it was a meth lab, chief."

Hal Bennetolli phoned a few minutes after Matt left. Alice told him, "The chief's not in, Mr. Bennetolli. May I take a message?"

"No, there's no rush."

When Matt returned to the precinct, Alice told him Hal Bennetolli had phoned and informed him that she had made an appointment for him to interview Dr. Passarelli on Wednesday.

"What time?"

"She has classes and office hours until 3:00, so I set it up for 3:30."

"Thank you. I hope we can wrap up this meth case by then."

16
Wednesday, October 3

Polly Ann tried to appear calm, but her hands refused to be still. She finally shoved them into her jeans' pockets. She smiled. Not one of her best efforts. "Hi, Matt. I thought I answered all your questions Friday night."

He didn't return her smile, but gestured for her sit in the chair opposite the desk he sat behind. "Could I get you anything? Coffee?" She started to say yes, but feared her hands would betray her nerves. She shook her head.

"What did you do, Polly Ann, before you got to your house Friday night?" She started to speak, but he interrupted. "Is that when your fingerprints got on Dr. Turner's doorknob and outdoor stair rail? We didn't find any elsewhere. Were you in Turner's bedroom?"

Polly Ann slumped. "I think I'd like that coffee now, please."

She drank half the contents, set the cup down, sat up straight, and folded her hands. "I had to stop running; my side hurt. I was across the street from Turner's house, in the shade of the big tree on the boulevard. I saw someone come out of Turner's front door, carrying a case of some kind. I could tell it was heavy; he was listing to one side. As he started down the steps, someone else walked up the sidewalk toward him. The first man swung the case at the other one's head, knocked him down, and walked casually away.

"I stayed behind the tree until he walked halfway down the street, got into a car, and drove away."

Polly Ann stopped. She picked up the coffee cup with both hands, steady now, and drained it.

Matt pushed a box of face tissues across the desk and waited.

Polly Ann pulled out a tissue and began twisting it in her hands. She took a deep breath and let it out on a long sigh. "I watched as the man who'd fallen got up and limped away. I walked up to the door. My knees were shaking so hard I had to hang onto the stair rail. I took hold of the doorknob. But, Matt, I couldn't make myself go inside. I turned away and came home."

Polly Ann dabbed at her eyes with the tattered tissue. "I knew someone had taken all the secrets Turner gloated about. Including mine!" Polly Ann put her head in her hands. Eventually, the sobs stopped, replaced by hiccups and then a deep breath. "I didn't kill him."

"Okay. Do you know who or what did?"

"I guessed it was poison. No one gasps like that, chokes like that over a simple sip of champagne. I don't know who killed him or how."

"Polly Ann, do you know what mead is?"

"It's a honey wine, isn't it?" She stiffened. "Is that what I thought I tasted in the champagne? But it didn't make anyone sick. It was kind of nice. It couldn't have killed anyone."

Matt waited while her thoughts caught up with her words before he told her, "Dr. Turner died of anaphylactic shock. Peanuts cause that for a lot of people. For a rare few, honey is the culprit."

"Someone spiked the champagne? As a joke? Or somehow knowing that it could kill Dr. Turner? Someone who wanted his files." Polly Ann's last words were not a question.

Matt stood up and came around the desk to put a hand on her shoulder. "Apparently, you didn't know about his fatal allergy. I wonder how many people did. I'll have to find out."

He lifted up the phone. "Alice, would you bring us some more coffee? And an ashtray?

Turning to Polly Ann, he asked, "You still smoke, don't you?" She nodded. "Me, too, but not often. This seems like a good time."

They sat smoking and sipping coffee in silence, thinking. "Do you want to talk about your secret? Was Turner blackmailing you?"

"Not really – or at least not yet. He told me several years ago that he knew what I was hiding and that there would come a day when he would ask me to pay for his continuing silence. He has – had – bits of evidence that could endanger someone I care about."

Matt's phone buzzed. He listened for a moment before hanging up. "I have to run, Polly Ann; crime in progress. I don't need to hear the details of your secret, but I want your promise that if someone contacts you demanding your cooperation on something in exchange for keeping quiet, you'll let me know immediately. Watch your back, and let's hope he didn't see you hiding beneath that tree."

Polly Ann promised that she'd let him know, but the fingers of the hand behind her back were crossed. *He still thinks I might be guilty. I hope one of his other suspects looks more so.*

Matt followed her to the outer office and held the door for her. Turning back, he said, "Alice, alert the DA's office and have them tell Marge that I'm on my way. Tomas and Javier have arrested the pair who rented that meth house, and she needs to know what we found at the site and what the suspects may have said to my guys."

17

Thursday, October 4

"Good morning, Alice. Apart from talking to Hunter Edwards, it looks like we have a quiet day. Maybe we can catch up on some of those pending files."

Alice nodded. "Let's hope it stays quiet." She spoke too soon. The phone rang. "It's for you, chief. Sgt. Ortiz sounds agitated."

"What's up, Rafe?" Matt listened while the tale tumbled out. "I'll be right there, and I'll call for more backup." He absently handed the phone back to Alice. "Put Mr. Edwards off until tomorrow if you can. Otherwise, juggle next week's schedule. There's a holdup in progress at the 7Eleven near the highway. Have George and Duncan meet me there."

It turned into a long day, but finally the suspects surrendered peacefully, the clerk finally could get up off the floor, unhurt but stiff and sore, and the other employees emerged from the storeroom.

Friday, October 5

Matt wrapped up the staff meeting and barely had time to dump the remains of his coffee and grab a bottle of water before Alice announced Hunter Edwards' arrival.

Matt hadn't previously met Edwards, although he'd seen him at university functions. Up close, the man's head seemed too large for his body. Perhaps it was the too-full hair, carefully teased on the top and sides, making his small eyes and mouth look pinched and emphasizing the large nose and its broken capillaries. His casual gray slacks, navy blazer, and tasseled loafers seemed designed for a younger man.

Edwards smiled and nodded, but did not reach for a handshake. "Detective Brophy, it's good to see you. What can I do for you?"

"Have a seat Mr. Edwards. Would you like coffee, tea, water?" Edward shook his head, took a chair, and put his hands on his knees. Matt thought he detected a faint tremor.

Matt went straight to the point. "I'm curious as to why your fingerprints were on the file cabinet in Stanley Turner's bedroom."

What faint color there'd been in the man's face drained. Matt imagined the synapses in Edwards' brain sparking madly and wondered if he'd tell the truth.

Edwards cleared his throat, started to say something, cleared his throat again. "Stan had some information about me that would have ruined me. I helped him out with a couple little things in exchange for his silence."

"So you went to his house to remove that information?"

"Yes." Edwards raised his hands, the shaking now obvious. His voice also shook as he said, "But someone was there before me. The file was gone. All his files were gone!"

"He was blackmailing you. Was the price you paid worth it?"

"Look at my hands! I'm a pharmacist. I need steady hands to do my job. In six months, I can retire, but if I do that before my time is up, I forfeit my pension. For now, I have medication that works pretty well most of the time, but the condition is getting worse. If my boss knew, he'd fire me instantly."

Matt felt sorry for the man, but he had to ask, "If the person who has that information about you offers to trade silence for a few favors, I want you to tell me immediately."

"I can't do that until it's safe."

"Until you retire or that file is in your hands?"

"Yes."

"Then I can't help you." Both men stood up and moved to the door. Matt added a final warning. "This person has killed once and may again. Please be very careful."

Hunter Edwards scurried to the safety of his car. Matt watched him go before heading to his office. He was due in court in half an hour.

Matt looked out the window in his office for a moment, watching an industrious squirrel hanging upside down from the bird feeder. At his desk, he quickly wrote down a few thoughts about Hunter Edwards.

A weasel. Successfully blackmailed by Turner and

obvious target for a successor. Could he have known about Turner's allergy? Did he have an opportunity to poison the champagne? He couldn't have used a syringe without spilling some of the contents with the shaky hands that he was careful to show me and tell me about, but he did say he has medication – medication he obviously did not take before our appointment.

Matt spent the afternoon at the courthouse, waiting for the verdict in a messy mugging case. Finally the jury was ready and they all could go home.

18
Homecoming weekend, October 6 & 7

Polly Ann picked up Patty and the Brophy kids and, knowing that parking anywhere near the parade route would be impossible, drove to the precinct. From there, they walked and found a good vantage point to watch the spectacle.

The kids oohed and aahed as the high school and university bands marched, the mounted police unit from Cheyenne trotted, the K-9 teams cruised the crowd ("they're sniffing for dope!"), the regular and volunteer firemen walked in formation, and the decorated wagons and flatbed trailers floated. The Ridgeview PD officers directed traffic, retrieved wandering kids that got too close to the horses or tried to pet the dogs, and passed out popsicles.

Polly Ann and her passengers wandered back to the precinct. As the Brophys got out of the car, Patty said, "Sure you don't want to ride with us to the game?"

"No, thanks. I'll find you in the parking lot. My contribution to the tailgate party will be ready when it feels like being ready, and I don't want to hold you up."

Polly Ann found a parking place two rows from Patty's station wagon. She started to get out of her car when she saw Katrina walking toward a group gathered around a minivan. Halfway there, Regent Edwards stepped out from a red Jaguar convertible to intercept the young woman. Polly Ann was close enough to overhear. "Well, hi there, young lady. Remember me? We met a couple weeks ago. I've heard a lot about you – mostly good, of course." He moved closer to her. "You're not here alone, are you?"

Polly Ann began striding toward them. Before either of them saw her, Katrina's friend Chad came up behind the girl and slung a casual arm over her shoulders. "Hey, kid, you're missing the party." He glanced at the man standing in front of her and then did a double take when he saw the red convertible. He reached out a hand. "Hi, Mr. Edwards. I'm Chad Norris. Your car is a classic, sir. And in beautiful condition. Who does your maintenance?"

Edwards smiled like a proud parent. "I do it myself. I'm very particular, and I know what I'm doing. In my youth, I worked in an auto repair shop. I learned everything I could about all makes of cars, but Jaguars were my favorites.

"You wouldn't believe how thoughtless some people are. Guys would drive in, tell us to fix the problem, and shove the keys in their pockets. I learned how to hotwire anything with an engine. Not for joyriding, you understand. Simply so we could get a car running and start to diagnose the problem."

Chad nodded. "You do good work. Well, enjoy the game. Is your wife with you?"

"I have no wife."

"Oh. I didn't know that. Still the hunter, huh?"

Kat pulled at her friend's arm. "Sorry to tear you away, Chad, but the gang is waiting for us. "Good to see you, Mr. Edwards." Neither of the young people saw the look of rage on the older man's face at the thoughtless comment as they moved away to join their friends. Polly Ann ducked behind the nearest van, not wanting to risk having Edwards see her in Kat's vicinity.

That Sunday afternoon, Polly Ann gathered her requirements for the weekly phone call: Bloody Mary, cigarettes, lighter, ashtray, Kleenex, memo pad, and pen. "Hi, Katrina. It's me. Tell me that Regent Edwards was not hitting on you yesterday."

"Could you believe it? He's old enough to be my father, if I had one, and I'm big enough to drop his skinny butt on the ground with one push. He gives me the creeps."

Polly Ann shook a cigarette from the package and lit it. "Has he ever pulled anything like that before?"

"Yeah, a couple weeks ago. I was waiting in line at the bookstore and all of a sudden he tapped me on the shoulder. He suggested I join him for a Coke to talk about my research, about my background."

"Do you think he's gay?"

STRIKE VOTE

"No. And it's really odd. He's peculiar, but not queer. It's like he's fishing to know more about me, where I come from, where I've lived."

The next day, Polly Ann experienced for herself what Katrina was talking about. She was in the cafeteria, drinking tea and grading papers when Edwards came up to her table and asked if he could join her. He asked a few awkward questions about her classes, naming a couple students and wondering what she thought of them. That led to the question, "How well do you know Katrina Tallfeather?"

Polly Ann hoped that her reply was casual enough and that her body language didn't show how startled she was. "I hardly know her at all. She and 115 other students took a class from me last year."

Polly Ann scrawled a brief note at the bottom of the last page of the last essay, gathered the pile together, and stuffed the collection into her briefcase. "Excuse me, Regent Edwards, but I'm late for a meeting." She managed to walk out in what she hoped was a dignified manner.

That evening, she received an unsettling phone call. A muffled voice said, "You had a little girl with you in Michigan. You came to Colorado in a hurry. If you came alone, where's the body?" The caller had to be in possession of Turner's files.

19
Monday, October 8

Matt's phone buzzed. "Chief, your next appointment is here, but it's two people. Ms. Giannetta and Mr. Martin insisted on coming together."

"That's all right, Alice. I'll deal with it." Matt had frequently encountered the elegant regent at various campus events. Today, instead of one of her habitual power suits and upswept hairdo, she wore an attractive pantsuit and her hair was in a casual pony tail.

Martin was also casually dressed, in a white short-sleeved shirt carefully tucked into pressed, belted jeans. Matt waved the couple toward his office. "Can I get you anything?" They agreed to coffee, which Alice brought as soon as they were seated.

Matt looked at the two, recalling that according to rumor, they loathed each other. Their body language said otherwise. Martin hitched his chair closer to the regent and crossed his left leg over the right, toe pointing toward her. The usually icy regent looked up at him with a soft smile.

Matt waited until both focused their attention on him rather than each other. "Jorge, would you tell me why your fingerprints were found in the bedroom of Stanley Turner's house?"

Regent Giannetta patted Martin's arm, still smiling, "That was careless, my dear. If you'd been on duty, you'd have had your gloves." Matt didn't know her very well, but he had observed her on many occasions, always scowling. The smile took years off her face.

"I sent him," she said, "to find something we didn't want known just yet. Stan occasionally asked me to do something for him, threatening to tell our secret if I didn't comply. I didn't care if he told everyone he knew, so I simply laughed at him."

"But," Martin interrupted, "when I checked, the file drawers were dumped all over the floor, bank statements, owner's manuals, tax documents and stuff spilling out. One drawer was empty and I saw no file folders. Someone else now has that information."

"Which is?" Matt asked.

Glynda Giannetta laughed, a lovely peal of glee. "That we've been happily married for ten years. Our respective positions at the university might make that look like a conflict of interest. I'm stepping down from the board as soon as a new president is in place, and we planned to go public then. But if anyone thinks we'd allow ourselves to be blackmailed over it, they're wrong. The charade has gone on too long already."

Matt had to laugh. These two dropped to the bottom of his suspect list. He couldn't imagine either of them as a killer. "Okay, but if you find out who has your file now, let me know. I have a murderer to catch before he – or she – targets someone else."

Matt heard the pair chatting with Alice and quickly wrote down his conclusions about the couple.

Very good at pulling the wool over everyone's eyes for ten years. But they intend to reveal their secret marriage soon, so unless they have another reason to kill Turner, it's not an issue.

He joined them in the outer office and watched as they headed to the parking lot. Giannetta's arm was linked in Martin's. They were probably happily debating where to go for lunch. He got his brown bag lunch out of the break room fridge and, resigned, settled into an afternoon of paperwork.

Getting out of his car at home, Matt saw Polly Ann watering the mums that glowed in rust and peach clumps across the front of her house. "Hi, neighbor," he called as he walked to his home.

"Hi, Matt. How's the investigation going?"

"Slower than I'd like, but it will get better. I've got a friend of Katrina Tallfeather's coming mid-week. Never met the young man, but I doubt he's my killer."

Polly Ann dropped the hose and hurried around her house to turn off the water. Matt heard her back door slam. "I wonder what that was all about," he muttered.

The bedside phone rang at 3:00 a.m. Charlie and Adam were on the scene of a carjacking. Charlie said, "Chief, I left my car at the scene and am riding with Adam. We're a bit north of the Walmart on 287, following a guy in a stolen minivan. The victim's dog is inside, fortunately safe in a travel crate in the back."

"I'm on my way."

A few minutes later, Charlie was back on the radio. "He's turned east on Carpenter, maybe heading for I-25."

"Okay. I'm coming north on the interstate. I'll take the Carpenter exit and head toward you. Maybe we can box him in. Is there any other traffic?"

"Negative. Maybe if you put your flashers on, he'll pull over. Then we can sneak up beside him."

The ploy worked and soon the carjacker was in handcuffs in Charlie and Adam's patrol car. Matt said, "Charlie, you can drive the minivan; Adam and I will follow you. Where's the vehicle's owner?"

"The manager at that emergency vet clinic a bit north of Walmart convinced her to go inside until they heard from us."

When they arrived at their destination, Matt got out of his car and approached the window of the van. "Charlie, she will recognize you, so we'll both go in and let her know her dog is safe. Then you can retrieve your car."

A tearfully grateful middle-aged woman hugged them both and, after checking that her pet was indeed all right, explained what had happened.

"Rufus had an abscess on his side that I didn't notice under all that hair until it ruptured. I got him into the van and drove here. They drained the abscess and cleaned it up and gave me some meds to use at home. I put him back in his travel crate and walked around to the driver's side. A hand came out of nowhere, grabbed the keys I had in my hand, shoved me to the ground, and drove away. Fortunately, I had my cell phone in my pocket so I called 911 immediately. Your boys were here in no time."

Matt raised an eyebrow and looked at Adam, who said, "We were having coffee at that Starbucks next to Walmart."

"Well, all's well that ends well. Ma'am, would you be willing testify when this comes to trial?" She nodded. "Okay, then. Would you like us to follow you home, make sure you feel safe?"

She grinned. "And make sure I obey the speed limit? Yes, I'd be happy to have an escort."

Once the lady and her dog were delivered safely to their doorstep, Matt asked Adam, "Do you want to go home, or go back to the office and get the paperwork out of the way?"

"Charlie's going to meet us there, and we're officially on duty until 8:00, so let's get the paperwork behind us. If you can stay awake a while longer, chief."

20

Wednesday, October 10

Patty rolled over and turned off the alarm when Matt finally got into bed. She'd slept in fits and starts, waking to an empty bed and praying that the emergency would soon be settled peacefully. Finally, they both could sleep soundly.

When Matt walked into the precinct a few minutes before one o'clock, Alice greeted him with what seemed like relief. "Detective Brophy, you're just in time. Your one o'clock appointment was with a young man, but this woman," she said, pointing to the inhabitant of the chair near the door, "insists you should be talking to her."

"It's okay, Alice." Matt turned to the statuesque young woman, admiring as always the smooth, pale copper complexion, aristocratic features, and long raven-black hair held back from her face by a beaded headband. "Ms. Tallfeather, we haven't met since the LGBT parade. Thank you for coming. Shall we go into my office?"

Katrina took the chair facing the detective and waited.

"Do you have any idea why a friend of yours would have been in Stanley Turner's house shortly after the man died?"

Katrina sat up straight, put her elbows on the desk, and leaned toward Matt. "I sent Chad to get a file from Regent Turner's house, but he didn't find it and doesn't even know what was in it. He certainly didn't kill the man. Neither did I."

"What was in the file that was so important that you had to have it? And why didn't you go yourself?"

She stared at him. "Chief Brophy, I'm not stupid or reckless. A six-foot tall Native American woman skulking around in that neighborhood after dark would have been conspicuous. When I told Chad that I had to find a file in Turner's house, he offered to go."

"You didn't answer my first question. What was in the file?"

Katrina fidgeted, uncomfortable for the first time. "It's not really my story to tell. And I don't believe Dr. Passarelli is ready to tell it. You'll have to ask her."

Matt glared at her. "Was she looking for the same file you wanted?"

Katrina kept silent, refusing to meet his eyes.

"Is there something in that file about you and Polly – Dr Passarelli — that police somewhere would find of interest?"

Finally she looked up, eyes flashing, mouth tight. "Of course not! Dr. Passarelli saved my life and helped me disappear. If that story were to reappear, we'd have to vanish again." Katrina stood up. "And that's all I'm going to say. I'm done here."

She was out the door before Matt could get around his desk. Alice stood behind her desk and asked, "What on earth did you say to that girl? She stalked out of here, totally on the warpath." Alice sat down. Hard. "Sorry, chief, that was politically incorrect."

"I think she was probably pleased that she gave the desired impression. I like that young woman. Next time she comes, offer her something to drink. Speaking of which, is the coffee fresh? I need a short break to collect my thoughts and finish up the reports from last night."

Matt took the coffee into his office and made a few notes about Katrina Tallfeather.

Freely admitted sending a friend to get Turner's file on her. Keenly aware that if she'd gone herself, someone would have noticed. She is striking. Not much upset at the file's disappearance. Bristly at suggestion that she and Polly Ann had something to hide from police. Were they close at one time? Are they now?

Matt turned to a fresh sheet of paper.

Polly Ann says she started to enter Turner's house, but chickened out after seeing a man leave with a heavy briefcase. It's true, we found her fingerprints only on the stair rail and front doorknob. She did not say what she would have tried to find. I suppose she could have taken all the files without leaving prints anywhere else. But why? She is an unlikely blackmailer – more apt to send each file to its proper owner. Could she kill? Anyone could with the right motivation. And poison is a woman's preferred weapon. But I believe she didn't know about Turner's fatal allergy. Find out how well she knows Katrina Tallfeather. Strong reaction when I mentioned her name.

Alice appeared in the doorway. "Mrs. Wilberforce just called – again. She said there were people walking across her roof again last night."

"I'll run over there and talk to her. I know you think she's just a lonely, paranoid old lady, but it never hurts to check.

"Some years ago, there was similar situation in the southern part of the state. One night, the local cops went over once again to have coffee with her. They arrived just in time to catch drug smugglers who for months had been tiptoeing across her roof and neighboring ones to get to their drop off spot. Anyway, I always enjoy a restful few hours with Mrs. Wilberforce. Call me if anything comes up, but if nothing does, I'll go home after I see her."

STRIKE VOTE

21

Thursday, October 11

Stanley Turner's murder wasn't forgotten, but on the Ridge U campus, other matters pushed it to a lower level of interest. Classes were well under way and the regents were in another meeting. William Brasseth was unanimously selected to be the new chairman.

"We need to send memos to the people we picked for the search committee. You may have heard that Wills Gladwin declined to serve."

"Don't tell me," Burt Lincoln growled. "He's going to apply for the presidency."

"We don't know that for sure," Brasseth admonished. "But we should think about a new member. However, our first priority is to get a posting in *The Chronicle*. A copy should be included with the memos to the search committee people."

"Can't we use the one from last time?" Joanie Jameson asked.

Burt shook his grizzled head. "Look what that ad got us. We don't need another Limbach."

Rick Gregory consulted his notes. "I asked all of you to give me your thoughts, and I looked up a few postings for other vacant presidencies. Here's the general outline of most of them. A lot of them post a deadline 'open until filled.' But their posting dates are January or February, so I'd guess they plan not to fill the position before summer. We need someone before that. If we can get an ad posted by the end of this month, how about a deadline of December 1 for applications?"

"Everyone okay with that?" Brasseth asked. After a bit of discussion, all agreed. "What's next, Rick?"

"Personal strengths like leadership, creativity, entrepreneurship, team building. Experience and smarts in academics, budgeting, fundraising, and administration. Then there's a bunch of brags about the institution – its mission, diversity, high powered faculty, and any awards the place has received.

"Some of them wax poetic about the setting. Scenery, access to cultural stuff. They all mention research excellence."

Brasseth had a question. "What about professional qualifications?"

"Some put that first, others at the end. Earned doctorate in an academic area from an accredited university. Responsibility for managing resources – human and fiscal. Supporting the mission of the university. Raising money. Proven ability to work with local, regional, and national corporations, charities, and other educational institutions.

"Finally, most of them explain how to apply: with a letter spelling out how they meet all the qualifications, a vita, and references – three usually. And that's about it."

Rick handed out sheets of paper. "I sent you all a draft of a possible ad that touches on all that, but here are extras if you need one. Have you had a chance to read through it?" Nods all around." "Any suggestions for revision?" No one spoke up. Rick looked at Brasseth as if to say, "Now what?"

The new chairman was noted for making quick decisions. "Send it, Rick. It should be posted by Halloween and anyone seriously interested isn't going to take more than a month to send in his or her stuff."

They all stood up, preparing to leave. Bill Brasseth said, "I'll meet with the search committee as soon as possible and get them to name a chairperson and set up a meeting schedule."

STRIKE VOTE

22
Friday, October 12

Patty Brophy stood by the bank of mailboxes and watched her neighbor stomping toward her, scowling furiously. "Hey, friend, who bit your butt?"

Polly Ann stopped abruptly. If Patty hadn't spoken, Polly Ann would have marched right into her, not looking where she was going. "Oh, hi, Patty. They've done it to me again. I am SO screwed! I should've known this would happen. I was so chuffed about Limburger's resignation, I didn't think ahead. I'm so mad I could spit tacks."

Patty smiled at her friend's nickname for the departed president. "Get your mail and come back to my place. You need to sit down and breathe deeply."

Polly Ann barely noticed the newest additions to the Brophy's front yard landscaping, mums gloriously blooming in shades of rust, apricot, and lemon. She marched into the house, down the hallway, and into the long expanse of dining room and living room. She plunked into a dining room chair.

"Coffee, tea, or . . .?" Patty asked.

"Brandy would be good." Polly Ann didn't wait for her friend to pour the drinks and return to the table. "They've put me on the search committee."

Patty took her time to walk from the kitchen, searching for the right thing to say that wouldn't wind Polly Ann up again. "That's good, isn't it? You're an obvious choice. I'd think you'd be pleased."

Polly Ann tossed back half her drink. She choked and spluttered for a moment. "Pleased? I can see that some people would consider it a good way to kill several pigeons with one golf ball – cover the diversity angle with a woman faculty member who's also union and keep me too busy to create a ruckus.

"But, Patty," she wailed, "everyone else will have flexible schedules. I'll have to fit meetings around my classes and office hours. And what happens with my research?" Polly Ann's voice hit the next octave.

"You know what's really dreadful? Wills Gladwin declined to serve. At first that was good news, but it isn't. His will be one of the first applications for the presidency as soon as the posting appears."

Patty put a hand on her friend's arm and patted it. "No one likes Dr. Gladwin. Who'd vote for him?"

Polly Ann reached up to take a hank of hair in her hands and pulled hard. The resulting tears might have been pain or pure frustration. "Anyone who thinks he can raise money for their pet project."

"But they picked you."

"Yeah. To shut up any faculty dissent."

Patty started to say something else, but Polly Ann finished her brandy and stood up to leave. "I can't talk about it. Thanks for the drink; I needed it."

"My pleasure. See you tomorrow at the block party."

Polly Ann had calmed down by the time she drove south to join Katrina for lunch at an out of the way café.

"Hi, Kat. You beat me. Did you have any trouble finding this place?"

"None at all. The run down 287 is both quick and scenic. I wonder how many people in Ridgeview know about all the neat looking restaurants Berthoud has. And this place is awesome! The gardens out back are lovely even now. Although it's too cool today, I'll bet that in spring and early fall, sitting out on the patio is blissful. The food looks good, too."

"Wait until you try their soup. Have you had time to look at the menu?"

"So many choices. But I think I've decided. The BLT with chicken and guacamole looks dreamy."

"It is." Their server stopped by with glasses of ice water and a plate of lemon wedges. Polly Ann pointed at the menu. "We'll both have the Berthoud BLT. And cups of the broccoli/cheddar soup."

"Good choice. I'll have your orders out right away. Be sure to leave room for dessert: our cream puffs are exquisite."

Polly Ann glanced around the room to ensure that no one was pay-ing attention to them. "So, what's new in your world?"

"Apparently the same as in yours. We're both on the search committee to find a new president. Is that going to be awkward? Or dangerous?"

"I don't think so. Over the next few weeks we'll all form connections, so it will seem normal for the two of us to develop a friendly relationship. Maybe we can even have lunch together in town."

23

Matt Brophy spent the morning dealing with the seemingly never diminishing pile of paperwork. On a whim, he phoned his wife. "Hi, Hon. Could you join me for lunch?"

"Sure. Can we go to the Sidetrack?"

In a mellow mood after enjoying one of the Sidetrack's famous Reuben sandwiches, Matt was ready for his meeting with William Brasseth. The man strode into the precinct, seeming to fill even more space than his solid build and considerable height would suggest. He looked like a bank president: carefully styled silver-gray hair, autocratic face with thrust-out chin, three-piece suit in charcoal with subtle stripes of ivory. Matt felt under dressed in his uniform pants and pale blue shirt, neck open, no tie.

"Come on in, sir. You want coffee or a bottle of water?"

"No thanks." He walked into Matt's office and seated himself. He barely waited for Matt to take his chair behind the desk before speaking. "You want to renegotiate the mortgage on your house? Rates are good right now."

"No, that's not why I asked you to come in. Your fingerprints were found Friday night in Stanley Turner's bedroom. Would you like to tell me why?"

Brasseth appeared to deflate, looking less like a prosperous businessman and more like a guilty suspect. "Well, um, I can explain."

"Please do."

"Stan Turner was a collector. Not of stamps or coins or rare items of one sort or another. He collected dirt, juicy bits of gossip, hints of scandal about everyone he came in contact with. He was a blackmailer, although not the usual kind. He wasn't out for money. He traded his silence on whatever skeletons a person had in the closet for 'a future favor.' But he regularly reminded his victims that he had a hold on them."

The banker put his hands on the desk. "I did nothing illegal, merely supported his application for membership in the Ridgeview Country Club. He was a lousy golfer, but paid his bar bills on time."

"And that was all he asked of you?"

"All so far. There would have been other requests. Probably my support of his candidacy for the Ridge U presidency. I'm wondering if one of the internal candidates for the job now has Stan's file on me."

"Would you let me know if someone contacts you about that? It could help me catch a killer." Matt asked.

"I knew he died suddenly, of course. Nothing I heard or read mentioned the cause. I assumed the usual, heart attack or stroke. So someone murdered the son of a bitch? How?"

"Did you know that Turner was dangerously allergic to honey?"

"I would imagine that everyone knew. Well, not students, but everyone else. Joanie – Joanie Jameson – served mead, a honey wine, at a regents-only party a few years ago and Stan threw a tantrum, hollering that she was trying to kill him. What's that got to do with his death?"

"The champagne at the reception was doctored – with mead," Matt told him.

"I thought it tasted a bit different – rather nice, actually. Well I'll be damned."

"You didn't do it?"

"No. No point now. And I would never have backed him for the presidency." Brasseth leaned back, a wistful smile softening his features. "You know my wife died a few months ago. Her past can no longer hurt her, and it was never an issue with me."

Matt waited a minute. "You want to talk about it?"

"Yeah. You're a friend and our closest friends know the story. Sarah ran away from an abusive home when she was fifteen. It's an old story, never gets any sadder. Piranhas wait at bus stations for runaways, promising to take care of them. She literally ran into me one day as I was walking into the bank. She was skinny as a rake, huge, terrified eyes, skimpy clothes. She grabbed my arm, pleading , 'Please help me; he's gonna kill me.'"

The man closed in on himself, lost in memory. Matt asked if he'd like coffee. He nodded. When Matt returned, Brasseth had shaken off the momentary lapse and looked like himself again. Taking a sip from the mug Matt handed him, he said, "Your predecessor arrested that pimp and many others, closing down a large prostitution ring that operated between Cheyenne and Denver.

"Sarah and I were married a year later. She was twenty, I was forty. Didn't matter to either of us. We had twenty five wonderful years before the stroke that killed her.

Brasseth stood up and reached across the desk to shake Matt's hand. "So whatever lowlife now knows that my wife was a teenage hooker may have done some people a favor by getting rid of Stanley Turner, but if he hopes to pick up where Stan left off, I'll do all I can to help you nail him before he tries to destroy someone else's life. I'm just sorry I couldn't retrieve the stuff about Sarah before he took it."

Matt walked him out before starting back to his desk to finish his interview notes. He watched the bank president walk to his car, head up, chin thrust forward, shoulders squared, determination in every step. Alice looked up from her computer. "Mr. Brasseth's rather full of himself, but underneath the bluster, he's really a nice man, isn't he?"

"Yes, he is. What you see isn't always everything." Matt stopped to get a bottle of water from the break room – he'd had more than enough coffee. He closed his office door and returned to his pad of paper.

William Brasseth. A dark horse. Possibly capable of murder. Knew Turner would react to mead. Apparently, so did a lot of people. If he was honest about no longer caring who hears about his dead wife's past, he wouldn't have a motive. Unless there's something else.

Matt pushed aside the papers. No one really proved innocent, but not obviously guilty, either. He looked at the desk clock. Not quite 4:00. He picked up the phone to call Hal Bennetolli.

"Hi, Matt. I was just about to call you. I showed a few pictures to my people. They identified two or three men. There was one they couldn't find a match for – maybe a student. Jock said Mr. Ferrett, the guy from Human Resources, came through the kitchen area shortly after the

STRIKE VOTE

EMTs arrived, looking like he needed a bathroom in a hurry."

"Regent Edwards, Jorge Martin, and maybe William Brasseth, the bank president – are those the others your people identified?"

"Right. How'd you know?"

Matt laughed. "Sorry, I'm not allowed to discuss police methods. Thanks, Hal. I appreciate your help."

Freddie Ferrett. Interesting. If ever there was a man who looked like a blackmailer's dream, he's it. Matt straightened his desk and put his notes into a drawer before going to the door. "Alice, we need to schedule another appointment. See if you can get Mr. Ferrett, the Human Resources director, in here next week."

"I could see if he's available now."

"No, that might freak him out. Anyway, I've had enough of people trying to avoid telling me anything useful. If I hurry, I can watch part of my son's soccer game. I'll see you Monday. I think we're all due for a weekend off."

24

Matt quickly found his wife in the bleachers at the park. Three minutes later, his son scored the goal that tied the game. Two minutes later, a teammate scored another one and the game was over.

"Dad! Did you see? I scored and then Vinnie scored and we won! Vinnie's dad is taking us for burgers. Is that okay, Mom ? I won't need dinner."

Matt hugged him. "Yes, I saw. You were great." Patty rumpled his hair and agreed that burgers would be fine.

One arm around his wife's shoulders, Matt walked with her to the parking lot. "See you at home?" she asked as she climbed into her station wagon.

"In a few minutes. I need to stop at Polly Ann's." Matt got into his patrol car and led the way home. He parked in front of his house, walked down to Polly Ann's, and rang the doorbell. She didn't look surprised to see him as she invited him inside.

"I won't stay long, Polly Ann, but I have a few questions. Miss Tallfeather phoned you, I assume. How long have you known her?"

Polly Ann straightened up to her full height, all 5'2" of it, barely up to Matt's shoulders. "We met a dozen years ago. Since moving here, it's been essential that no one is aware that we share a bit of history. She thinks it may be time to stop hiding. I don't agree. I've told her that we must keep quiet until Stanley Turner's killer is found. Then we will tell you the story and you can decide if it needs to go public. Meanwhile, she needs protection. Can you do that?"

Matt took a minute to consider. "She's in witness protection?" Polly Ann nodded. "Well, sort of. She was a witness to a crime and she's been in my protection ever since."

"All right," he said, "I will continue to look for a killer and probable blackmailer and will watch over Miss Tallfeather. But I want your promise – and hers – that if either of you feels threatened, you will get hold of me immediately. Promise?"

"Cross my heart and hope to die. No, I don't hope that. I'll trust you to make sure that doesn't happen. If anyone threatens Kat, I will do whatever is necessary."

Matt patted her on the shoulder and started for home. *Has she already done something? I don't think Polly Ann is a killer, but she sure is a mama bear defending her cub where that young woman is concerned.*

Polly Ann closed the door and picked up Simba, who was weaving around her ankles. "Pussy cat, I think my mouth just put me back near the top of Matt's suspect list."

"Dinner's on the table," Patty said as Matt walked in the door. "You don't look very happy. Bad day at the office? Or has Polly Ann been giving you a hard time?"

"Some of each. I started the day with a half dozen suspects. I think I can take one or two off the list, but – damn it, Patty, people keep so much of their lives under wraps that they can do something evil for reasons I never imagined. Motives for murder are few, but each one is incredibly complicated. Fear is a biggie, but trying to figure out what triggers it is nearly impossible. Jealousy, greed, power, love, and hate aren't much easier.

"Sorry, dear. I try not to bring the office home with me, but today was frustrating."

"Sit down and eat. I'll open a bottle of wine. Food and booze usually help quiet the mullygrubs."

25

Monday, October 15

"Chief, you have time for a quick coffee before Mr. Ferrett arrives," Alice told him as Matt entered the precinct, hoping that this day would go better than the previous one.

Minutes later, right on the dot of 9:00, Frederick Ferrett scurried through the door. Matt set down his coffee to shake the man's hand. He'd not seen Ferrett up close before. As he ushered the man into his office, Matt realized – not for the first time – how unkind some names were. Too many people, those who had never encountered a real ferret, imagined a sneaky, weasel-like creature and wrongly assumed a person with that name would also be sneaky and untrustworthy.

Like a four-legged ferret, Freddie had a long, slender body and quick movements. His face was narrow, with bright, soft, inquisitive eyes. His blondish hair would have been sleek if it hadn't been wind-tossed. Freddie was somewhat effeminate, but that didn't detract from his charm. The open, yet nervous look on his face invited confidence – the kind of face that would say, "How can I help you?" and mean it.

"Would you like some coffee?"

"Thank you, no, but water would be nice." Ferrett's voice was a pleasant tenor.

Matt led the way to his office and pointed to what he thought of as the witness chair. He sat behind his desk and looked down at the notepad in front of him. "I believe you were at the reception Friday night, Mr. Ferrett. Is that right?" Ferrett nodded.

"When did you leave?"

Ferrett's eyes darted from one wall to another, never to Matt's face. Finally, they stared at the floor. In a near whisper, he said, "I wasn't feeling well. I left maybe half an hour after I got there."

"That would have been about 6:30?"

"I guess so."

"And you went through the kitchen."

"It was close to the men's room."

"And from there, you went to Stanley Turner's house."

Ferrett bolted to his feet. "No! No, I didn't! I went straight home!"

"You left the reception about 6:30, but didn't reach your house until 7:20, according to your housemate."

Ferrett paced the room, obviously distressed, twisting his hands together and clutching his head. "You talked to Ivan? Where is he? He was gone when I got back from the office yesterday and didn't come home last night. He's gone! Someone's taken him."

Matt waited until the man stopped pacing and sat down, curled over, his head in his hands. "I phoned him yesterday afternoon before my secretary called you to make this appointment. Talk to me. Did you find what you were looking for in Turner's bedroom?" Matt waited to take more notes

Not quite hysterical, Ferrett talked fast. His eyes were closed, as if he was reliving the scene. "I didn't get that far. The front door was open a crack so I started to push it with my shoulder when suddenly it was jerked open from the other side and someone came out carrying a briefcase. He saw me and swung the thing at my head, knocking me to the concrete stoop. And then he was gone."

Ferrett finally looked at Matt. And Matt understood why the man had been chosen for his job. Freddie's eyes were dark brown pools of warm, caring vulnerability. Holding the eye contact, he continued. "I knew he had private information about my family. There was no point to my going inside. I picked myself up and drove to that service station on the corner by my place to clean up before Ivan saw me. My nose was bleeding, my trousers were torn, and my knees were scraped."

Ferrett sobbed the last words: "And now Ivan's gone."

Matt now knew why Ferrett's fingerprints hadn't been found in Turner's house. But he was no further ahead in his search for a killer. Ferrett could be guilty. So could several others. If Ferrett wasn't his man, had he seen who hit him? If not, might his attacker believe he had?

Matt walked around his desk to place a hand on Ferrett's shoulder. "We'll do all in our power to find your friend. Meanwhile, I want you to be very watchful. Don't go anywhere alone, and make a conscious effort to observe your surroundings. Get in touch with me if you notice anything that seems a bit off."

He walked Fred Ferrett to the door, noting that the man straightened his spine, squared his shoulders, and walked toward his car with his head up.

Alice asked, "Is he all right? He seemed dreadfully upset."

"I think he's going to be fine."

STRIKE VOTE

26

Freddie Ferrett drove very carefully, aware that in his present state he was an accident waiting to happen. "Please, please, please let Ivan be there when I get home."

The house had that empty feeling houses get when no one is there. Freddie walked from room to room hoping to find his friend, his lover, his everything, but knowing that the search was futile. The red light on the phone in the den was flashing. Hands shaking, Freddie picked it up and clicked Play to hear the messages. There was only one. A robotic voice said, "I have Ivan. You've talked to the police. Do not do that again or you will never see your friend alive."

A click. Silence. Freddie played the message again. It hadn't changed. How long was he supposed to avoid Chief Brophy? What if he accidently encountered him on campus? He had to do something. He had to find Ivan.

The silent house was giving him the willies. He would go to the office. If he couldn't work, perhaps he could think.

Crossing the street from the parking lot to the student union, his shortcut to his building, he saw Polly Ann Passarelli entering ahead of him. She was one of the few people he trusted. She always treated him like a friend.

"Polly Ann, have you got a minute?" She paused inside the building and turned to look at him.

"Freddie, what on earth is wrong? You're white as a sheet. Can I do anything for you?"

"Let me buy you a coffee."

They went to the faculty lounge where Freddie got two mocha lattes and took them to a corner table. Polly Ann mopped up the spills with napkins she'd picked up on entering the room. Freddie took a sip of his coffee and several deep breaths. He leaned close to Polly, although he spoke so softly she had trouble hearing him.

Freddie told her about his abortive attempt to retrieve material from Stanley Turner's file cabinet. "I didn't see him clearly, but he may not know that. Brophy warned me to watch my back. But Polly Ann, he's got Ivan!"

"Oh, Freddie, I'm so sorry! What can I do to help?"

"He said that if I talked to the cops again, I'd never see Ivan alive. But Brophy has to know. You're friends. You could tell him. Couldn't you? Would you?"

"I can and will. But you and I should not be seen together. I'll leave now. Wait a few minutes, go straight to your office, and stay there."

Polly Ann tried to walk naturally to the ladies' room without looking furtive. She checked to make sure the place was empty before pulling out her cell phone. "Hi, Alice, it's Polly Ann. Is Matt available?"

"He's alone in his office doing paperwork. I'll put you through."

"Polly Ann, did you think of something else?"

Two women entered the powder room, chatting while they primped, still chatting when they left.

"Polly Ann? You there?"

"Sorry, Matt, someone came in. They're gone now. But this will have to be fast. You know Fred Ferrett's housemate, Ivan. He's been kidnapped and Freddie's been warned not to talk to the police. So I'm doing it for him."

"Okay. I'll take it from here. If it's possible, don't be seen talking to him until we find Ivan. And, of course, don't tell anyone else. How's Freddie holding up?"

"Not well, but I think he was feeling a bit better when I agreed to talk to you."

"You don't happen to know Ivan's cell phone number, do you?"

A student came in and shut herself in a stall. Polly Ann said, "I'll call you back in a couple minutes." Another student entered. Polly Ann checked her phone's directory. She vaguely remembered inputting Ivan's number several weeks earlier when he was organizing a surprise dinner for Freddie.

For the moment, the room was clear. She punched in the precinct number and told Alice the information Matt needed. Polly Ann watched enough TV cop shows to know that if Ivan had his cell phone, Matt could discover where the man was being held and perhaps avoid a tragedy. She sent a little prayer heavenward: "I know Freddie's a wuss, but he's not a mean wuss, so please give Ivan back to him."

While Matt waited to hear back from Ahmed and Dana, who were attempting to trace Ivan's phone, he swung by Freddie's house. Freddie opened the door and whisked him inside. "Did anyone see you? He told me not to tell the cops."

"I drove my personal car and no one followed me. I need to be quick. Can you get me a recent picture of Ivan so my folks will know who they're looking for?"

'Sure. Come this way."

Matt had been in the house only once or twice before – a surprise birthday party for Polly Ann the previous year and some other occasion he couldn't remember. However, he had not seen the area beyond the living room and kitchen. Freddie led him down a hallway to the back of the house, where a full wall of windows and a skylighted ceiling revealed an artist's studio. Paintings leaned against two walls and a large easel held a work in progress.

Matt was stunned. "I guess I knew Ivan was a painter, but I had no idea he was famous. I've seen wildlife paintings like these on signs all over the area and in Rocky Mountain National Park. Didn't he also do illustrations for several children's books? That chipmunk looks like a twin to a character in one of my Kate's books."

Freddie's face lit up in the proud smile seen on parents of precocious children. "Yes, Ivan has paintings in several galleries around the country. But you can look at your leisure some other time. Here's a brochure from the Alliance Gallery with a recent picture. Go find him! Then you can come back and stay longer."

27

Tuesday, October 16

Freddie wasn't much of a drinker, but he was gradually working his way to the bottom of a bottle of Jim Beam. The day had crawled by. At least work put his frantic concern about Ivan on hold. He looked with distaste at the still half-full bottle. Pounding on the front door startled him out of his gloom.

He shuffled to the door and looked through the peep hole. He fumbled at the locks in his hurry and flung open the door. Ivan stood there, unshaven, rumpled, red-eyed. To Freddie, his friend had never looked better. Speechless, they embraced and without letting go, entered the house.

Ivan told his story in fits and starts while Freddie could only repeat, "Oh, my god! How awful! My dear, did they hurt you?"

Ivan never saw his abductor. He'd opened the door to a man in a balaclava that covered his entire head and face. He'd tried to close the door, but a smelly cloth smashed into his face and that was the last he knew until waking up in a seedy motel room.

"Freddie, the toilet and sink were stained with rust and who knows what else, the bedding smelled of mold, the wallpaper was peeling off in spots, and the ceiling was patterned in water stains. I couldn't sleep on that bed. I pulled the spread off of it and laid it on the floor. Not that I could sleep. I kept hearing skitter noises in the walls. I guess I dozed off for a while."

Ivan continued to tell what details he could remember. The masked man had returned when the outside dark turned to a dim light filtering through the draped window. He brought coffee and two plain donuts. Ivan asked why he'd been kidnapped, how long they planned to keep him here, where he was. His captor left without answering.

Hours passed. The room had no TV, no radio, no stationary, nothing to write with, only a Gideon Bible whose blank pages were covered with phone numbers, women's names, and filthy comments.

"When I heard a key turning in the lock on the door, I thought he'd come back. Freddie, I've never in my life been so happy to see cops! They tracked my cell phone to the motel."

Freddie frowned. "If you had your cell phone, why didn't you simply call me?"

Ivan scratched his head and rubbed his stubbly chin. "They took it away from me." He thought for a minute, trying to remember. "Oh, yes! You know Matt Brophy, the detective? Well, he said they tracked it to a dumpster out in the parking lot here. Then they talked to the desk clerk."

Ivan spotted the bottle and the nearly full glass on the coffee table. "Freddie, since when do you drink whiskey?"

"Since you disappeared and someone phoned me to say they'd kill you if I talked to the police. Would you like a glass?"

They finished the bottle and, exhausted from a traumatic day, went to bed.

The next morning Freddie waited until he got to his office before phoning Polly Ann. The house was filled with cops looking for bugs and phone taps and evidence that might lead to Ivan's kidnappers.

"Polly Ann Passarelli, I can't thank you enough for what you did. Ivan is home safe and sound, thanks to you."

"And to the Ridgeview police. You're very welcome, Freddie. I talked to Matt this morning. Until this whole mess is cleaned up – Turner's murder, the blackmailing, and Ivan's kidnapping, we are not to talk about this with anyone. You didn't tell anyone except me that Ivan was missing, did you?"

"No."

"Well, don't. Since we're both on the search committee, it would look odd if we stopped talking to each other. We simply will be careful not to talk about blackmailing and kidnapping."

28
Wednesday, October 17

Polly Ann's campus mail included an envelope from the Ridge University Board of Regents. The enclosed letter was on board stationery. William Brasseth's name, with his new title of chairman, headed the list of members. *I wonder,* Patty Ann thought, *what they did with all the old stationery? Probably using it for scratch paper. If they're too cheap to put a stamp on this and send it through the postal service, they're too cheap to buy notepads.*

The letter explained that the attachment was the text of the advertisement in *The Chronicle of Higher Education* and instructed her to read it carefully. It also informed her that she was summoned to an introductory meeting of the search committee the next day. *Obviously, he didn't bother to check my schedule. I'll have to reschedule an office hour, but at least I don't have a class that day.*

Thursday, October 18

Regent Brasseth took attendance at the first meeting of the presidential search committee. Polly Ann muttered to herself, not so quietly that Jorge Martin, sitting next to her, couldn't hear. "Taking attendance? Really? We are no longer in grade school, Toto." Martin stifled a smile.

"As you know," Brasseth announced, "I'm a very busy man, so if you quickly choose a chairman – or woman, of course – I will leave you to your deliberations. When it's ready, send me a copy of your meeting schedule between now and Christmas. Once a week should be sufficient. Any nominations?"

Jorge Martin spoke up. "I nominate Dr. Passarelli."

Katrina Tallfeather seconded. Hearing no other names, Brasseth asked for a show of hands. Polly Ann glared at her colleagues and fisted her hands in her lap.

"Congratulations, Ms. – er, Dr. Passarelli. I hereby turn the meeting over to you. Good luck." Polly Ann wasn't sure if the wish was for the whole committee or just her.

"Thank you, Mr. Brasseth, for taking time out of your busy day to get us started," she said. He left the room, showing no sign that he caught the sarcasm.

Polly Ann stood up and looked around at her fellow committee members. "He assumed you all know each other. In case that is not so, allow me. I'm Polly Ann Passarelli from the English Department and president of AAUP, the faculty union. Sitting on my right is Jorge Martin, chief of the campus police and president of their union. Next to him is Katrina Tallfeather, grad student in the sociology department and chair of the campus LGBT organization. Most of you know Fred Ferrett, Director of Human Resources. And next to him is Harold Profit, Dean of the College of Business.

"You've all read the ad in the *Chronicle of Higher Education*. Any suggestions for revision?" Head shakes all around. "Okay. I see no reason for us to meet every week until we have some applications to talk about. I'll let you know when Mr. Brasseth sends me some.

"As for day and time of meetings, I have classes and office hours on Monday, Wednesday and Friday and an evening class on Wednesday. For me, Tuesday afternoons at 1:00 would be best. Would that be a problem for anyone?" Polly Ann expected at least two people to have objections. Polly Ann invariably expected the worst. It was in her DNA. To her surprise, Martin said Tuesdays would suit him and the others all nodded their agreement.

She smiled and clapped her hands. "Wonderful! I hope we can agree on everything else we talk about. Halloween's coming up. Get ready to scare little kids."

Polly Ann hurried to the parking lot, relieved that the first meeting had gone better than she expected.

Simba greeted her return home with muted chainsaw purrs and wound himself around her ankles until she picked him up. "So far so good, Simba, but it won't last. Each of those people is going to have a favorite candidate that someone else finds abhorrent. I foresee long, tedious, abrasive discussions. Let's go check the liquor cabinet – the supply may be getting low."

Judie Freeland

29

Wednesday, October 31

Freddie never outgrew his distaste for Halloween. The other kids in his childhood, in their fancy, store-bought costumes, had made fun of his ghost costume, nothing more than an old bed sheet with holes cut out for his eyes. One year, they pushed him into a mud puddle, spilling his candy and sending him home in tears.

Ivan, however, loved dressing up and insisted that Freddie join him. Last year, their Raggedy Ann and Andy attire delighted the little kids and their parents. This year, Ivan would be Luke Skywalker and Freddie, Darth Vader. Their light sabers lit up like the real thing. Ivan insisted that they practice some fencing moves.

By the time they greeted the third group of kids at the door, even Freddie was enjoying himself. As the giggling children left, a sheeted figure approached, waving its shrouded arms, and speaking in a whispery spectral voice. "I am Death. I've come for you." Instinctively, Freddie waved his saber, which flared into a wonderful, ominous blue light. Beside him, Ivan thrust his pale green saber at the intruder and snarled, "Bug off!"

The apparition backed away, missed the step, and fell, exposing gray slacks, Argyle socks, and tennis shoes. The man managed to right himself, clutched the sheet around his waist, and staggered off down the sidewalk.

Freddie started to follow him, but Ivan held him back. "He'll be gone before you can catch him, and there are more kids coming. We don't want to scare them. I'll phone Detective Brophy."

Polly Ann had mixed feelings about Halloween. People had always been appreciative of the costumes Polly Ann's mother created – Snow White, Rapunzel, a Barbie doll – but something always went haywire. Apples outnumbered candy bars for Snow White. (Her mother made an apple pie and a lot of apple sauce.) One of the neighbor boys stepped on the Rapunzel wig, pulling it off her head and wrapping it around a light pole. One of the grapefruit halves taped to her chest fell out and the corset her mother dug out of an old trunk to create Barbie's tiny waist was so tight she couldn't breathe, never mind bend over to retrieve the grapefruit. And it was always dark by 6:00.

As an adult whose mother had stopped making costumes, Polly Ann settled for the same costume every year. Her black academic robe, required for commencements and such, a pointy black hat she'd picked up at a yard sale, a huge warty nose, and judiciously applied makeup turned her into a believable witch. The ratty broom from the garage completed her costume.

Simba was the wrong color for a witch's familiar, and he didn't much care for the fuss of Halloween, so he retired for a nap in the bedroom.

Polly Ann had filled the basket of treats a second time when the doorbell rang yet again. Instead of cute little people dressed as Minions, princesses, and trolls, this was a big man wrapped in a sheet. Polly Ann clutched her broom and cackled, "Aren't you a little old for this?"

The would-be ghost whispered, "I am here for you. I am Death."

Polly Ann shrieked and, without thinking, jabbed at the creature's midsection.

He took one step toward her before a miniature cyclone of fur flew down the hall, snarling with every hair upright, tail like a bottle brush. The man apparently was not about to challenge an attack cat. He turned and soon disappeared into the dark night.

Polly Ann picked up her quivering cat. "Simba, that was so brave! You scared him witless. Clever boy. Let's go to the kitchen and find you a treat."

Polly Ann reached for her phone, mixed a Stinger, took both to a side table, and sank into her recliner. Simba soon jumped into her lap. Polly Ann paused to take a sip and light a cigarette before punching in her neighbor's phone number.

Matt listened without interruption as she described her evening adventure. When she finished, he told her that Fred and Ivan had the same visitor. Matt laughed as he described how the Star Wars characters scared off the ghost. "They weren't able to identify their caller, apart from what he was wearing. I guess you couldn't, either. A sheet does make a pretty good disguise. Could you recognize the voice?"

"No. He had a growly kind of whisper, wasn't using a normal voice. He was obviously trying to sound spooky, and it worked. I was scared even more when he started moving toward me, through the open door. That's when Simba proved what a really big cat he is."

An hour later, Polly Ann's phone rang. "Where's that little girl now, Dr. Passarelli?" She'd heard that voice not long ago. She started to ask the speaker to identify himself, but he'd hung up. Damn! This was beginning to really piss her off. The good news was that obviously he had no idea that the little girl was right under his nose, no longer little, no longer helpless. She immediately called Matt again to tell him that she'd received a call that she considered a threat.

STRIKE VOTE

30

Saturday and Sunday, November 17-18

The third weekend in November brought the first snow storm of the season, and it was a doozy. Polly Ann gave up on her new snow blower after ten minutes, realizing that it was not able to cope with a foot of heavy, wet snow. She grumbled all the way into the garage to get the trusty snow shovel, but it was a half-hearted grumble. She actually enjoyed shoveling snow.

She finished the first path down the driveway and leaned on the shovel to catch her breath. Matt, Patty, and their kids were making a snowman family. Their driveway and front sidewalk were already cleared.

Patty waved. "You want some help and then some hot chocolate?"

Polly Ann figured it would take her another hour or more to finish clearing her area. "Sure! I'll bring brownies."

Once the driveways and walkways were clear, coats hung to dry on the hall clothes tree, boots and mittens parked on radiators, the adults sat around the Brophy's kitchen table, nursing their mugs of hot chocolate.

"Are you going to Wisconsin for Thanksgiving?" Polly Ann knew that Patty's parents usually had their entire family come for at least one of the holidays.

"No, we're staying here this year. We'll fly there for Christmas – more time to visit. So, you'll join us next week, I hope? And provide the stuffing, rolls, and pumpkin pie?"

"Of course. I have extra folding chairs, too, if you need them. Who else is coming?"

Polly Ann spent the weekend making a huge batch of her grandma's famous stuffing and stashing it in the freezer. Then the pies. *Let's see. At least 24 hungry people and maybe a couple extra waifs, so four pies. No, better do five. All pumpkin? Maybe one apple. And I have grandma's mince pie recipe. If no one else likes mince, that's more for me.* While the pies were in the oven, she used her trusty bread machine to prepare the dough for two dozen dinner rolls.

She'd just taken the pies out and put the roll pans in the oven to rise when the phone rang. "Polly Ann? It's Freddie. You really busy?"

"Not at the moment. I'm waiting for my Thanksgiving rolls to rise before I bake them. I can talk for a few minutes."

"I'd rather not do this on the phone."

"Oh. Well, can you get through the storm and come over here?" The thought of having to deal with Freddie's nerves put a damper on her spirits, but the poor guy needed her.

As soon as Freddie calmed down a bit, helped by a generous glass of wine, she asked, "You haven't heard anything from a new blackmailer, have you?"

"No, but I'm afraid it's only a matter of time. Stan would have forced me to vote for him. Now he's gone and someone else has his files. That someone took Ivan to remind me where I'm most vulnerable. I'm scared that I'll be forced to support another unsuitable candidate. There's sure to be a bunch of new applications right after the holiday. What am I going to do?"

"Freddie, all I can say is vote your conscience and watch your back. Not to change the subject, but what plans do you and Ivan have for Thanksgiving?"

At that, Freddie brightened up. "His mom has invited us to join the family for dinner. Now that her husband is gone, she feels free to welcome Ivan – and me – back home."

"That's wonderful. I'll see you on the 27th. Between now and then, you can enjoy the visit and forget all the bad stuff"

STRIKE VOTE

31

Friday, November 23

Polly Ann checked her campus mailbox morning and evening on the days she was in her office. She pulled the fat envelope from the Board of Regents out of her box, muttering, *Too cheap to use regular mail. Don't they know that anything in an office box can be retrieved by anyone? If they want search committee business to be confidential, this stuff should come to my home via registered mail.*

She deposited the envelope in her briefcase and waited until she got home to open it. The note on top of the pile said, "Please make copies of these applications for the other committee members."

She re-read the note, debating whether to scream or laugh. *Those turds! They have a budget any department would kill for and they stick me with the expense of making copies! I wonder what they'd do if I presented them with a bill for copying costs, coffee, and donuts when this is all over. I'll do it! They can only refuse and if I tell the student newspaper editor, they'll look like pikers.*

Polly Ann made the copies at the Kinko's in the student union, carefully putting the receipt into her briefcase. She wrote cover notes, paper-clipping them to the four packets of applications, asking the committee to meet in the faculty's private dining room the following Tuesday. Then she phoned the facility and asked that coffee and cookies be available.

Tuesday, November 27

"I trust you've all had time to read the five applications we've received so far. Let's go around the table and decide which are viable. Mr. Martin?"

"Call me Jorge, please." With a smile, he looked at his notes. "I like the CEO of the rehab center for problem teens. He has a Ph.D. in psychology from NYU, he was promoted to full professor before being selected as a dean. Two years later, he moved to the center. He's raised a lot of money for its programs.

"I'm not so sure about the two academic vice presidents, and the admiral may think that running a ship is like running a university, but I don't."

Polly Ann jotted down a few notes before calling on Katrina. "Whom do you like?"

"That rehab guy sounds good. And the woman vice president from Montana meets the qualifications. So does that other one, but there's something fishy about his application."

Freddie Ferrett interrupted. "I say we wait until the deadline to make any decisions about who's in and who's out. There's got to be someone better than this lot."

Harold Profit cleared his throat, stood up, and folded his hands across his ample abdomen. "You're all ignoring the obvious best candidate, the DBA from Texas. As head of the Accounting Department, he knows how to create and supervise budgets, and his fund-raising record is stellar."

"Has he ever taught a class?" Jorge asked.

"No, but he's run numerous seminars and workshops. Madame Chairman, what do you think?"

Polly Ann asked, "Did any of you phone the references these people provided?" Only Jorge nodded. Polly Ann continued. "I talked to the retired dean from Montana and two department heads who've been there for years. This woman vice president froze the faculty positions of four retired faculty and hired part-timers. Some of you may approve of that particular economy, but our union contract doesn't.

"I know the other vice president by reputation. He's solid. And stodgy. Very old school, which is not, I think, what Ridge U needs. The head of that rehab center sounds interesting. I'd like to know more. I'd suggest putting him at the top of the list for now, and wait to see if more people apply."

Polly Ann stood up. "By next week we will have all the applications. Until then, have a happy and safe holiday. Do I hear a motion to adjourn?"

It was the usually silent Harold Profit who said, "I so move."

A chorus of voices said, "Second."

32

Tuesday, December 4

Thanksgiving food and fellowship seemed a distant memory. Polly Ann stopped by her office mailbox on her way out of the building. A fat envelope from the Board of Regents promised last-minute applications. She puzzled over a ratty-looking white envelope that appeared to have been dropped in a mud puddle. No return address, no stamp, her name and campus address in block letters. She ripped it open and unfolded the rumpled sheet of paper inside. Also in block letters, the message read, "VOTE FOR OUR FOUNDATION VICE PRESIDENT OR YOU'LL REGRET IT."

A momentary shiver of fear was quickly replaced by anger. "We'll just see about that," she growled, causing a passing graduate student to turn around and walk away.

She kicked the closed elevator door and stalked off to the stairwell, down the six flights of stairs, out the doors, and all the way to the Union. She stopped inside the main door, bending over to touch her elbow to her knee to relieve the stitch in her side. Jorge Martin came up behind her. "Are you all right, Polly Ann?"

"No, I'm not. I'm furious. Let's get to that meeting."

Jorge held the door for her, perhaps, she thought, afraid that she would simply tear it off its hinges.

Waving the offending message in her hand as she looked around at her committee and reading it aloud, she asked, "Did all of you receive one of these and are they identical to mine?" When Katrina and Jorge nodded, she said, "That's good. It suggests that the writer is not specifically targeting one or two of us. I'd guess that he – or she – has no juicy secret knowledge about any of us. It's an empty threat."

Freddie dropped his head. Dr. Profit observed that if anyone was targeted, it was Wills Gladwin. "I've known Wills for years. He wouldn't pull a dumb stunt like this. Sounds to me like someone is trying to hurt his chances, if, indeed, he has sent an application."

Polly Ann picked up the other envelope. "I think he may have. Let's see what's in here." She ripped it open, tearing a corner of the envelope in her haste. She pulled out several fat files. "Here's an application from our academic vice president, Dr. Angelocci, and one from Dr. Gladwin." She skimmed the first page of each of the others. "We also have two deans, a bank president, and three department heads.

"The board evidently took my hint that they should pay for copies. They've sent enough for all of us." She passed around the extra files. "We'll need time to evaluate these, so let's plan to meet next week. I'd like each of you to rank your top five so we'll have something to talk about.

"Now, has either of you who got the warning message called the police?" Jorge nodded; Katrina shook her head. "Okay, Mr. Ferrett and Dr. Profit, please check your mail and let me know if you also got it. I'm assuming you did. I will phone Detective Brophy. This meeting is adjourned."

On his way out, Freddie Ferrett asked, "Polly Ann, do you think Dr. Gladwin sent those notes?"

"I have no idea. And I'll leave that question up to Matt Brophy."

"Well, if Gladwin didn't, who else could it be?"

"Almost anyone, Freddie. I know you're scared. Keep your eyes open; don't go anywhere alone; and keep your doors locked. Tell Ivan to do the same. And keep those light sabers handy."

Katrina waited until she and Polly Ann were alone. "You really believe what you said?"

"Pretty much. He may think he's got something on us, but he's not sure. I wish I knew what was in Turner's files."

As Polly Ann turned to drive into her garage, she saw her neighbor walking from the mailboxes, skimming through the collection of catalogs, flyers, and perhaps a piece of real mail. She stopped her car and got out. "Hey, Matt, got a minute?"

Matt looked up and continued walking past his house toward her. "Sure, Polly Ann, what's up?"

She fished inside her briefcase for the Ziplock bag she'd put the nasty note in and handed it to him. "Each of the members of the search committee got one of these. My fingerprints will be on it, and the department secretary's will be on the envelope, but I bagged it as soon as I saw what it was." *And if I'm still on Matt's suspect list, he might decide I sent the notes myself.*

"Thank you for that," he said. "What's the note say?"

She told him and added, "We got more applications today, both from Ridge U people."

"Wills Gladwin being one of them?" She nodded. "Well, Polly Ann, either he's not very bright or he's crafty enough to realize we'd assume he's not that dumb and conclude he's being set up. And maybe he is. I think all of your committee members are safe for now. Will you let me know when you are close to making a recommendation to the regents?"

"Sure." Polly Ann turned away to the safety of her home. She needed a warm body to hold and Simba was waiting. Normally the cat didn't like to be held tight for more than a few seconds, but this time he seemed to understand that she needed solace.

She carried him into the kitchen, filled his dinner dish with kitty kibble, poured herself a stinger, and moved to the living room. She eased her taut body into her recliner and waited for Simba to finish his dinner and join her.

He soon jumped into her lap, turned around twice, lay down, and licked a paw before using it to clean his whiskers. Stroking his soft fur, Polly Ann felt her tension ease.

"Dammit, Simba, this is always my favorite time of year. And now it's spoiled. Turner died, horribly, and Matt thinks I could have done it. The search committee will go through the motions, but a couple of them will push for Gladwin because they're scared. And the regents like him – or some of them do. But he'd be a dreadful president. All he thinks about is money. He hates the faculty because they are expensive. He loathes scholarship students, preferring the offspring of rich parents who pay full tuition and often donate to the foundation."

She finished her drink and started to get up. Simba jumped off her lap and she headed for the kitchen. She wasn't in the mood for cooking, so she pulled a container of lasagna out of the freezer and put it in the microwave. A salad and glass of wine completed the meal.

Simba started for the dining room and looked over his shoulder when he realized she wasn't following. "Just a minute, kitten, I have to get my stuff."

Polly Ann ate quickly, pushed her plate aside, and emptied the contents of her briefcase onto the table. Her notes for the rest of the week's classes were finished and, for once, she had no student papers or tests to grade. She pulled out a yellow pad and a couple pens and looked with dismay at the pile of applications.

She made a list of all the specifications in the *Chronicle* ad down one side and, across the top, wrote the names of the three candidates she'd already tentatively approved plus the two new ones. Her ranking system was simple: stellar to mediocre.

She read each application with great care. When she finished, two hours later, she added up the totals for each candidate. "Time for coffee, a cigarette, a shower, and bed, pussy cat."

Simba raised his head for a moment, but stayed on his cat bed next to her chair until she headed toward the bedroom a half hour later.

33

Thursday, December 6

Matt Brophy studied the man sitting across the desk. Carefully styled hair made to look casual, manicured hands with one bandaided finger – probably from a recent visit to his racquetball court – tailored navy sports jacket over a pale blue shirt, no tie, tan slacks. Matt hadn't noticed as the Ridge University Foundation director walked in, but he'd bet the socks were navy and the shoes had tassels. Matt knew Wills Gladwin was in his late 50s, but he obviously worked hard at looking a decade or two younger.

Matt slid a copy of the note across the desk. "Dr. Gladwin, you can tell me if you sent this or had someone do it for you."

Without touching it, Gladwin read the note before raising his head with a look of surprise and anger that might have been real. "I did not. Who received it?"

"The members of the university search committee. I assume you are a candidate for the presidency?"

"I am, but only the committee and the chair of the Board of Regents are supposed to know that. Who told you?"

"No one. As I said, I assumed. If you aren't responsible, who might be?"

Gladwin didn't bother to tamp down his anger. "Either some idiot who thinks something like this would actually help me or, more likely, someone who really dislikes me." He stood up. "Is that all? I have an appointment in half an hour."

"Just one more question. Did you go to Stanley Turner's home the night he died?"

To Matt's surprise, Gladwin laughed and sat down again. "No, but campus scuttlebutt suggests that a parade of folks did, looking for the dirt Stan had on them."

Matt shook his head. Nothing like a small university town for rumors running rampant. He wondered who'd let that cat out of the bag.

"Did he have dirt on you?"

Gladwin was still smiling. "He thought he had evidence that someone had embezzled several thousand dollars from the foundation several years ago. He knew that an envelope in possession of the bank manager at the First Ridgeview Bank was missing. It contained a check from the foundation to the bank. It was never recovered. Stan leapt to the conclusion that there was hanky panky between my foundation and Bill Brasseth's bank."

"What happened to the bank manager?"

"She was killed in an auto accident on her way back to the bank from a lunch outing with one of my people. That's why she had the check. We saved the cost of a stamp. It cost her her life. I still think to myself, 'What if. . .?' "

"I'll need her name." Matt passed over a pen and notepad. "And before you ask, yes, I'll keep the matter confidential. I simply need confirmation." The two men stood up and shook hands. Matt walked the director out and watched as he strolled to his car. He glanced at the name on the scrap of paper Gladwin had given him.

Half aloud, he muttered, "I wonder how accidental that accident was?"

"You talking to me, boss" Alice asked.

"Nope, just myself. There are too many possible suspects in this case. It keeps getting more and more complicated, and I get more and more paranoid."

34

Tuesday, December 11

Polly Ann looked around the table at her fellow committee members and smiled. They all seemed eager to share their conclusions about the applicants. All, that is, except Freddie. His eyes darted around, dropping to his hands, clenched on the pile of papers in front of him, when he saw her looking at him.

Polly Ann decided the kindest thing would be to ignore his nerves. "Okay, let's get to work. Let's go around the table so each of you can discuss your rankings and the reasons for them. I'll take notes." Turning to her right, she said, "Jorge, would you start?"

The campus police chief stood up, rubbing his hands together. "I really like that rehab center guy. He's got it all: academic credentials, teaching experience, management, fund raising, and what I'd call vision. I'd put our Dr. Angelocci as a close second — he doesn't have much fund-raising experience, otherwise he'd top my list. Then that dean from Wyoming. She's solid, but she's been in administration for only a year. Dr. Gladwin sounds okay on paper, but his one semester as a part time lecturer in accounting isn't very impressive; student evaluations were abysmal. I'm not really sold on that other academic vice president. Apart from arrogance, he's a lightweight in all areas."

Katrina Tallfeather was next. She looked down at her notes, cleared her throat, and declared her choices, sounding a bit defensive. "My top pick is Cecelia Cantrell, the Wyoming dean. She's young, full of ideas, and a real mover and shaker. Dr. Angelocci would be my second choice. My only reservation about him is that he's never worked anyplace else but Ridge U. Started here as an assistant prof and moved up the ladder quickly, but most department heads and deans who aim higher go elsewhere. My third choice is the rehabilitation CEO. He sounds like a terrific counselor, but not much of a team player. Any one of those three would be okay. I don't care for the others."

"Freddie?" When Polly Ann called on him, he bolted to his feet. In a too loud voice, he insisted, "It's got to be Gladwin," and abruptly sat down, looking at no one.

Harold Profit stared at him, started to say something, but – catching Polly Ann's head shake – picked up the stack of applications. He waited a moment. "I support the same people you all do. Each of them is strong in all but one area: Angelocci has little experience with fund raising; Cantrell is too young to have had a whole lot of experience at anything; as Ms. Tallfeather observed; Cohen seems too fond of running the whole show single-handed; Gladwin is okay, in my book."

Polly Ann passed around copies of the grid she'd made that showed her rankings of the candidates. "As you can see, my assessments agree with yours. I guess we're ready to forward these four names to the regents and wait until we get the interview schedule from them. Now we can get on with final exams, Christmas parties, and the holiday break. We'll meet again next year!"

Polly Ann had served on numerous search committees, for faculty members, department heads, deans, and even one vice president. All had been long drawn out, vituperative exercises in how ill-behaved grown men and women can be. She was stunned by how easy this had been. She beamed at them all before noting that Freddie still looked miserable.

"Freddie, would you walk out with me?" She dawdled enough getting her coat on and putting the briefcase contents back where they came from to give the others time to leave.

"Freddie, obviously something is very wrong. I know you intensely dislike Dr. Gladwin and feel that he would not be a good choice to run the university. So what's going on?"

Freddie's eyes filled with tears. "Someone phoned me. I don't know if it was Gladwin or someone else, but whoever it was has Stanley Turner's files and told me the 'dirt' he had on Ivan would be released to the news media if I didn't make sure Gladwin got the nod from our committee."

"What could anyone possibly know about Ivan except that he's a respected artist, not just here, but nationwide?"

"His father died in a Cuban prison. Turner added two and two and came up with seven. He assumed both Ivan and his father were terrorists. They weren't. Ivan's dad made the mistake of protesting against Castro in public. Ivan is a naturalized citizen, but if that rumor about his being a terrorist were made public, it would take forever to prove it false. I have to protect him."

Polly Ann was flabbergasted. She couldn't imagine that Ivan's status could be threatened, but she didn't trust the government to agree with her. She had to pacify Freddie somehow.

"Freddie, nothing is going to happen until we've interviewed all the candidates. You'll just have to vote your conscience as will all the rest of us. But remember, Matt Brophy is still determined to identify Turner's killer and the blackmailer. The regents won't get our recommendations until January. Have faith in the Ridgeview police. Ivan will be safe."

"If you say so."

"I do say so. You and Ivan will have a wonderful Christmas. Don't let this spoil it."

Freddie straightened his shoulders and managed a shaky smile. "You're right. I think I can stop stewing about this for at least a couple weeks." He took Polly Ann's face in his hands and kissed her gently on the forehead. "I don't normally kiss girls, but you're special. Merry Christmas."

35

Saturday, December 15

Dozens of rows of chairs in the auditorium were removed following the mid-year commencement ceremony. Polly Ann and Anne McGregor stood near one of the numerous groups of recent graduates and their parents. However, they had to leave the area before disgracing themselves by bursting into laughter. The source of mirth? A comment to a cap and gowned young man from his proud papa. "Son, you done good."

"Anne, please tell me that boy isn't one of our English majors."

"Thank the powers that be, no. Check the tassel color. He's an engineer."

Christmas break, December 21, 2013 - January 7, 2014

After the flurry of finals, term papers, and almost too many Christmas parties, Ridge U was ready for the two-week break. Anne McGregor, Polly Ann's department head and long-time friend, invited Polly Ann to join her and her husband plus a few others for the Christmas feast. Polly Ann offered to bring sherry trifle, a wonderfully boozy concoction handed down from her teetotaler grandmother.

Snow was still drifting from the sky, adding to the three or four inches already covering the streets, walkways, and yards. A blanket of white bedecked the trees and shrubs. Polly Ann decided that shoveling now would be pointless.

As she started to leave, Simba raised his blue eyes to her face and patted her leg with a soft paw, clearly reminding her that he expected her to return with a VIP bag for him – turkey, of course.

Four hours later, after marvelous food and conversation eased along by eggnog and wine, Polly drove into her garage. The snow had stopped, so she could work off some of the excess calories by shoveling. Simba greeted her at the kitchen door, but not with a purring welcome: he was agitated. He turned to walk away, looking over his shoulder to make sure she was following. She stopped only to slip off her boots and set the bag of goodies on the kitchen counter.

Simba led her to the back door and meowed. She couldn't see anything through the pane of glass in the top half of the door, so she pulled the door open, giving her a view through the storm door of the back porch and patio. Her heart stuttered and she grasped the doorknob to steady herself. Footprints, large ones, showed that someone had come from around the corner of the house up onto the porch and stood there, probably peering through into the house before going back the way he had come. Polly Ann assumed it was a man – the footprints were huge.

She shut the door. "Let's take a look at the front walkway, Simba." The cat's agitation had lessened, but he seemed eager to help her check everything before enjoying his Christmas dinner.

The front porch revealed more footprints. Polly Ann started to step out, but stopped abruptly, afraid to disturb the evidence, afraid the prowler might be lurking in the shrubbery. She saw tracks leading up from the street to the porch, back down, and to the corner of the house. Another set cut across the yard back to the street.

"I may be paranoid," she muttered to herself, "but this time locking all the windows and doors may have avoided a break-in. I wish Matt and Patty were home. I'm scared. I don't want to be alone. I'll phone the precinct. Someone will come." She explained the problem to Alice, who assured her that help was on its way. "I'm sending Eric and Ahmed – you know them, don't you?"

Polly Ann watched through the peephole in the front door. *Thank goodness I didn't rush to clear the walkway for them. They would not have been pleased if I'd obliterated the evidence. Maybe I am learning to think before I act.*

The two Ridgeview PD officers arrived a few short minutes later. They parked two houses down where undisturbed snow lay in the street and on the walkways. They carefully skirted the footprints leading to her front door. She opened the door. "Thanks for coming so quickly. Do you want to come in?"

"Later. We'll check out the trail first and take some pictures. Maybe try to get a cast of a couple footprints. We'll check the door handles for fingerprints, but he was probably wearing gloves or mittens."

Polly Ann wanted to go with them to see for herself the violation of her home, her refuge. She was too nervous to simply stand around waiting. She had to do something. "Would you like some coffee when you're finished?"

"That would be great. Thanks."

The two men rang the doorbell some time later. Simba had scarfed down his turkey and tiny helping of squash and waited to greet the visitors. They both paused to remove their boots and stroke the cat, who led them into the dining area.

"Cream and sugar?" Polly Ann inquired. They shook their heads and Eric said, "No, thanks. Good fresh coffee will be a nice change from the stuff at the office. Matt still likes it when it's been sitting around all day, but the rest of us drink it only because it's there."

They chatted about their Christmases and plans for New Year's Eve. As the men were leaving, Ahmed said, "Matt will be back the day after tomorrow. By then we'll have whatever information we can find on the footprints. I'm afraid there won't be much, if any. The chief will let you know. Happy New Year!"

"Thanks, guys. Happy New Year."

Matt did phone her a few days later with the news – or rather, the lack of news. "Your intruder wore gloves or mittens, so no fingerprints, and his boots were size 11 Sorels – expensive, but too common to trace. Half the men in town own them."

36

Monday, January 7

A two-hour break between classes allowed Polly Ann to get coffee and a chunk of fruit cake that someone had donated to the department. Polly Ann liked good fruit cake, and this one was almost great – someone's grandmother's recipe, made lovingly from scratch.

She retrieved the stack of mail from her box and retreated to her office. Class lists, a late term paper from a grad student who'd opted to take an Incomplete, notice of an upcoming department meeting, the agenda for the dean's monthly meeting with the Arts & Sciences faculty, and a missive from the regents detailing the schedule for interviews with the four recommended applicants for the presidency.

Assuming that the regents would normally compose a schedule that suited no one but themselves, when Polly Ann had forwarded the search committee's picks, she'd attached a note spelling out which days and times were available for her committee. She had classes and office hours that she refused to cancel. Jorge Martin had required meetings and regular patrol hours. Katrina Tallfeather had classes. Harold Profit and Freddie Ferrett set their own schedules; both said they'd be available whenever the others were.

Polly Ann scanned the list. Angelocci first – tomorrow. Cantrell and Cohen the following week. Gladwin the week after that. Apparently the regents believed that the last person the committee interviewed would be the one they best remembered and would recommend. From her experience on searches, Polly Ann knew that rarely worked. Each prospect would have to be better than the one before. She smiled.

She looked over the list of questions the regents had prepared for the search committee to ask each candidate and was gratified to note that most of the questions her people had submitted were on the list with no additions.

Tuesday, January 8

Polly Ann met Dr. Angelocci at the main door to the Union and walked with him to the faculty lounge. She was pleased to see that all members of her committee were present, coffee cups and croissants on the table in front of them. They all stood as soon as the academic vice president entered. "Good morning, all," she said. "The nice thing about early meetings is that parking is plentiful. You all know Dr. Angelocci."

She pointed at the buffet. "May I get you some coffee?"

"Thanks, Polly Ann. I can get it for myself." He filled his cup, put a pastry on his plate, and carried them to the head of the table where an empty chair awaited. "It's good to see you all – Mr. Martin, Miss Tallfeather, Dean Profit, Mr. Ferrett, Dr. Passarelli."

Polly Ann waited until everyone had finished eating. Angelocci chatted with each one, obviously knowing more about them than merely their names and their jobs. He asked Katrina how her master's thesis was coming; inquired about Harold's new faculty member's search for housing for his family; discussed the revised parking regulations with Jorge and commented on the department's newest recruit – a canine named Slug; and congratulated Freddie on getting all the paperwork done for the benefit packages for new hires.

Polly Ann pushed her plate aside. "Okay, everyone. Get more coffee if you wish and let's get started with our list of questions for Dr. Angelocci. Kristina, would you start?"

The questions covered all the required qualifications. To avoid skipping from one topic to another, unrelated one, the group had agreed that each member would focus on questions relating to one area. Kristina volunteered to deal with the vice president's academic background and efforts to attract more minority students and faculty.

"Your application lists the institutions where you got your degrees, and spells out your experience as a professor and then a dean, but I'd like to know in what ways you encouraged minority hiring." Angelocci put his hands on the table and leaned forward. "As a faculty member, I had no real clout, but I did encourage friends and acquaintances from my graduate student days to apply for positions they qualified for. Our problem wasn't prejudice; it was getting a broader pool of applicants.

"As a dean, I persuaded my department heads to extend their searches for faculty members to include women and minorities. I sent back one list of potential interviewees to the committee suggesting that there must be some non-white, non-male applicants for faculty positions in his department."

"Which department, if I may ask?"

Angelocci laughed. "Social Work, if you can imagine."

"Thank you, sir. We know your record here at Ridge U has been pretty good. That's all the questions I had." Kristina turned to Harold Profit, sitting on her right. "I guess you're next."

Profit cleared his throat and sat up straight. "I don't see much evidence of fund-raising in your application."

"Ah, well, the posting referred only to fund-raising for a college or university, so someplace in my application, I mentioned chairing the United Fund in Minneapolis – I did that for five years – and here in Ridgeview for the past six years. But I didn't go into detail. Since you ask, I doubled the budget in Minneapolis and have come close to that here. I can provide references, if you wish."

Profit relaxed. "That would be good. I have nothing to add. Jorge?"

"I assume you're familiar with the university's mission statement. Do you think we're achieving it? If not, do you envision ways to do so?"

Angelocci frowned. "I doubt that more than a handful of people, whether they're teaching, learning, or maintaining Ridge University – or any other college of university in the country – can recite the mission. Those things are full of platitudes about commitment, excellence, and leading the way for the world. I think our mission should be both simple and profound: to foster and reward excellence in teaching and learning at all levels of the university, from the regents to the custodians."

All around the table, committee members voiced their approval. "Hear, hear." "Wow." "Bravo." Harold Profit reached out to shake the vice president's hand.

Freddie surreptitiously pulled out a handkerchief, dabbed his eyes, and looked at his watch. "We have another 45 minutes, so could we take a short break before continuing?"

As soon as they reconvened, Polly Ann said, "Freddie, do you have any questions?"

"I think everything's been covered. You meet all the qualifications, sir. Finding someone to fill your shoes won't be easy."

Angelocci laughed. "You do have other candidates, so I may be staying right where I am."

Polly Ann stood up and smiled. "I, too, think all our questions have been answered to our satisfaction. Thank you, sir, for your time, and good luck with the other groups who'll be interrogating you."

Angelocci bowed slightly and shook everyone's hand. "Thank you for having me. You've been very gracious."

Polly Ann walked him to the door and watched as he greeted several people on his way down the corridor. Turning to her committee, she said, "I'll see you next Tuesday for our chat with Dr. Cantrel."

"She's the dean from Wyoming, right?" Profit asked. "And that CEO – Cohen – is here Thursday?"

"Right you are."

Freddie waited for her to put her briefcase in order and put on her coat. By then, the others had left. "He's really a great guy, Polly. He'd be almost as good as Gladwin, I think." Polly Ann raised an eyebrow, but said nothing. Poor Freddie, still terrified that if he didn't support Gladwin, the sky would fall.

37

Tuesday, January 15

Cecelia Cantrell was a delightful surprise. Job applications were not allowed to ask for ethnic identification nor a picture, so meeting the petite woman with café au lait skin and the lovely lilt of a slight Jamaican accent had the committee members smiling and perhaps holding her handshake a bit longer than courtesy required.

"You're probably wondering how a girl from New York whose parents came to the U.S. from Jamaica wound up in Wyoming. I guess you could blame it on the riding lessons my mom signed me up for when I was little. Horses were my first love and still are."

After a bit more chit chat, they got down to business. Cantrell's academic credentials were excellent: Phi Beta Kappa as an undergraduate, M.A. in 18 months, Ph.D. in three years. Her field was biology, specifically equine disease.

Katrina started the interview. "You've been a student, faculty member, department head, and now dean. How do they compare?"

Cantrell thought for a minute. "Well, whatever the label, you're always a student, always learning. As an actual student, you answer to no one but yourself. And, of course, somewhat to your professors. As a faculty member, you have a responsibility to your students. All of them, gifted or not, earning their own way or supported by their parents. It's an awesome responsibility to get through to each and every one. Sometimes you fail. That hurts, so you try harder.

"The hardest thing about being a department head is realizing that although you consider yourself still faculty, your colleagues don't. You aren't exactly the enemy, but when you can't give them everything they want – more research support, more time for research, more travel funding – they blame you. As a dean, your department heads expect the same things for themselves and their departments. No one admits that it's those on the next rung on the ladder who set the budgets for underlings."

Katrina smiled and nodded at Polly Ann. "Your turn."

Polly Ann said, "I have only one question: do you think a president has that power?"

"No, but he or she is closest to the real power – the Board of Regents. I can be pretty persuasive. I'd like to try."

Harold Profit didn't wait to be called on. "What fund raising experience have you had?"

"Apart from selling Girl Scout cookies? Not much, I'm afraid," she replied. "I've been a dean for only two years, and my focus had to be on program review and restructuring to deal with an out of control budget. I was able to get alumni funding for ten years for two visiting professorships."

Freddie wanted to know if she'd succeeded in making Wyoming U a more diverse campus.

"As you can imagine, it's slow. We've been lily white and majority male for a long time, but my arrival got people thinking about the need to attract minority students and faculty. I chaired a committee to revise the mission statement to emphasize national outreach, and our student body has gone from 1% minority to 5%. The faculty is now close to 7% minority and 25% women. Not there yet, but we're progressing.

"One of our big problems is broadening the kinds of research we do. When I looked up what you're doing here at Ridge University, I realized that to attract a more diverse faculty, a wide range of research has to be supported in every department."

Polly Ann nodded, looked around, and checked her watch. "We're about out of time. Does anyone have other questions?" No one did, so with smiles all around, Dr. Cantrell left.

"What do you all think?"

"She's impressive. And our administration could use another minority female."

"No fund-raising experience to speak of, though."

"Give her another year or two and she'll be ready for at least a vice-presidency."

"Okay. That's my feeling, too. I'll see you all Thursday for Dr. Cohen."

STRIKE VOTE

38

Thursday, January 17

Dr. Jonathan Cohen strode into the room ahead of Polly Ann, nodded to the others without offering to shake hands, declined coffee, and sat down in the designated chair at the head of the table. "Let's get started, shall we? I think my application speaks for itself. However, if you have additional questions, I will respond."

Polly Ann waited for someone else to speak, but heard only silence. "I have one question. Did you work directly with the faculty, department heads, and the dean of your college concerning program development?"

"No. Our program review committees in each department dealt with that."

Cohen did not elaborate. Polly Ann had another question. "I assume your students completed annual evaluations of their professors. How did you rate?"

"Not very well at all. Students want professors who will entertain them and give easy exams so everyone gets a high grade. I was there to teach. If students chose not to learn, that was not my problem."

Polly Ann shuffled through Cohen's letters of recommendation, all from members of the board of his foundation. "Dr. Cohen, you are obviously doing a wonderful job managing the complexities of your charity and improving the lives of at-risk young people."

She looked at her watch. Twenty minutes to go. She stared beseechingly at the others. *Please, somebody, say something!*

Sensing her desperation, each of them asked a couple questions that clearly annoyed the candidate. After one, he actually harrumphed. After each innocuous question, he referred them to his application and expanded on each point for a few minutes. Polly Ann tried not to squirm. Finally she was able to say, "I think that's all the time we have. I believe Dean Profit is assigned to escort you to your next meeting with the student government representatives."

"Thank you. I hope to hear from the Board of Regents soon." With that, Cohen left the room, glancing behind to verify that his escort was following.

Jorge broke the silence. "If he treats all his underlings like drug addicts in need of rehabilitation, they aren't going to be impressed.'"

The others stood up, preparing to leave. On her way out, Katrina said, "Already, I'm not impressed."

Freddie held the door for Polly Ann and started to walk out with her when his cell phone rang. "Let me get this; I'll catch up with you in a minute." Polly Ann turned to nod in time to observe what color there was in Freddie's face disappear. He fumbled to reach for something to hang on to, dropping the phone in the process. Polly Ann reached out to steady him. He looked at her with pain-filled eyes. "How did he get my cell number?"

"Who?"

"I don't know who he is. The voice was muffled. He said, 'Choose wisely, Freddie. It would be a shame if someone suffered a fatal accident.' Polly Ann, if we don't pick Gladwin as our top pick, something dreadful could happen."

"Freddie, let's go back in the room and phone Detective Brophy. We can't deal with this by ourselves."

Matt listened intently. "Polly Ann, you two stay put for a few minutes. I'm going to get hold of Jorge Martin and ask him to wander over to where you are and casually walk Mr. Ferrett back to his office."

Matt summoned Alice into his office and closed the door. "Alice, call all available officers in for a lunch meeting. Then phone an order to the Pizza Palace – you know what everyone likes."

"You can listen while you eat. We have a problem." Matt explained Ferrett's disturbing warning and said, "I have a couple ideas, but you may have other, better ones. Adam?"

"Yeah, chief. It's probably not likely that anything will happen until the search committee and the other groups finish all the interviews and make their recommendations, by which time the out of town applicants will have left. After that, we can warn the two in-house candidates and make sure they're never alone."

Ahmed shook his head. "I dunno. Seems to me there could be an attack on any one of the chairs of the various groups that have done the interviews before they send their votes to the regents."

Charlie frowned. "The regents make the final decision, right? And if I remember past history, they don't always accept the recommendations of anyone else. Maybe we need to talk to each of them."

Matt was frustrated. "I don't want too many people knowing about this or we'll have a campus-wide panic. I'll talk to Regent Brasseth and ask him to give me the sense of the board without scaring them. And I think I'll have another chat with Wills Gladwin."

39
Friday, January 18

Alice approached the door to Matt Brophy's office. "Dr. Gladwin is here, chief."

Matt stood up and reached across his desk to shake hands. "Thanks for coming in."

Gladwin moved his chair back a few inches before sitting down. "No problem, although I thought we'd covered everything during my last visit."

"Almost. There are just a couple of loose ends. The cause of the accident that killed your secretary is still an open hit-and-run case, perpetrator unknown. No bank envelope was found in her car. Did it ever turn up?"

Gladwin shrugged. "No, it did not. It was cancelled immediately, of course. Possibly it fell out of the car at the time of the accident and someone grabbed it, only to discover it would do them no good. I never got that check. However, I can't prove I didn't put it in a bank in the Caymans. You asked about my being accused of embezzlement. I explained what actually happened. End of story. Is that all?" He started to rise.

Matt gestured to him to sit back down. "Not quite. A member of the presidential search committee received a phone call threatening repercussions if that member didn't persuade the others to recommend you as the top choice in their report to the Board of Regents. All the members received notes to that effect."

Gladwin's face turned red and he clenched his fists. "Brophy, I swear to you that I did not write threatening notes or make that phone call nor do I know who did. Or why. As I told you before, someone either hates me and is determined to prevent my presidency or has a sick crush on me and is too stupid to realize that these tactics will do more harm than good."

"I think you may be right. The tactics this person is using are strange.

If you were chosen, can you think of anyone who would benefit?"

Gladwin thought hard for a minute. "No, I really can't."

Matt stood up and walked around the desk to stand by the door. "You do want the job, don't you?"

"Sure, but I want to win fair and square, not by subterfuge or threats. Find out who's doing this, Brophy. You might ask the regents if they've received unusual mail."

"I plan to. Your interview with the committee is next week I believe? I wish you well. If anyone should contact you suggesting some kind of payoff, let me know."

As soon as Gladwin left, Matt picked up his phone and called Jorge Martin. "I need you to do something for me. Your wife knows about the threats the search committee has received, I assume. I also assume she hasn't gotten one, or she'd have told you. Would you ask her to determine if any of the regents has?"

Jorge agreed, although he did mention that the regents did not have a scheduled meeting for two weeks.

"That's okay. The committee members have their last interview next Tuesday and they'll meet a week later, possibly ready to make their recommendation. The board meets on Thursdays, if I'm correct. Thanks for your help."

40

Tuesday, January 22

Polly Ann looked forward to the final interview. Juggling her classes, office hours, meetings, and her own research with the demands of chairing the search committee had left her short-tempered and frazzled. She reviewed both Angelocci's and Gladwin's applications, reminding herself that personal likes or dislikes must not affect her decision. She'd have to bend over backwards to be fair to Gladwin. Both men were good – really good. However, she respected and genuinely liked Angelocci; she could respect but never like Gladwin.

She had met him shortly after Ridge U hired her. He'd asked about her background and ended the conversation by saying, "Would you agree with the old saying, 'Those who can, do; those who can't, teach?' " and walked away before she could speak. The man had a reputation for assuring donors that their contributions to the foundation would be used for worthwhile endeavors, not faculty budgets. More than once he'd remarked that professors were paid too much. "They're in their classrooms for what? Ten or twelve hours a week?"

Polly Ann deliberately arrived early for Gladwin's interview, hoping that the familiar room would help her to be impartial. To her surprise, Gladwin was there before her.

"Dr. Passarelli, I would like to discuss a matter of concern with your group before the actual interview begins."

Polly Ann frowned. "I can arrange that, sir, but it is rather unusual."

"Fine." Gladwin dismissed her with a nod and moved to the head of the table. He remained standing as the others entered the room.

At the other end of the table, Polly Ann sat down and called the meeting to order. "Before we start with questions, our guest has something to say. Dr. Gladwin, the floor is yours."

"I have twice been summoned to the Ridgeview police chief's office, as you may or may not know." Judging by the looks on several faces, they had not known. "I was told that all of you have received notes sent and one of you got a phone call threatening dire consequences if you do not forward my name to the Board of Regents as your preferred candidate for the presidency."

He made eye contact with each member in turn, holding his gaze until, one by one, they looked away. "I did not write those notes. I did not send those notes. I did not make that phone call. Someone is trying either to cast doubt on my integrity or – if that person is deranged – to help my candidacy in a misguided belief that I can't win on my own merits.

"Now, I assume you have all studied my qualifications and perhaps have questions to clarify a few points." At that, he sat down and smiled. His eyes remained cold.

Only Harold Profit appeared unrattled by Gladwin's opening remarks, so Polly Ann called on him first.

"Dr. Gladwin, I've seen the Ridge U Foundation's books, and it's obvious you're very good at squeezing money, if not blood, from stones. Speaking of stones, why were your attempts to get a sizable donation from Caleb Stone unsuccessful?"

That question finally elicited a real smile from Gladwin. He shrugged. "Even I can't win them all. I told him I could not change the graduation requirements to allow his grandson to walk away with a diploma, and I could not guarantee that the regents would name a building after him. I trust none of you will share that information, although it's hardly a secret."

Jorge Martin was next. "As you may know, sir, the campus police force is understaffed. Our budget remains static while enrollment continues to rise. Would you support an increase?"

Gladwin frowned. "Your people seem to be handling the misdemeanors pretty well and it's not like Ridge U is a hotbed of real crime, but I would carefully review your requests."

Martin wasn't finished. "Are you aware that student suicide is an increasing problem? Two years ago, there were two. Last year there were five and three attempts we managed to stop. We've asked for a suicide prevention program and training for our people in dealing with potential suicides, but those requests were denied."

Gladwin said, "I would look into the problem. Anything else?" Jorge shook his head.

"Freddie, do you have questions?" Polly Ann asked. He didn't. "Katrina?"

"I looked up the foundation staff and noticed that there are five clerks and secretaries, all white women, and the rest of your people are white men. Why is that?"

Gladwin grimaced and repositioned the cushion on his chair. Hemorrhoids? Polly Ann was sufficiently distracted to miss part of his answer. ". . . those people were there when I arrived. All I can say is that we have the best people we can find. Perhaps we need to try harder."

Gladwin looked at his Rolex watch. "Dr. Passarelli, I see that we have about ten minutes left. Did you have a question?"

"Just one. How do you feel about part-time faculty?"

"You mean the poorly paid, over-worked lecturers with larger teaching loads than regular faculty? Some are better than one would expect. Most are not. But then, that's true of the faculty, too. I think we need better evaluation mechanisms, higher expectations for both. Tenure and promotion should require more than a certain number of years on the job."

Polly Ann stood up, resisting the urge to stretch. "Thank you for your time, Dr. Gladwin." She walked him to the door, shook his outstretched hand, and watched him stride away. She turned to the others. "I assume you have places to go and people to see – and time to think. We'll meet next week and perhaps have a recommendation for the regents."

STRIKE VOTE

41

Thusday, January 24

The regular meeting of the Ridge University Board of Regents had been postponed a week. Glynda hadn't checked her campus mailbox since Christmas, but her husband had showed her the threating note he got and told her that everyone on the search committee had received one like it. "Would you check your box and ask around? I'm thinking board members may also have been threatened."

Glynda overheard Burt Lincoln spouting at Regent Gregory. "Rick, I'm telling you, Wills Gladwin is trying to fix this appointment."

Rick appeared suitably concerned. "It does look that way, Burt, but I don't think Gladwin's behind it. He isn't that stupid. Let's see who the search committee favors and find out what other groups that interviewed all the candidates thought. There's no need to panic yet."

Glynda raised her voice to get everyone's attention. "Correct me if I'm wrong, but do I assume that all of us, not just me, Burt, and Rick, got notes threatening dire consequences if we don't support Wills Gladwin?"

Bill Brasseth the new chairman, nodded. Joanie Jameson burst into tears. "I got this nasty note – I can't believe Wills would stoop so low and anyway, he's always been real nice to me. But I can't vote for him until we know who's officially recommended. Maybe I should just resign."

Brasseth patted her on the shoulder. "Don't worry your pretty little head. We'll wait until we get all the reports and then we'll decide who to hire. Nobody's going to bother you. They're just bluffing."

"If you say so, Bill."

Glynda didn't say anything, but she knew from past experience that recommendations from deans, students, union members, and even vice presidents were sometimes ignored. Each group believed their input was vital. However, even the search committee's pick had been set aside at least once in the past. The final decision rested in the hands of the Board of Regents. This board made a bad mistake with the last guy. They'd be more careful this time.

Glynda reported back to Jorge. "The members all got one, but no one – except Joanie – seems very bothered about it. I got one, too. I agree with those who don't think Wills is stupid enough to have sent them himself."

"What did Edwards say?"

"Hunter? Oh, he wasn't there. Called in sick with a cold."

It wasn't the generic threat notes received by all the regents that sent Joanie Jameson into a meltdown. Just when she thought there'd be no more phone calls, another one came to disturb her morning yoga session. Like the one yesterday that she couldn't get out of her mind.

"Your husband wasn't riding his bike on the right side of the road. Was it because he lost his rear reflectors?"

Like the other calls at seemingly random intervals, this one ended immediately, giving her no time to respond. She sank into a chair, shaking uncontrollably. Ernest laid his head in her lap and gazed at her with love-filled eyes, doing his doggie best to help her feel better.

"Ernest, how would he know? Unless he was there. If he saw the accident, why didn't he come forward?" Joanie thought about that for a minute. Ernest put a paw on her knee and whined.

"Unless . . . oh, my God! Unless he was driving the car that hit Robert. Maybe he panicked and fled, not knowing Robert was still alive. But there was no evidence that the car swerved or braked. Was it deliberate? Who would do that? And why?"

Ernest left her side to get his favorite squeaky toy, a purple octopus missing two of its eight legs. He dropped it at her feet.

"Okay, I'll stop fussing, for now anyway. And I won't mention this to anyone." She squeezed the toy and tossed it into the kitchen.

42
Friday, January 25

Polly Ann's office phone buzzed. "Polly Ann? It's Freddie. Can you invent a good reason to come to my office? It's urgent. I'm on my cell phone, so no one will know I called you."

Polly Ann hung up the phone. She wasn't so sure about that. Freddie's phone might be safe, but hers might not be. It could be hiding a bug. Granted, her phone rang non-stop during her office hours and for someone to listen to hours of student problems in hopes of catching one particular call would be obsessive. But the person trying to fix the presidential selection was obsessive, wasn't he?

"I'll think of something, Freddie. Give me half an hour."

She looked over the list entitled "Pending Matters." Not much was urgent. But maybe that one recommendation for tenure. She dug through her files. Ah, yes. Professor Brown. Glowing student evaluations, good comments from colleagues and department head, but there was a disquieting note from one student alleging sexual harassment. Furthermore, the dean recommended further investigation.

Polly Ann squirmed into her parka and boots, slid the file into her briefcase, and headed out. Ridge University's library, dormitories, and a few offices peeked out from the trees covering the east facing slopes of the foothills. The climb up the icy walkway past the library to the HR office was treacherous. Not for the first time, Polly Ann wondered how a handicapped person was supposed to navigate.

"Hi, Belinda. Is Mr. Ferrett in?"

"Let me see." The receptionist punched a button on the desk phone. "Dr. Passarelli is here. She does not have an appointment." A moment later, she told Polly Ann, "Go right in." Polly Ann left Freddie's door open a crack and had to strain to hear the woman's low voice say, "Dr. Passarelli just went in to see Mr. Ferrett. She didn't have an appointment. She was carrying a big envelope." Polly Ann waited for the click of the phone returning to its cradle before shutting the door ever so cautiously.

She raised her voice so the sound would carry to the spy on the other side. "Thanks for seeing me at short notice, Freddie. I brought the relevant papers." She reached across Freddie's desk for a note pad and pen and quickly scribbled, *Your receptionist is spying on you. She's just informed someone that I'm here.*

Freddie took a deep breath. "How can I help you, Polly Ann?"

She opened the envelope she'd brought and pulled out the contents. "I think your office needs to talk to this student and then confront the professor. It looks to me like sufficient cause for termination." She handed over the copies of the tenure recommendations. In a lower voice, she asked, "What's so urgent?"

Freddie set the papers aside and whispered, "I've studied the applications of Angelocci and Gladwin and I took lots of notes. What am I going to do, Polly Ann? I'm scared. Scared for myself. Scared for Ivan. But I have to vote for Tony Angelocci. He's got it all, and most important, he cares about us. All of us. Students, faculty, staff, everyone."

All Polly Ann could say was, "Wow! Okay, Freddie, let's see how the others vote. If it's unanimous, I'll alert Detective Brophy that we all need police protection. And I'll send our report to the Board immediately."

43
Tuesday, January 29

Polly Ann entered the little bistro in the student union and looked around for members of her committee. From the back of the room, Katrina stood up and waved. She was with Jorge Martin, so Polly Ann joined them, figuring no one would suspect she was actually meeting Katrina.

"I'm guessing today will be our final official meeting, although I hope we'll all continue to be friends."

"Serving together on committees tends to encourage that," Jorge said. "Could I get you something?"

"Yes, thanks. A hazelnut latte, please." Polly Ann turned to Katrina. "I guess you'll be happy to have more time for your own work."

Playing along with her friend, Katrina replied, "I will. My thesis is nearing the end, so I really need to concentrate on it." She glanced over to make sure Jorge was still at the serving counter and lowered her voice. "Are we still on for lunch next Wednesday?"

Polly Ann waved at a colleague coming in the door and stood up. "Yes. I remember. I need to talk to Tricia. I'll see you in a few minutes."

Polly Ann called the meeting to order. "Well, here we are again. Everyone ready to vote?"

Her friends smiled at her. Friends? Yes, they had all become friends, some dearer than others. How would they decide? Tony Angelocci or Wills Gladwin?

Polly Ann studied each person around the table – Katrina and Harold on her right, Freddie and Jorge onto her left. The sixth chair, the one across from her reserved for the applicants, sat empty, as if waiting for the committee to decide who should sit there.

In keeping with the gravity of the situation, Polly Ann chose formality over familiarity. "Miss Tallfeather, how say you?"

Katrina smiled and winked at her. "I say Dr. Angelocci. He has what we need without the attitude of a couple others. If, God forbid, he should refuse, Gladwin could do it, I suppose."

"Dr. Profit?" Polly Ann resigned herself to at least one Gladwin supporter.

Profit looked down at his notes, then raised his head. "I've known Wills Gladwin a long time. I admire his successes with the Ridge University Foundation. And I believe that's where he should stay. I vote for Angelocci. I doubt he'd back out, but if he did, I'd advise reopening the search rather than going for one of the other current applicants."

Polly Ann picked up a pen and appeared to write a short note. Actually, she sought to hide her look of joy. It wasn't over yet. "Mr. Martin?"

"I'm with Harold. Tony Angelocci or no one. Gladwin talks a good talk, but I don't trust him to follow through."

Polly Ann sent a silent prayer that Freddie could remain brave. She put her right hand in her lap and crossed her fingers. "Mr. Ferrett?"

Freddie stood up and raised his chin. "I've come to the conclusion that once the Board members announce the winner, whoever it may be, the threats will stop. Angelocci is head and shoulders above the others. He's going to be exactly what Ridge U needs. Madame Chairperson, how do you vote?"

Polly Ann felt delighted, surprised, humbled by the basic good sense of human beings. Why had she been so perpetually negative? Choking back happy tears, she said, "I make it unanimous for Dr. Angelocci." She needed a moment to compose herself before getting back to business. "Shall we meet tomorrow or the next day to do the paperwork?"

Silence greeted her suggestion. Finally, Harold Profit said, "This week's really busy for me and I have family plans for Saturday. Couldn't we do it now? It shouldn't take long. I assume the computer and printer over there in the corner are for us to use?"

It took only a few minutes for Polly Ann to type out the committee's report to the Board, print out three copies, and have everyone sign them.

"Why three?" Jorge asked.

Answering him with a shrug, Polly Ann dismissed the meeting and followed the group out. Two others moved toward the Union bookstore, which also housed an office with a copy machine. She glanced around and seeing that the coast was clear, made copies for her committee.

She then ducked into the post office, set off in a small alcove at the back of the store. She pulled pre-addressed envelopes from her briefcase. One original she sent snail mail to the Board, another to her English Department mail slot, and the third went back into her otherwise empty briefcase. She wrote a brief note on each of the copies for her committee members and dropped them in the campus mail slot. The notes read, "Put this in a safe place and, if I go missing, do not discuss our deliberations with ANYONE."

I am not paranoid, but there's a killer out there who is not going to be happy if he knows he's lost. If I drop dead in the next couple hours, at least the Board will have our recommendation.

Polly Ann didn't drop dead, but she got only as far as the parking lot where her car waited before gloved hands jerked the briefcase from her hand and clapped a stinky cloth over her face. Her last conscious act was to throw her car keys into the shrubbery.

44

Still Tuesday, January 29

Before any of the committee members reached their respective homes, snow started coming down in huge, fat, wet flakes. The streets were merely sloppy at first, but the temperature plummeted suddenly and the wind began to howl. The weather station had predicted snow, but now the forecast changed. A major storm was on the way.

"On the way, hell," Matt muttered, looking out his office window. A few soft, white flakes drifted past. "It's here." Alice handed him a list of businesses, schools, and scheduled events that were being shut down, closed, and cancelled. Ridge U was cancelling classes for the first time in over a decade.

Matt had spent most of the morning catching up on the endless paperwork. By 11:00, he was nearly finished. "Alice, I'll be heading for home soon. You should go now, before the storm really starts winding up. Cancel any appointments for the next couple days and stay safe."

As Matt stacked the results of his morning's labors into tidy piles, Freddie Ferrett cautiously drove home. A frantic Ivan met him at the door. "Freddie, there was another phone call. I'm to tell you that he's got Polly Ann and as long as you keep your mouth shut, he won't kill her."

"Did you call Chief Brophy?"

"No. I was afraid our phone might be tapped."

Freddie might be timid where his own well-being was concerned, but a threat to Polly Ann aroused a bit of superhero in his psyche. "I'll use my cell phone. Matt's gotta know about this.

"Detective Brophy? I'm glad I caught you before you left. We've had a phone call. He's got Polly Ann and threatens to kill her if I don't keep quiet."

"Who's got her? Where? How long has she been missing?" Matt

could hear the anger, frustration, and fear in his voice. He could be calm and professional most of the time, but this was Polly Ann! The neighbor and friend who'd been part of his and Patty's life for years. He clenched his teeth.

"Freddie, what are you supposed to keep quiet about?"

"About the search committee's recommendation for the presidency. We voted today." As Freddie continued, his voice rose higher into the realm of hysteria. "I don't know who's got her. Or where. Our meeting ended about 10:00. She went across the hall to the bookstore to mail our decision to the Board of Regents. A few minutes later I saw her going out the door to the parking lot. Ivan got the phone call at 11:15."

"Matt," he wailed, "if the regents accept our advice, he's gonna kill her!"

Matt forced himself to calm down. "We've got at least a few days, Freddie. The bookstore's closed and no mail is going out of there until this storm ends. And when the regents do get your report, they will take a day or two to deliberate before making an announcement."

Freddie caught his breath on what sounded like a sob. "Okay, Matt. But you've got to find her before that happens."

"I'll do my best. You and Ivan stay put. This is a serious storm, and you won't accomplish anything by running around in it trying to find her."

Matt looked at his watch. 11:45. He'd been looking forward to a comforting lunch at home – tomato soup and grilled cheese sandwiches. Instead, he went into the break room and hit the vending machine harder than it deserved. Peanut butter crackers would have to do. He phoned his people to ask them to be on the lookout for the missing woman and to be ready to move as soon as any leads surfaced. Then he called his wife.

"Patty, I'll be on my way home in a few hours. I have to go someplace else first. If you can get over to Polly Ann's, get Simba in his carrier and take him to our house. Polly Ann's missing. I'll tell you what I know when I get there."

"Oh, dear." Patty was quiet for a full minute. Matt could picture her absorbing the frightening news. "Yes, I'll get Simba. You drive carefully."

Matt's final call was to the dorm where Katrina Tallfeather lived, hoping the approaching storm had kept her there. He was in luck. "Miss Tallfeather, may I come up and talk to you?"

"If you can get here safely, that would be fine."

"I can sure try. Look for me in about an hour." He contacted the department car barn and requested that the snowmobile be prepared for action.

STRIKE VOTE

45

Earlier, Polly Ann had come to, fuzzy headed and nauseated. She started to sit up, but decided it wasn't a good idea. Maybe she could slowly roll over onto her side. She almost rolled off the bed. This was not her comfy queen-sized bed. It was a ridiculously narrow cot.

Her stomach roiled at the sight of a bucket on the floor. She swallowed hard, refusing to upchuck, although she understood why the bucket was there, next to the cot.

Without moving her head, she let her eyes roam the room. Room? Barely larger than her walk-in closet. One high, skinny window near the ceiling with a view of ridged metal – a window well. Two doors, probably locked. When she could move without barfing, she'd check.

Oh, shit. There's a peep hole in that one door. Whoever put me here can see me, but I can't see him. What does he want? I guess he got my briefcase. Maybe he's dumb enough to assume he's got the only copy.

She heard steps approaching. Coming down stairs, she guessed, further evidence that she was in a basement. She eased over onto her back and lay still. The steps halted at the door on the opposite wall from her cot. He spoke through the closed door. Afraid she was ready to attack him if he opened it?

"You should be awake by now, probably feeling sickish. Sorry about the chloroform, but I couldn't let you scream." Polly Ann had heard that voice before. When? Where?

"You're a smart girl. Too smart for your own good. You're going to have to stay here until the board members make an announcement. Can't have you telling them your committee's decision, can we? I've made sure your colleagues won't talk.

"If you haven't already used the bucket, you won't have to. One of the doors leads to a bathroom. I'm going to open this door and leave you some lunch." She didn't answer.

A moment later, she heard a key turn in the lock. The door opened a few inches, enough for her to see a huge form enveloped in black cloak, wearing a Halloween face mask – a grinning Richard Nixon. He dropped a MacDonald's bag on the floor, slammed the door, and re-locked it. "See," he called through the door, "I'm not heartless. I have to leave now. I'll bring more food when I return. You will be good, won't you?"

The footsteps faded. A door latch clicked, ceiling high but further away. She was alone. She was exhausted. She slept, unaware that frantic friends were already trying to find her.

46

It had been a few years since Matt had been on a snowmobile, but he hadn't forgotten the jarring his body got when bouncing over bumpy terrain. The roar as the beast climbed up the hill to the dorms drowned out even the din of the storm.

Katrina heard it coming and opened the main door of the sprawling building to the snow-covered police chief. "How'd you get here?"

"The department owns a snowmobile. It comes in handy a couple times a year."

"Well, come in." She led the way down a hallway, around a corner, and through a door that opened into a small foyer. "And let me take your wet clothes. I'll put them on the coat rack next to the heat register." She waited while he removed his boots, parka, waterproof pants, and heavy mittens. "The living room's this way. Can I get you anything?"

"No, thanks. Maybe later."

"Make yourself comfortable," she said, pointing to a recliner. She seated herself on the edge of a well-worn couch.

Matt got right to the reason for his visit. "Katrina, Dr. Passarelli's been abducted and you may know something that would help us find her."

Katrina sat unnaturally still for a moment. Only her hands, clenched together in her lap told of her shock. She leapt to her feet, sheer rage on her face, teeth bared, eyes flashing. "When? Where? And what are you doing here? You should be out looking for her!"

Matt remained seated to avoid the appearance of confrontation. "I'll tell you everything I know, Katrina. I'm here seeking background information that can help us figure out who has her and why. Every man and woman I can spare is out gathering information, seeking witnesses. Two of my men got to the parking lot where she was snatched before the snow covered up what little evidence there was."

Katrina paced to the window where there was nothing to see but blowing snow. "How long has she been missing? Where was she when she was taken? What if she's dead, her body dumped in a snowbank?" she wailed.

Matt got up and walked over to join the girl at the window. He put a tentative hand on her shoulder. When she wheeled to face him, he braced himself. Her rage visibly dissipated as she began to sob, great gulping outpourings of grief.

Matt put his arms around her and let her cry it all out. Katrina might be a big woman, almost as tall as he and solidly built, but he held a devastated child.

Finally the weeping stopped and she backed away. "I'm a mess. Let me go wash my face and then we'll talk."

When she returned to the couch, her face was blotchy, but her eyes were clear. Matt saw that her previously bare feet were now encased in intricately beaded moccasins. She noticed the direction of his gaze and held up a foot. "Polly Ann got these for me. They make me feel braver, stronger."

"They're beautiful," Matt said. "Now, if you're ready, I'll answer your questions and ask you some." He began pacing the floor.

"Polly Ann disappeared close to 11:00, shortly after your meeting ended. She got close enough to her car to unlock it. We found the keys in a nearby snowdrift. I'm guessing she tossed them there."

"Why?"

"Why do I assume that? Because I think her captor would have moved her car if he could have done so. I'm positive she's still very much alive – and madder than hell. If he meant to kill her, he'd have done it right there in the parking lot. There were no witnesses. For some reason, he wants her alive, at least for now."

Katrina tucked her feet under a couch cushion. "While we were all still at the meeting, she put together our final report and had us all sign three copies. She put one in her briefcase, but I know she intended to stop by the campus post office and mail one to the Board of Regents and one to herself. I guess she wanted to make sure they didn't get lost – or stolen."

Matt returned to the recliner and sat down. "The campus shut down before noon when news of the impending storm was announced, and I doubt that the Board will see that report until the blizzard is over. I think whoever he is will keep her hidden until the Board gets the committee's recommendation and makes a decision."

The young woman had calmed down and her mind was obviously working logically. "How did you discover she'd been grabbed if there were no witnesses?"

"Fred Ferrett's housemate got a phone call threatening to kill Dr. Passarelli unless Ferrett promised to tell no one what your committee was recommending. He'll probably issue the same threat to the rest of you. So we have time to find her and apprehend her kidnapper. I will share with you any information we get.

"Now it's your turn. How long have you known Polly Ann?"

Katrina sank back into the sofa pillows. "Years. She saved my life." Katrina took a deep breath and sat up straight. "It all started when a bunch of us kids from the Tecumseh School – that was a boarding school in Michigan for Indian orphans – a bunch of us were taken on a holiday to a forest camp in northern Michigan. Polly Ann, a student volunteer from the university, served as one of the counselors.

"We were playing hide and seek in the woods. I went too far and got lost. We'd been told that if we ever got lost, we should get up high enough to see further than the next tree. I climbed a hill and saw three guys in hunter camouflage carrying shotguns. One of them, several yards from the others, was peeing on a big pine tree. When I saw one of the others raise his gun and shoot him, I started to call out. Right as he lowered the gun, he saw me. I turned and ran."

Matt could only imagine the terror a little girl would have felt, lost in the woods and witnessing a murder. "Did he chase you?"

Katrina looked up, surprised at the question. "Yes, he did. Terror put wings on my feet. I ran as fast as I could, but I could hear him crashing behind me. I was all scratched and bleeding, my nose was running, and I was bawling myself sick.

"I literally ran into Polly Ann. No one else was around – the kids and their counselors were all in their cabins, packing to leave. She took me to her cabin, calmed me down, and cleaned me up before she started asking questions."

Katrina smiled and leaned back, finally relaxing. "She's really good about fishing information out of people. That's why she's such a good teacher; she makes her students think things out rather than telling them the answers before they have time to use their own minds."

Matt nodded. "Yeah, she's really good at helping people remember details that might seem unimportant at first. Scared as you were, did you remember if you recognized any of the men you saw?"

Katrina tensed up again. "I'd never seen the shooter before, but I'll never forget that face. He had a really scruffy beard and black streaks – camo, I guess – all over his face. It's the other man who's the reason Polly Ann and I wound up here in Colorado, pretending we'd never met. It's kind of a long story."

"I have all afternoon. And I need as many details as you can give me."

Katarina stood up. "You want a Coke?"

"That'd be great. Can I help?"

"No, thanks. Stay put." She walked over to a little fridge Matt could see in the kitchen alcove of the suite and took out two cans. "Do you want a glass?"

"Can's fine."

She twisted off the tabs and picked up a box from the counter. "I hope you like pretzels. I usually have crackers and cheese on hand, but I wanted to get here before the snow piled up, so I skipped my usual trip to the grocery store." Her eyes filled with tears. "I would have driven right by the Union and maybe I could have saved Polly Ann." She struggled to compose herself.

47

"Miss Tallfeather," Matt said, "I wish I could go back a couple hours and change this story, but I can't. My people are all over the city talking to people. If anyone saw anything, we'll soon know. I'd be out there myself, but the background you can share with me will be invaluable."

"Chief, please call me Kat. 'Miss Tallfeather' sounds so formal and official, and I like feeling that I'm talking to a friend.

"The story's needed telling for a while, but until now, the timing was wrong." Katrina took a long sip of her Coke and collected her thoughts. "The man who was shot in the back, Clarence Hunter, was the owner of a drug store near the University of Michigan campus. The other one I could identify operated a family business in town, Turner's Tours."

That got Matt's attention. "Stanley Turner?"

"None other. The tragic story of the so-called accidental death of Clarence Hunter was front page news for over a week. When asked about the third man, one article quoted Turner as saying something like, 'Clarence introduced him to me as a young friend from Ohio. Didn't mention his name. The guy was real broken up about what he'd done, couldn't even look at the body. I told him I'd stay put while he went to the ranger station and called the police. They showed up about half an hour later, but I never saw Clarence's friend again. I guess he went back to Ohio.'"

"And that was the end of it?"

"Pretty much. There was a short report after the inquest that upset Polly Ann, because Mr. Turner said there'd been a rumor about another witness, a little Indian kid, but that he hadn't seen anyone."

Katrina got up to take the empty Coke cans to the kitchen alcove. "Chief Brophy, do you want to stay here for dinner? The dining room is still open."

Matt looked at his watch. "I didn't realize it was so late. I would like to hear the rest of the story. If I may use your phone, I'll call my wife. Is it okay if I go to dinner in my stocking feet?"

Katrina said, "Given the circumstances, I don't think anyone would notice, but the guy next door is about your size. He's not here, but I have his key so I can get in to water his plants. He won't mind if you borrow some shoes. You can wash up while I pop over there. The bathroom's just through that door and next to the bedroom."

Matt was already moving when she left. His face in the mirror gave him a start. His cheeks were wind-burned from the driving snow he'd encountered on his way here. He'd skipped his shave that morning, expecting to be in the office all day catching up on paperwork. The stubble look might be okay for Hollywood, but not Ridgeview. However, there was nothing he could do about it.

Gingerly, he patted his face with warm water and ran his fingers through his hair, wetting down the cowlick on his forehead. He tucked in his shirt and buttoned the top button.

Katrina was waiting when he emerged. She set a pair of black dress shoes on the floor. "Let's see what's for dinner."

The imposing young man approaching their table frowned as he studied Katrina's face. "Kat, you look upset. Hello, Chief Brophy. You're not here to arrest us, are you?"

"You must be Chad. Although we've never met, I've seen you on the basketball court – you're impressive. No, she's not in trouble, nor are you, despite the fact that I have your fingerprints on file. My jail doesn't have room for all the people who were marching through Regent Turner's house that night, and Katrina assured me you were simply trying to do her a favor. I've been picking her brain, and she's been a big help."

Chad visibly relaxed. "That's good. When she told me what was going on, I told her she had to tell you. But she said it was too soon and too dangerous. What's happened?"

"Chad, Polly Ann's been kidnapped! Chief Brophy has all his people out in this ghastly storm talking to anyone who might have seen her or might know something. The details of what happened in Michigan all those years ago may help him find her."

Chad put an arm around her and leaned over to whisper "You okay?" She nodded.

Chad resumed his waiter posture. "I assume you're here for dinner? As you can see, we don't have a whole lot of customers. The menu is pretty limited, but I can offer hamburgers, fries, salad, and some birthday cake left over from a couple days ago. Kat, I know you like your beef rare. Chief?"

"Me, too. Chad, if you haven't already eaten, why don't you join us?"

As they ate, Chad asked what, if any, progress was being made in the search. Matt told him about his people finding Polly Ann's car keys and added, "We're assuming he's taken her someplace in town. The blizzard started late this morning, but warnings were already out for drivers to stay off the highways and urging them to stay home except in an emergency."

"Do you have any suspects?"

"Not really. We need information. We have some ideas about where to look for it. By tomorrow, we will know more."

As Chad cleared away their empty plates, he asked if they wanted cake and coffee. Katrina declined the cake, but asked for two coffees to go.

"No cake for me either, Chad. Thanks for a wonderful dinner. And I'm pleased to have met you."

Back in Katrina's suite, Matt removed the borrowed footwear and traded them for the Styrofoam cup Katrina handed him. "I'll return these shoes to Barry's room," she said. "He'll never know they've been on a walkabout."

They settled back into their accustomed places. Matt drank half his coffee, hoping the caffeine would keep him alert until he got back home. "So, did you really run away? And did Polly Ann help you do that?"

"I quit running when Polly Ann found me. We didn't have to run or hide. Camp was over and all the kids and counselors were climbing into buses for the trip back to school. So we merged in with the others.

"I don't know what Pol said to the principal, but she got permission to take me to her place, and I stayed there for the whole next week."

Matt drained his coffee and excused himself for another trip to the rest room. His wind-burned cheeks were still ruddy, but not as vivid as before.

While he was out of the room, Katrina had changed out of her Ridge U. sweatshirt and jeans into a caftan. "When did you come to Colorado?" he asked.

"The weekend after we left the camp. Pol got hold of a friend who practices law here in the area. She told my story to colleagues of hers, a Native American couple with a whole tribe of kids, and they adopted me. Their name was Tallfeather, so I changed my old last name and became Katrina instead of Katherine.

"A couple days before I left, Polly Ann got an offer from Ridge U, so she came here just a couple weeks after I did. We spent a lot of time together at first, but when Mr. Turner arrived in town we avoided places where anyone we knew would see us. We couldn't be sure that he didn't suspect that she had talked to me before I disappeared. And we couldn't afford to believe that he hadn't witnessed the murder and helped the other guy escape.

"The first time Polly Ann met him here on campus, he was overly friendly, asking all kinds of questions, including a few about that camp and if she'd known the runaway Indian kid.

"Good thing he didn't move to Colorado until I left for college. I went to Ft. Collins public schools and if he'd been looking for a specific Indian kid, he'd have spotted me in no time."

Matt stood up to stretch and put his now empty cup in the trash. He'd have to leave soon or he'd be in danger of falling asleep on the snowmobile.

"So you started out at CU Boulder and eventually transferred to Ridge U and got active in the LGBT movement. Why?"

Katrina laughed. "Why what? Transferred or led folks to think I was gay? Boulder's nice, but Ft. Collins is home. And Polly Ann's here. The LGBT thing is personal. I'm not gay, but because of that assumption, guys rarely hit on me, and girls know better than to try. The real reason is that I knew a guy at CU whose sister was raped and beaten to death by a bunch of homophobes. It made me furious and gave me a cause to fight for."

Matt's respect for her intensified. "Good for you. Possibly also dangerous, since it's brought you a lot of attention, not all desirable. I assume Turner did eventually meet you. Did he ever suspect that you were that 'runaway Indian kid'?"

She shook her head. "I don't think so. Last spring when the Board had a reception for our club, he made a point of chatting up every Native American woman there, but he didn't pay any more attention to me than to anyone else. He would never have seen Polly Ann and me together off campus."

Matt took a while to process the complicated story. "Do you think Turner knew the shooting was deliberate?"

"I don't know. I'm sure the killer insisted that it was an accident. But maybe Turner saw something and realized the potential for causing trouble."

"Yeah, he would. And it may be why he was killed. Well, Katrina, I've overstayed my welcome. Thank you for all the information, for dinner, and for Barry's shoes. You've been really helpful."

Katrina got to her feet and walked to the door with Matt. She lifted his parka off the clothes tree and patted it. "Good. This is dry. Chief Brophy, I wish I could identify the shooter. Maybe he's here in Colorado, too, and if he's got Turner's files, he has a motive for taking Polly Ann. I'll be praying that you find her soon."

"We will. How many middle aged men associated with Ridge U came here from Michigan in the last 10-15 years? That shouldn't be too hard to find out."

48

Evening, Tuesday, January 29

The glimmer of grey light from the tiny window disappeared as the window well filled up with snow. *Oh, great. Just great. I get to sit here in the dark until I starve. Umm, why isn't it dark?* Polly Ann looked up at the ceiling; recessed lights blinked back at her. She hadn't noticed them previously.

Hours earlier, she had nibbled at the salad and hamburger her captor had left, but her stomach rebelled. Now, she was hungry. She also needed the bathroom. It, too, had a ceiling light, but might have been less disgusting if there'd been no light.

She raised the toilet seat. Rust colored water filled the bowl, but she saw no alligators or other horrors. It was that or the bucket. The sink faucet delivered more rusty water. She dried her hands on her jeans and left the tiny room. She moved around the walls of her prison, knocking on the paneled walls.

The studs appeared to be evenly spaced every 16 inches if the builder had done the job to code. Although they would be far apart enough for her to squeeze through, it would take a more effective tool than her bare hands to break through a panel. She paid special attention to the exit door.

Thumping on it proved it was solid. Oak, perhaps. What she had originally thought was a peep hole proved to be nothing more than a small blemish in the wood. She was relieved to learn that he couldn't spy on her through the closed door.

She was still hungry, but not yet desperate enough to finish the cold, greasy burger and limp lettuce. She looked at her watch. She'd left the Union that morning at 10:30. It was now nearly 7:00. She had slept most of the day!

When she heard the stamp of feet coming down the stairs, she quickly stood up. She refused to look submissive. She heard a key undo the lock and saw the door open barely wide enough to allow the cloaked figure to poke its garish head inside. Who was this person?

The voice was muffled. She might have heard the man speak in her previous life, but she couldn't remember.

"I brought you food. Enough for several days. I managed to get through this blizzard today, but Ridgeview is shutting down and anyone on the streets unnecessarily will be ticketed.

"You can't identify me, but I know you. Didn't get a Mrs. degree in college, so you settled for a Ph.D. No children, so you kidnapped one. That makes you as crooked as I am. Well, I need to go. We'll talk later."

He dropped a large, obviously heavy backpack on the floor and closed the door. Polly Ann heard a key turning to lock her in.

Polly Ann sank back onto the cot. She thought hard about what he'd said. *He didn't know everything. Maybe, probably, he didn't know who or where Kat was.*

For sure, he didn't know she had been married. Hardly anyone did. Her husband was in his third year in medical school when the war in Afghanistan began. He was still listed as MIA, all these years later. Someday, he would come home.

Patty and Matt didn't know the whole story about Kat, but she'd told them about Trevor. The first time she saw Matt Brophy, her heart skipped a beat. Like Trevor, he was very tall, well over six feet. Not really handsome, but with nice features, the same dark crew cut that hid the curl wanting to spring forth, the same intense blue eyes, the same character lines.

Polly Ann had been disappointed to see the ring on Matt's finger, but then she met his wife. In a few short weeks, she formed a deep bond with both of them. If anyone would search until they found her, it was Matt, with Patty cheering him on.

For a few minutes, she felt better, thinking about her friends. However, her thoughts returned to the evil person who'd locked her in this place. *He's probably poisoned the food. That's his preferred method.* She sulked for a few minutes before giving herself a pep talk. *C'mon now, Polly Anti. Negativity is not helping. He wouldn't have brought a ton of food if one bite would kill. Let's see what's for dinner.*

No longer dizzy and weak-kneed, she walked over to the backpack. It took both hands to drag it over to the cot, her temporary table. She pulled out half a dozen familiar containers designed to heat the contents simply by pulling the recessed ring to remove the lid. *Well, well.*

The man knows something about camp food. She checked the labels: one each of stew, lasagna, and chicken pot pie.

She set them aside and reached back into the backpack, finding a bag of lettuce, sliced tomatoes in one small Ziplock container, small heads of broccoli and cauliflower in another, and three packets of salad dressing.

Under the salad makings were sandwiches: ham and cheese, roast beef, deli chicken, and – she smiled – PB&J.

I must admit he thought of everything. What's to drink? She reached into the bottom of the back pack. No wonder it felt so heavy. There were bottles of water, cans of Pepsi, V-8 and grape juice, and four half pint cartons of 2% milk. Tucked in the corners were four granola bars.

She fished around a bit more and came up with ready to drink lattes. She sat down on the floor and began to laugh. The laughter turned to tears before she shook herself out of the doldrums. *No need to get hysterical. He's buying time. Maybe he believes that the report in my briefcase carefully addressed to the Board of Regents is the only copy. He can probably get my committee to keep quiet if he threatens to kill me. But the Board's going to get our recommendation anyway.*

Okay, quit thinking the worst. There's food for at least a couple days. Someone will be looking for me or at least tell Matt that I'm missing. He and Patty will look after Simba. And I'm not going to sit here contemplating my navel. If there's a way for me to get out of here, I'll find it.

Polly Ann scarfed down the container of stew and used the empty bowl to put together a salad. Either the grape juice was laced with a sedative or her system had yet to recover from the chloroform, but in either case, her body craved more rest. She cleared the remains of her dinner off the cot and was asleep in minutes.

49

Visibility was almost zero as Matt left the Ridge U campus. The snow and wind had intensified. However, home was straight downhill and he arrived safely. Patty heard the snow machine coming and waited at the open front door. "I assume it's you, Matt. You're a twin to the snowman the kids created in the back yard. Come in and thaw out."

He stomped his feet, leaving on the porch most of the snow that had stuck to his clothes. He shed the parka, ski pants, boots, and heavy mittens in the entry way and limped into the living room. Patty handed him a tall glass of Royal Velvet. He wasn't much of a drinker, but he did enjoy an occasional sip of good Canadian rye.

"You look like you need this," Patty said. "Knowing you would be late, I had my dinner, but I can warm it up for you. Meatloaf, if that's okay?"

Matt took the glass and gave his wife a one-armed hug. "Comfort food sounds good, but I've already eaten. Save the meatloaf for tomorrow's sandwiches. Speaking of comfort, where's Simba?"

"After roaming the entire house, crying for Polly Ann, he curled up on the ledge in the living room looking out the window for her to come home."

"Patty, what am I going to do? Polly Ann's been kidnapped; we're in the middle of a major blizzard; and the interstate is a parking lot with several smash ups snarling traffic. Even if I knew where to start looking, the town will be socked in and my people will be tied up with storm complications."

"Bring your drink to the living room. Then I'll listen while you vent and brainstorm." Patty watched in helpless sympathy as he drained the whiskey. "Do you want a refill?"

"Yes, but no. I need a clear head. Put on the local news, would you? At least they'll tell us how long and how bad this storm will be. Where are the kids?"

"They wanted me to make pizza and let them take it upstairs to watch *The Avengers*."

"Again?"

"They love it. You go sit. I'll bring coffee."

They settled into the love seat, stocking feet resting on the coffee table. Simba, finally resigned to his person's absence, curled up in Patty's lap and closed his eyes. Matt put an arm around his wife's shoulders. "Thanks, dear. I'm sorry this case has made me such a grump these past few months."

Patty snuggled closer, careful not to disturb the sleeping cat. "Remember, dear, my dad was a cop. I knew what I was getting into when I married you. So. What do you know? Never mind right now what you don't. Stick to the positive."

Matt finished his coffee. "I'm pretty sure the person who killed Stanley Turner and made threats is one of the people who was in Turner's house the night of the murder. That's when he got the files."

Patty detached herself from his arm. "I'll be right back. I'll need paper and a pen so I can keep notes."

Matt grumbled, "I've got a desk full of notes."

She gave him a gentle thump on the head. "Well, they aren't here and anyway, those are old notes. These will be new notes." She quickly returned. "Okay, so who was at Turner's house that night, and which ones are still on your suspect list?"

Matt got up and started pacing. "I think better on my feet. Right. There's Fred Ferrett. He's no killer and Polly Ann is his best friend. He's been the target of the threats and he may eventually be able to identify our perp."

"Did you just say 'perp'? I thought only TV cops used that term."

Matt laughed and stopped pacing long enough to plant a kiss on Patty's forehead. "I think we borrowed it from them. Anyway, if Freddie's on the list at all, he's way at the bottom.

"I felt that Katrina Tallfeather was hiding something tied up with a past connection to Polly Ann. That's where I've been most of the day. Her story explained a lot and definitely removed her from the list of suspects."

"Who's a suspect, Dad?" Dan, Matt and Patty's son, appeared in the living room doorway.

"Are you eavesdropping?"

"Nope. The show's over, we finished the pizza, and Mom was making brownies when we went upstairs."

Patty headed into the kitchen. "C'mon, Dan. I'll cut the brownies and you can take a plate upstairs for you and Kate."

"With ice cream?"

"Okay. Matt, you want some, too? And more coffee?"

A few minutes later, Patty and Matt finished their desserts. Patty picked up her pen. "Who's next?"

"Regent Brasseth. He's slick. He and Wills Gladwin may have committed fraud, but the only witness was conveniently killed in a car accident. Hunter Edwards is another puzzle. The question is, what's his motive? He's either scared spitless or is one hell of an actor.

"The only others on my original list are Glynda and Jorge Martin, and I crossed them off the suspect list almost immediately."

"Well," Patty said, "that's a start. Let's see what the storm update is and go to bed."

"Woman, are you propositioning me?"

"Well, sort of. I'll run a bath for you. And there's chicken noodle soup you can have while you're soaking."

The bath and the soup collaborated to ease his pain – riding a snowmobile in the middle of a storm was like riding a bucking bronco. Patty offered to rub him down with liniment. "Thanks, dear. Just this once, I won't mind smelling of wintergreen. What's the latest on the storm news?"

"Beginning to taper off by late Thursday. The city plows have been running all day and will keep it up as long as necessary. They're doing only the main streets, of course, so smart folks will stay home. You won't try to get to the precinct, will you?"

"No. I'll work on the phone. Katrina gave me some possible leads, so I'll get available officers to do some computer searches. We can't physically look for Polly Ann, but we might get a hint as to her whereabouts. Speaking of Polly Ann, how's Simba doing?"

"He's curled up on Dan's bed. He and the kids are sleeping soundly."

"I hope Polly Ann is where she can sleep safely tonight. I wonder how her day went."

50

Wednesday, January 30

Hard as the cot was, Polly Ann slept soundly. Something woke her up. There it was again. She breathed a sigh of relief; it was the alarm on her watch. She'd gone to sleep at 9:00 and the hands now showed 7:30, so it must be morning. Wednesday. She swung her feet off the bed and squiggled into her boots. A shower would be good; brushing her teeth even better, but the bathroom offered only a threadbare washcloth.

She decided not to wash her face, grubby as it felt. She'd reserve the little washcloth for cleaning her teeth. Even in captivity, priorities were important. Back in the other room, Polly Ann did a few stretches and knee bends before hunger could no longer be ignored.

She took two sandwiches out of the Wendy's bag – PB&J and ham with cheese. She put a bit of lettuce inside the ham one, wishing she had a dill pickle. Breakfast was accompanied by V8 juice and a latte. Fond as she was of hazelnut lattes, for breakfast she preferred regular, black, hot coffee. Lukewarm latte couldn't compete.

When she finished eating, she removed the contents of the bag and put them on the bed. If she couldn't figure out an escape, she'd have to start rationing her food. "And I'd better eat the beef sandwich and the chicken one for lunch. Food poisoning would not be good. I hope it's not too late to worry about that. And I'm not really talking to myself; I'm pretending Simba is here as my faithful listener."

She replaced the food in the bag, ready to search for tools and weapons. The main room of her prison offered little in the way of hardware. The walls were bare. She crawled under the cot, hoping the mattress was supported by a network of wires. It wasn't. A slab of plywood rested on the metal frame. The frame itself was held together by rusty bolts that might respond to a large screwdriver, but she didn't have one.

Perhaps standing on the cot would get her high enough to reach the ceiling, where there was probably a metal grid holding up the ceiling tiles. If she could trust the cot not to collapse under her weight. She'd try it later, if she got desperate.

Let's see what the bathroom has to offer. Polly Ann was familiar with the innards of toilet tanks. With any luck, this one would have a metal arm attached to the plug. And she knew how to detach the lever and remove the toilet seat.

The slimy water in the toilet bowl should have warned her, but she grimaced in distaste when she lifted the lid of the tank. "Yuck! I am not putting my hands in that. There's so much gunk coating the innards that I can't tell if the fittings are metal or plastic."

Most people talk to themselves occasionally. People with pets do it often in the firm belief that the pet listens to every word. If Simba had been present, Polly Ann would have discussed at length her plans to repurpose the plumbing fixtures into tools of escape. Without Simba, the words echoed forlornly in the silence.

She turned to the cupboard under the sink where she found an unopened bottle of Clorox and – halleluiah! – a long -handled brush and a pair of rubber gloves.

She flushed the toilet and as soon as the tank began to fill, she poured in half the Clorox. It could sit all day, loosening the rust-colored goo. She replaced the lid and turned to the shower. Black smudges of mold speckled the inside walls, but it was the shower head that attracted her attention. Her shoulders slumped. This thing was useless. Unlike modern fittings with a flexible hose and the shower head cradled in a wall bracket, this one had no hose and was firmly attached to the wall above her head. *Lord, if Matt can't find me, show me how to get out of here by myself.*

Polly Ann left the bathroom and sat down on the cot. She pulled the next to last latte from the backpack and opened it. She thought better over coffee.

She didn't want to attack the toilet tank before the bleach had time to work, so she ate her lunch. She wasn't sleepy; there wasn't a magazine or book in sight, but she had to something while waiting for the gunk to loosen up. Book lists were always good for killing time and she would need ideas for next fall's classes. She had no writing paper, and no implement to write with, but the backpack held enough paper napkins for a family picnic. She explored the pockets of her parka and found a stubby eraserless pencil.

The only surface hard enough to serve as a desktop was a piece of heavy cardboard that stiffened and gave shape to the bottom of the backpack. She removed it, leaving the bag to collapse.

For the spring term, she'd be teaching a science fiction/fantasy class. Her personal list of favorite books was several pages long; in a single class, only half a dozen could be discussed in any depth. She covered several napkins with three times the number of titles she would need. It took half the afternoon for her to narrow the list. Next, where would the bookstore find sufficient copies? Heinlein's *Stranger in a Strange Land* was widely available, but Herbert's *Dune* had been out of favor for years. A couple others would require contacting used book dealers and out of print sources.

She considered a few of Heinlein's other novels. His heroes and heroines were amazingly creative when it came of getting out of tight spots, especially Lazarus Long. Of course, it didn't hurt that he could add or subtract years from his body almost at will. She tucked that thought into the back of her mind.

By the time Polly Ann finished her lists, which she put in an inside pocket of the parka, it was nearly 5:00. The Clorox should have had time to loosen some of the gunk. She returned to the bathroom and removed the lid of the toilet tank. She donned the rubber gloves and grabbed the brush. Soon, she could see the inner workings of the toilet. All plastic, except for two metal bolts at the bottom of the tank, the source of the rust color of the slime.

She was disappointed, but not surprised. And while part of her mind had been on science fiction, another part had come up with a better idea for escape.

She turned to the cupboard under the bathroom sink. Sitting on the floor, she reached in to remove the nut holding the metal strip that connected to the drain plug. It took several hefty yanks with her bare hands to break off the attached end, but when she was finished, she triumphantly held up an eight-inch shiv.

However, she couldn't use it to force the door open; it wasn't strong enough. What else would work? Her eyes drifted up to the ceiling tiles. She had once – only once; it was not a job for amateurs – installed ceiling tiles. The metal grids supporting the tiles were thicker, stronger than her little improvised knife.

She stood in the middle of the cot, fingertips on a tile. She was able to lift it an inch or two. To get it a bit higher, she raised herself on her tiptoes, lost her balance, and fell, twisting her ankle. Inching to the edge of the cot, she tried to stand up. "Oh, ow! Shit! That hurts. Please, Lord, it isn't broken." She fell back. Why the hell hadn't her captor put an ice pack in the backpack?

Okay, I'm done for today. She pulled the lid off the pot pie, ate it and the salad, and drank another bottle of juice. She ached all over. A hot shower would have helped, but even if there was a working hot water heater someplace in this basement, she didn't trust the plumbing. Maybe her ankle would recover by morning. As she nodded off, she wondered if the storm still raged outside.

STRIKE VOTE

51

Thursday, January 31

Patty, bearing a mug of coffee, woke Matt up. "It's nearly 9:00, and Charlie just phoned, bored and eager to do something."

"Thanks, love. I'll get to work as soon as I'm dressed."

"You don't have to get dressed or shave if you'd rather not. You could work in your bathrobe for all we care. No one else would ever know."

Matt grinned. "Can I trust you or one of the kids not to take a picture and post it on the internet for the whole world to see? I suppose I could put my badge on the lapel of my robe."

"Drink your coffee. As soon as you're feeling official, breakfast will be ready."

Pushing aside his empty plate, previously filled with waffles and bacon, Matt returned Charlie's call. "Charlie, I hope you're not one of the many people who've lost power." Assured that the officer still had lights, heat, and a functioning computer, he explained what he wanted. "I need you to track down accounts in Michigan newspapers from 12 to 15 years ago of a hunting accident and the disappearance of a young Indian girl."

Matt hoped that at least one account would have the name of the third man.

Next, he phoned Human Resources. Perhaps someone had braved the storm to man the office and could give him Fred Ferrett's home phone number. It was in the directory in the office, but not here. Maybe Fred could trace the backgrounds of Bill Brasseth and Hunter Edwards.

An unfamiliar voice answered the phone. "Human Resources. This is Caroline. If it's urgent for you to speak to Director Ferrett, please phone his cell. That number is 555-3233."

"Thank you. I'll try that."

"Freddie, it's Matt Brophy. What happened to Belinda?"

"I fired her. Don't worry. She doesn't know the real reason. I told her she spent too much time on her computer on personal business. What else is on your mind?"

"Are you and Ivan okay? No threatening calls?"

"No. We're just bored. I hope you have something for us to do."

"Indeed I do. I assume your new girl is trustworthy?"

Freddie laughed. "She'd love being called a girl. She's my seventy-five year old great aunt, and she'd go to hell and back for me. She's temping until we find a permanent replacement for Belinda. She lives across the street from campus. I think she used snowshoes to navigate the drifts."

"That's great. I need someone with access to your office files. Would you ask her to pull all the records you've got on William Brasseth, Wills Gladwin, and Hunter Edwards? Where were they born, where'd they go to school, where were they living ten, twenty years ago, when did they show up in Colorado? Have her fax or e-mail everything she can find to me – and to you as well. You might see something I would miss."

"E-mail will work. I don't have a fax machine at home. Do you?"

"You're right. I don't. It's at the precinct. So, e-mail it is."

"May I ask what you hope to find?"

"I can't share everything, but there was a murder in Michigan many years ago, declared an accident. Stanley Turner knew about it and thought he recognized someone now here in Ridgeview as a witness to what actually happened."

"You want what we've got on Turner as well?"

"Sure. You have all the background on current and past regents?"

"We do. I'll get Caroline working on this right away."

An hour later, Matt laid the reports from Fred Ferrett's Aunt Caroline side by side across his desk. Huntington Edwards III (aka Hunter Edwards) on the far left, Bill Brasseth next, Wills Gladwin in the middle, Stanley Turner on the right.

He expected to confirm his suspicion that all four had been in southeastern Michigan/northeastern Ohio in the relevant time period. The reports belied that. Only Stanley Turner had lived and worked there.

STRIKE VOTE

The records confirmed Katrina's account that the man had owned and managed Turner's Tours, a travel agency in Ann Arbor, for several years before he relocated to Colorado.

Despite the evidence that neither Brasseth nor Gladwin had ever lived east of the Mississippi River, Matt was still convinced that there was something linking the four men.

However, the real eye opener was that Hunter Edwards had not existed until a dozen years ago. Matt studied the man's file, his vita, accompanying newspaper clippings, and various notes. The vita – compiled, of course, by the man himself – declared that Edwards was born in 1970, earned a B.A. and Ph.D. in economics from the University of Minnesota, and taught for four years at Mankato State.

A handwritten note from Ferrett said, "Matt, I've contacted people in Minnesota. There's no record of a Hunter or Huntington Edwards, with or without Roman numerals after the name. I'll dig deeper; maybe Google will help. I'll call you when I have something."

Matt almost asked, "Who's Google?" before remembering that it had something to do with getting information from a computer. Both Patty and Alice teased him regularly about his refusal to learn how to do anything on the computer except e-mail. His only defense was that other people were geniuses at coaxing information from machines the size of small TVs and he didn't have time to learn.

He forced himself to spend an hour with the newspaper, wondering how the delivery person managed to get around the paper route when hardly anything else was moving. He read the editorials, disagreeing with Cal Thomas' insistence that climate change was a hoax, agreeing with the editor's plaint that the city needed more snowplows. He read the comics, finding most of them not very funny. It took him twenty minutes to solve the Jumble. He didn't feel desperate enough to try Sudoku.

Patty came in twice to refill his coffee mug, but didn't stay. The second time, he asked, "What are you doing today?" hoping that perhaps there was something they could do together to pass the time.

"I'm cleaning out the kitchen cabinets and washing all the stuff on the top shelves. We should donate most of that to Goodwill – it's serving no useful purpose, just collecting dust. Would you like to help?"

"Ah, no thanks. I think I'll dig out my old snowshoes and see if anyone in the neighborhood needs help getting out of a garage. You need anything from King Soopers? If I get that far?"

"I'll put together a list. There's nothing urgent, but we're always nearly out of something."

Matt was able to help a couple neighbors. He got to the corner of Ridgeview Road and Maple in time to help two of his officers untangle the vehicles involved in a fender bender. The earliest snow had turned to ice on the once-warm pavement and the succeeding six or eight inches of snow hid the danger beneath. Until the plows and salt trucks got to the side streets, driving was going to be treacherous.

He continued on to the grocery store, picked up the milk and bread flour Patty requested, and headed back home. He cut through the alley behind the houses on Ridgeview, passing behind Stanley Turner's former home. He was surprised to see a dim glow of light reflecting off the snow at the foundation of the house. Curious, he moved closer. The light was coming from an invisible window, discernible only because he could see the metal rim of a window well filled with snow. *That's odd. Whoever is checking that squatters or vandals don't get in must have left the basement lights on. We'll have to check that out.*

By the time he got home, Patty had a pot of split pea soup bubbling on the stove and he could smell a new batch of brownies. "Give me time to have a hot shower, honey, and I'll be right back."

The unaccustomed exercise and the hot soup combined to make him aware that he was bone tired. He hadn't been sleeping well lately; perhaps a nap was just what he needed. "Patty, you need me to do anything?"

"No, thanks. I've started a new book, and it's a good one. You look tired. Go lie down for a while. I'll wake you if anything interesting happens."

Matt woke up hours later and spent a minute wondering why a cat was curled up under his chin and licking his ear lobe. "Simba?" The cat purred and began to knead his chest.

52

Thursday, January 31

Polly Ann woke up slowly, wondering why Simba was not curled up near her or patting her face with soft paws to get her to open her eyes. Then she remembered: she was not in her own cozy bed and Simba was not sharing her prison.

Still, she was reluctant to get out of her cocoon of musty blankets. The cot had not become any softer, but it was warm. And she felt weak, sore all over. The previous day's gyrations under the bathroom sink had activated long dormant muscles.

She refused to admit that she was afraid – afraid that he would come back. Or that he wouldn't. Afraid that despite the previous day's little triumphs, the door would stay locked, she would run out of food, the lights – were they flickering? – would go out, leaving her to starve in eternal darkness.

I'm Polly Ann, not Pollyanna. I do not see the positive in situations. A forlorn tear spilled onto her cheek. Then another. She sniffed and squared her shoulders. *It's up to me to escape. I can't depend on anyone else.*

She wiped away the tears, threw back the consolation of warm covers, and put on her sweater and boots. Gingerly, she set her feet on the floor and tested the injured ankle. It seemed to be okay. Tender, but okay. She made a quick trip to the bathroom, remembering to scrape the night's fuzz from her teeth with the threadbare washcloth. She ate the remaining peanut butter and jelly sandwich, drank the last V-8 juice, and wished there'd been another latte.

Once fortified, she returned to the bathroom. Removal of the metal strip that could become a weapon had revealed something of greater possible value.

Freeing the thin, 4-inch long rod left hanging where the metal strip had been was easy. Polly Ann had repaired more than one faulty sink drain in her time. She examined the little rod fondly. It might, it just might fit the keyhole of her prison.

She took it to the door and aimed for the old-fashioned keyhole, thanking her lucky stars that it wasn't designed like modern ones. Her hand shook so hard she dropped her fake key, perilously close to the narrow slit under the door. "Get a grip, girl," she admonished herself.

The second try was better, but the thing got stuck before it was fully in. Polly Ann had to twist and tug hard to pull it out. The third time was the charm. It was a tight fit, but not so tight she couldn't feel something moving inside the lock. She wiped her damp hands on her jeans before resuming her efforts. She didn't dare hope, but she could pray. "Here goes nothing. Lord, if you're listening, I can't do this alone."

A sudden click startled her. *Oh, crap! He's back. He's right outside and his key is in the lock. Where's my shiv? Damn. It's still in the bathroom.*

When nothing happened and her heart rate returned to near normal, she realized what the click was. She turned the doorknob and pulled. Inch by inch, the door opened. The light shining through the door from her prison let her see the staircase straight ahead. The rest of the basement was dark. She didn't care. "I've done it! Thank you, Lord."

Polly Ann pushed the backpack through the opening, preventing the door from swinging shut and leaving her in the dark. She hurried back to the bathroom, grabbed her only weapon, and returned to the exit. She pulled on the parka, stuffed the remaining food and the shiv in its pockets and started toward the stairs.

She turned back and took her homemade key from the lock. She smiled. "He'll drive himself nuts trying to figure out how I escaped."

53

That same morning

Matt finished his bacon and eggs, mopping his plate with the last bit of toast. "Patty, you're spoiling me. That's twice in two days."

"You rarely have time for a proper breakfast, so it's fun for me to show off my culinary skills. You finished just in time. Mr. Ferrett is on the phone."

"Morning, Matt. I googled Hunter Edwards and Huntington Edwards and when that got me nothing useful – only a sentence about his being a regent at Ridge U and a little squib about the university – I tried Edward Hunter and Theodore Hunter. And I got a hit."

"What made you think of that?"

"Well, I've got a rather dorky cousin named Carter Clark, who thought it was funny to sign his name as Clark Carter. Spending the time I do looking at various documents, I've always found it interesting to see first and last names that could be reversed.

"Anyway, since Hunter Edwards didn't seem to exist before he showed up here, I started thinking. 'Ed' is often a nickname for both Edward and Theodore. And there it was: Theodore Hunter. So I phoned an old friend in the state police and he made some more calls, and got the whole story."

"So tell me about Theodore 'Ed' Hunter."

"Born and raised in northern Ohio. Ne'er do well kid – swiped cars for joyrides, arrested for drunk driving several times, suspected drug dealer, spent a couple years in prison for forging the signature on a few of his grandmother's Social Security checks. What do you bet his uncle Clarence – Stan Turner's friend – invited him to go fishing, and let him take along a rifle?"

"Why would he kill the pharmacist?"

"Drugs. I did some checking there, too. Clarence Hunter was under investigation for cooking the company books and selling drugs to suppliers in Ohio and Michigan. Maybe Eddie was one of his dealers and Uncle Clarence was ready to ask for a plea deal."

"You're a wonder, Freddie. I think I'll call on Mr. Hunter."

Matt phoned Judge Forbisher and explained why he wanted a warrant for Hunter Edwards' home. Next, he asked Alice to track down two or three of his officers and tell them he'd meet them at the precinct. He retrieved his ski pants and parka from the clothes horse near the hall register and prepared to go back out into the blizzard.

Adam, Charlie, and Dana were waiting at the precinct. "Thanks for coming so quickly, guys. We need to make three stops. Adam, would you drive? Take us to Stanley Turner's house. I have a strange feeling." Matt was remembering the light in Turner's basement the day before.

"Okay, Boss. Then where?"

"The judge's place to pick up a warrant, and then Regent Edwards' house. Watch for drivers who should have stayed home. Time is critical and we can't afford an accident."

STRIKE VOTE

54

Polly Ann clutched the bannister and cautiously planted her left foot firmly on the next stair before lifting the right one. Part of her wanted to surge up the stairs, fling open the door into whoever's house this was, and dash out the front door to safety.

But what if, once outside in pure, clean air she didn't know where she was, didn't know which way to go? What if the blizzard still raged and she could only see a few feet in front of her?

All staircases had twelve steps, she'd heard. So one more to go and a door would be in front of her. What if it was locked? She could see nothing. The light from her prison that had guided her this far had flickered and gone out. Probably one of the modern systems programmed to quit when no one was in the room.

She reached out a hand. Empty space. Reach further. Good. Instead of space in front of her hand, there was solid wood. Polly Ann fumbled until she felt a long crack – one side of the door. She moved her hand up and down, seeking a knob. Instead, she found a hinge.

She wanted to pound on the door in frustration, but forced herself to take deep breaths before sliding her hand across to where a knob had to be. Another long crack. She held onto the bannister with one hand while moving the other carefully up and down, not right near the edge, but where a doorknob ought to be. And was. She turned it and pushed.

The sudden light blinded her. She waited for her eyes to adjust. It wasn't all that bright, but after the gloom of the stairwell, it was almost painful.

Her knees shook. She shuffled through the door, found herself in a kitchen, stumbled into the next room, and dropped into the nearest chair. She was facing a picture window with partially open drapes.

Outside, snow continued to blow, seemingly in every direction. She couldn't tell if it was old snow caught up in the wild wind surges or new snow continuing to fall and making it to the ground far away. She could see the fuzzy outline of trees and houses, so perhaps the storm was beginning to let up.

She looked around the room, then looked again. She began to laugh, not quite in hysteria. "I don't believe it," she said to the flocked wallpaper and chintz-covered sofa. "The gall of that turd! He locked me up in Stanley Turner's basement."

Polly Ann had been in the house a few times before Turner's death – for a sherry party or some such – and noted the incongruity between some very nice antiques in the lovely century-old house and the frankly tacky upholstered chairs and sofa.

She wanted to open the door and dash across the street to her own cozy house and hug her cat. She pulled aside a corner of one of the drapes across the picture window. She couldn't see the street; the trees on the boulevard appeared to be ghosts. The snow was still coming down hard and the wind still whipping it every which way. With her luck, she would get hit by an unseen car in the middle of the street or get blown so far off course that she'd wind up in the park and snow would cover her body until it was found weeks later.

It would be foolhardy to risk the storm. She would find one of Turner's phones and pray that it was still connected. As she started to let go of the drape, she glanced out the window one last time. And froze. A car stopped right in front of the house. A hooded figure got out. Polly Ann fumbled through her parka to find her homemade knife and tiptoed to the door.

55

"You three stay here while I check inside the house," Matt said. "If I find anything, I'll call you."

He waded through the thigh-high snow and nearly tripped on the steps. He took off his gloves and fished Turner's house key out of a pocket. The driving snow chilled his bare hands, but he didn't want to risk dropping the key where finding it would be like searching for a needle in a very cold, wet haystack.

He unlocked the door and pushed it open before abruptly falling backward. The snow slightly cushioned the insult to his tailbone. He looked up in wonder at the woman in the doorway waving what appeared to be a knife. "Polly Ann, is that you?"

'Matt! Is it really you? I am so sorry. I thought you were him – he. That awful man."

"Uh, Polly Ann, would you put the knife down please?"

It dropped from her hand. She started to cry. Matt extricated himself from the snowbank, waved at his officers, and held out his arms.

He held her safe and murmured as if to an injured child, "There, there, it's all right now."

Polly Ann's sobs turned to sniffles and she pushed herself a few inches away. "I don't have a hanky."

Matt produced a large handkerchief. "Here. As soon as you feel better, we'll go."

"I can make it across the street if you'll watch for cars. When I get home, I'm going to make a cup of tea." She hiccupped. "I've had nothing hot to drink for days!"

"There's coffee in the car. Sorry, Polly Ann, but we have to make a couple stops before I get you to safety and warmth. I'll explain as soon as we're on our way." He zipped it her parka and pulled up the hood. "Do you have mittens?"

Charlie saw them coming and got out of the car to open the back door. "Dr. Passarelli, are we ever glad to see you! Chief, you want to get in back with her? Dana can squeeze up front with me and Adam."

"Sure. Where's that thermos of coffee? The lady needs a hot drink."

As soon as they started slipping and sliding on the treacherous street, Matt explained to Polly Ann where they were going and why. They stopped a few blocks away in front of Judge Forbisher's home. "You all sit tight. I'll be right back with the warrant."

Polly Ann took one last sip and replaced the cap on the thermos as they began to move again.

Matt stowed the empty thermos in a cup holder. "Polly Ann, are you feeling brave and full of righteous indignation? I think seeing you will shock our suspect out of any complacency he may be feeling."

"Ready when you are, chief. I'm not just indignant, I'm furious."

56

Hunter Edwards' house was five blocks north of Judge Forbisher's, half a mile from Turner's. They went slowly on streets still ice-covered and hazardous. Matt rang the doorbell. Edwards opened the inner door and peered at the officers, looking surprised at seeing Polly Ann with them. "Ms. Passarelli, you ought to be indoors someplace warm."

"That's Dr. Passarelli to you. I got tired of being shut in."

"May we come in?" Matt asked.

Edwards hesitated for a moment before nodding and turning away, leaving them to open the storm door and let themselves in. Edwards continued moving through the entry alcove. He watched with a faint smile as Polly Ann removed her boots and the others wiped their feet before joining him in the living room.

"Do sit down, ladies and gentlemen. To what do I owe the – ah – pleasure of your company?"

Matt held out the warrant. Instinctively Edwards reached out and took it. "What's this?"

"A warrant permitting me and my officers to search your house."

"For what?"

"Let's see." Matt scanned his copy of the warrant. "The first few items include note paper on which we can print a few lines from your computer to see if we have a match. Not quite as good as fingerprints, but it'll be a start. Your cell phone. A black cloak of some sort. A Halloween mask with a distinctive face. There's more, but that will give you rough idea."

"Adam, would you take Mr. Edwards into the kitchen? Charlie, Dana, we'll start here and work our way through the house. Polly Ann, you'd better follow us, just to be safe."

They found Edwards' computer in a small nook off the living room, a basic home office. As Dana turned on the computer and began typing, Polly Ann asked, "Are computer fonts really almost as good as fingerprints?"

"No, of course not. But it'll give him something to think about." Matt looked through the drawers and shelves of the desk, stacked neatly with office supplies. "Nothing suspicious here, and I didn't see any obvious hiding places. We'll check more thoroughly later if we don't find anything upstairs."

At the top of the stairs, the first door opened into a guest room, rarely used, judging by the layer of dust on the dresser and bedside table. The bathroom cupboards held nothing but linens and a few cleaning supplies. Charlie lifted off the top of the toilet tank. "Nothing here." Instinctively, Polly Ann caught her breath and peered over Charlie's shoulder, expecting to see another tank full of slime. This one was a whole lot cleaner than the one in Turner's basement.

The next room had to be Edwards' – unmade bed, bathrobe on a hook over the door, and soiled clothes trailing over the sides of a tall wicker hamper. Matt opened the closet and pushed the clothes aside, one hanger at a time. Encased in a dry cleaner bag was a black gown, size XXL.

"No wonder you thought he was huge, Polly Ann; this would fit nicely over heavy outdoor gear. Now, where's that Nixon mask?"

Matt lifted four shoeboxes off the closet shelf. The first two contained nothing but shoes. He took the top off the third one and was holding up the Nixon mask when he heard a loud "Stop!" from downstairs and the sound of a door slamming shut. He dropped the mask and ran to the window, Polly Ann right behind him.

They were in time to see a red convertible, top sensibly up, back rapidly out of the driveway and disappear up the street. Dana and Charlie were already out the door, racing down the stairs and to the front door. Matt tore after them and stopped abruptly at the kitchen doorway. "Adam, what the hell happened?"

Adam sat on the floor, holding his head. A trickle of blood leaked through his fingers. "The son of a bitch – sorry, ma'am – decked me with a teakettle full of water. I guess I'm lucky it wasn't boiling."

Polly Ann grabbed a wad of paper towels from under the sink and handed it to the injured officer. "Here, Adam, you're bleeding."

Adam struggled to get to his feet before Matt told him to stay still. "You may have a concussion."

"Aw, shit, chief. He got away, didn't he?"

"Afraid so, but I don't think he'll get far in that excuse for a car. Those little things will skid on an ice cube and get stuck in a snow flake. We'll find it in a snowbank in the next block."

"What do we do now, chief?" Dana asked.

Matt was already fastening his parka. "We split up. I want this house thoroughly searched from top to bottom – Turner's files are here someplace. We need them. And we'll try to figure out the most likely place or places he'd try to get to, if he's still on the move."

Polly Ann sat at the kitchen table, her head resting on her hands. She looked up, frowning. "Matt, maybe he would go to see if he can threaten Dr. Gladwin, assuming he has something to threaten him with. More likely, and this really scares me, he'll head for Freddie's house. "Freddie and Ivan have no suspicion that Edwards is the one who's been threatening everyone, the one who kidnapped both me and Ivan, the one who murdered Dr. Turner. He knows Freddie would do anything to keep Ivan safe, so he might force Freddie to hide him or help him escape."

Matt nodded his approval. "Good thinking. Okay, here's what we'll do. Charlie, you come with me. We'll take Polly Ann home – I'll phone Patty to look after her – and then we'll check on Ferrett and Gladwin. Dana, I want you and Adam to take this place apart – and you can monitor Adam for a possible concussion."

Polly Ann pushed herself away from the table, exhausted but resolute. "I'm coming with you to make sure Freddie's all right."

"No, you're not. Charlie and I can't protect you and simultaneously try to apprehend a possibly armed fugitive. Let us do our job. For now, you've done yours – magnificently, I might add."

Resigned, Polly Ann put her boots back on, wincing a bit, and zipped up her parka, wrinkling her nose at the olfactory evidence that she'd lived in the same clothes for three days. Three days without a shower.

She fell asleep before the police cruiser pulled away from the curb. Matt shook her shoulder when they stopped in front of his house.

"We're there. Can you walk?"

The ankle nearly betrayed her, but Matt supported her on the short distance to his front door. Patty took over, helping her to the nearest chair.

Simba, who did not like getting wet, carefully avoided the puddles left by the snow melting off Polly Ann's clothes. As Patty removed Polly Ann's boots, mittens, and parka, the cat sniffed disapprovingly as each item was added to the heap on the floor.

He followed as Patty led his lost person to the bathroom, saying, "Polly Ann, your bath is ready. Can I help you out of your clothes?"

Polly Ann slumped against her friend, too tired to cry. Between the two of them, they managed to banish the sweater, jeans, t-shirt, bra, briefs, and smelly socks to the hamper.

"Patty, you could just put them in the trash. I never want to see them again."

"Pity the poor trash collector!" That got a real smile from Polly Ann. Patty helped her into the tub. "I'll start the washing machine as soon as you're settled. Don't slide down too far. I'll be right back. Simba, take care of her."

Simba levitated onto the edge of the bathtub and sat down, big blue eyes firmly fixed on Polly Ann. She felt like a noodle, gradually going limp as the hot water did its job. Patty returned, bearing the mug Polly Ann had given her one year for her birthday – the one with a Siamese face looking straight ahead and the caption saying, "You're in my chair."

"The soup's chicken noodle," Patty said, "guaranteed to cure sniffles, banish bacteria, and restore the world to proper balance. Drink up. I'll wash your back."

"Would you start with my hair, please? And give me a minute to finish the soup. Right now, it's more even important than soap."

Once Polly Ann was soaped all over, Patty helped her stand up while the tub drained and she could use the shower head on its flexible hose to rinse the dirt down the drain.

Wrapped in a thick terry robe, Polly Ann limped to the Brophy's guest bedroom. Patty tucked her in, Simba curled up beside her, and she slept.

57

Charlie drove slowly as he and Matt scanned the side streets, looking for Edward's little red car. "Charlie, you know where Mr. Ferrett lives?" Matt asked.

"I think so, chief. Ponderosa Place? Barn red ranch house with white shutters?"

"That's right." As they turned the corner, the red sports car in the driveway of Freddie and Ivan's house answered the question of where Edwards had run to.

Someone had shoveled the walkway, but a layer of ice lay under the two or three inches of snow that had fallen since then. Matt shuffled up to the front door and rang the doorbell.

Freddie opened the door, eyes as big as saucers when he saw who it was, and began to speak. Matt interrupted him. "Hi, Freddie. Have you heard from Polly Ann? She hasn't been in touch for the past day or two, and Patty and I are a bit concerned."

Freddie's eyes blinked and darted from Matt to the cruiser and back again. Matt covered his mouth with a gloved hand and pretended to cough while saying softly, "She's okay."

Freddie relaxed in relief. "No, we haven't heard from her. It's great to see you, Matt. We have another visitor. I believe you know Regent Edwards. You want to come in and warm up?"

"Yeah, thanks. Just for a minute. I should remove my boots before I drip all over your floors."

"Don't worry about them. It's only water. Here's a towel for you to wipe some of it off. Come on into the living room."

Matt followed Freddie as carefully as he could. "Hi, Ivan. Sorry to interrupt. I didn't realize you had company. Hello, Mr. Edwards. Good day to be indoors with friends, isn't it?"

"Mr. Edwards arrived a few minutes ago," Ivan said. "We were just getting acquainted. Freddie and he have met, of course, at university functions, but I try to avoid those things."

Matt realized that Freddie and Ivan had no idea who Edwards really was and why Matt was there. He thought fast. *How do I get Ivan away from him?*

"Ivan, since I'm here, could I borrow that new Grisham book you were talking about?"

Ivan nodded, got to his feet, and walked over to an end table near where Matt stood, Freddie behind him. Matt watched for any move from Edwards that would suggest he was armed. Seeing no sign of threat, he said, "Mr. Edwards, would you come with me, please? I think we have a few things to discuss."

Edwards hesitated, but he was outnumbered and although Matt had said "please," the expression on his face did not allow a refusal.

Ivan said, "I'll get your coat." Matt took it from him, checked the pockets, and, without being seen, removed a small pistol. He held the parka for Edwards to put on. "Ivan, Freddie, would you take his arms so he doesn't fall going out the door? Those sneakers he's wearing are not quite the thing for this weather."

Once outside, Matt told Freddie and Ivan to stay in the house. "It's too cold out here to be standing around without coats." Taking Edwards by the elbow, he said, "Let's go, shall we?"

Charlie walked up from the patrol car, leaving the engine running. He handed Matt a pair of handcuffs. "Thanks, Charlie. Mr. Edwards, if you'd be so kind, put your hands behind your back."

They should have looked more closely at Edwards' sneakers. They weren't slippery-soled tennis shoes; they were golf shoes, complete with sharp spikes, intended to provide traction on grass and sand, and – in this case – ice and snow. They were also potential weapons. Edwards stomped one foot on Charlie's instep.

The sudden, sharp contact caused Charlie to stumble into Matt, and the icy sidewalk finished the job of sending the two men crashing to the ground. As they attempted to right themselves, Edwards jumped into the patrol car and roared away.

"Aw, shit! Not again. Matt, that freaky guy is slicker than a greased pig." Matt was already on his cell phone, calling in BOLO and APB alerts, furious and embarrassed that Edwards had outmaneuvered him again.

That done, he called to check in with his other two officers. He told them about the latest fiasco and said, "I'll give you all the gory details when I get there."

As soon as Matt had left them at Edwards' house, Dana and Adam agreed that they should finish the search upstairs before tackling the kitchen. Edwards didn't seem the sort who would keep incriminating evidence in the flour or sugar canisters.

"Why don't you sit in that chair and go through the dresser drawers, Adam? I'll finish what the chief started in the closet."

Dana pulled the remaining shoe boxes from the closet shelf along with a file-sized box. Once the shelf was clear, she set everything on the bed. "Shoes. More shoes. Let's see what's in this big box." She lifted out one folder at a time, briefly checking the contents of each one before setting it aside.

"Looks like we've got a treasure trove here, Adam. Somebody – maybe Turner –carefully labelled every file. There's one for Limbach, the ex-president; one labelled 'Regents'; and individual ones for Gladwin, members of the search committee, and a few names I don't recognize. Matt will want this entire box.

"How are you doing on the dresser, Adam?"

"Slow going. This one drawer seems to be a catchall for bank statements, receipts for everything from gas to garden mulch, unfilled prescriptions, and a bunch of loose cryptic notes like '50 oxys, $5000, LL.' Drug records, maybe?"

"We'll bag it all for Matt to examine. I'll see what the bathroom has to offer, especially the medicine cabinet."

Adam's cell phone chimed the opening bars of the Hallelujah Chorus. "Yeah, boss. We found all sorts of goodies: files, receipts, notes maybe referring to drug deals, and a box full of syringes and unlabeled vials of some liquid. We're about done upstairs. You want us to start looking through the fridge, freezer, and any open boxes of dry goods? Dana already checked the liquor cabinet. Guess what? A couple bottles of mead."

As soon as Adam paused for breath, Matt told him about the latest setback. Adam said, "Oh, shit. Okay, we'll wrap it up here and we'll be ready when you get here . . . Oh, thanks. My head's fine. Hard as ever."

Adam put his phone away. "Hey, Dana. Edwards slipped the noose again. The boss sounds really pissed off. He'll give us the details when he gets here. He's on his way."

"Good. It's getting late and I'm hungry. You sure your head's all right? Tell your wife about your situation. Have her watch for signs of concussion."

"No problem. She's a nurse. She fusses."

Matt and Charlie looked at Edwards' Jaguar. "Charlie, can you drive this thing?"

"Probably. He's left the key in the ignition. Hop in."

"Give me a minute to let Ms. Tallfeather that Polly Ann's okay."

Freddie and Ivan stood in the open doorway of their home, no doubt wondering what they'd just seen. Matt waved and called, "I'll catch up with you two later."

It was close to 5:30 when Charlie drove up to Edwards' house. He sat in the now warm little car while Matt went into the house, where he briefed Adam and Dana on Edwards' most recent escape. Neither cracked a smile. Matt said, "I'd like to keep driving all over town in hopes of finding something to help us find her, but I don't need to add to the chaos on the roads. All I can do now is wait for news, and I can do that at home as well as anywhere. I'll drop Charlie and you guys off at the precinct and trade that red thing out there for a proper car. Unless you'd rather come with me. Patty's got a turkey in the oven."

"Turkey? Dude, Christmas was weeks ago, remember?"

"So? Turkey's good anytime. Patty and the kids and I will have sandwiches to take for lunch all week."

Patty met him at the front door, holding the phone. A highway patrol car coming north on the interstate had sighted the RPD patrol car, going south, far over the posted speed of 75 mph. "Sorry, Chief Brophy, I lost him. The interstate's clear now, so he was flying. By the time I reached the next turnaround and started trying to catch up, he was long gone. Could have turned off almost anyplace, or he may still be racing toward Denver. I alerted everyone I could think of."

Despite numerous law enforcement agencies from Berthoud to Boulder and the Denver suburbs, no one spotted the black and white car until the next morning, abandoned in a rough area of Longmont and missing its tires, radio, license plates, GPS, and the contents of the glove box.

The next day, Edwards' picture was displayed on TV stations and several newspapers in towns along the interstate. Every patrol car in the state carried a copy. Matt received more than a bit of teasing from his colleagues around the state for having a suspect swipe an official car and disappear with it. But cops stick together: no one leaked that part of the story to the media.

Joanie Jameson opened her front door to let Ernest get the newspaper from the driveway. She followed his tail plume into the house and held out a hand. "Release." She set the paper on the counter and gave Ernest the expected treat before pouring herself a drink – two fingers of bourbon, a splash of water, and two ice cubes.

She nearly knocked the drink over when she unfolded the paper and saw the headlines. "Ernest! Listen to this! Hunter Edwards is not the kind, caring person I thought he was. If he could do this to Dr. Passarelli and run away when they tried to arrest him, he could do anything! I have to talk to Burt."

58

Friday, February 1

Matt was in his office at 6:30 the next morning, in time to hear that his patrol car had been found. No sign of the man himself. The Longmont police were checking for reports of cars stolen overnight. Glowering at the picture of Hunter Edwards on his desk, copied from a recent Ridge U yearbook, Matt had a eureka moment. "Alice, please call my wife in about an hour – this early, we'd both be in trouble – and tell her I need to speak with Dr. Passarelli."

Katrina arrived on the Brophy doorstep before eight o'clock. Patty said, "I think Polly Ann's had enough sleep and what she needs most right now is to know you're all right. Let me get some coffee for her." She tapped on the guest room door and entered, Katrina almost stepping on her heels. "Polly Ann, here's coffee. I'll leave you two to catch up on the events of the past few days."

"I'd hug you, Polly Ann," Katrina said, "but I don't want to risk spilling coffee on you and Simba." The cat raised his head, eyed the mug in his person's hands, and wisely jumped off the bed.

Polly Ann set the coffee on the bedside table. "Now it's safe. Come here. Kat, I was so afraid I'd never see you again."

"You were scared! Imagine what it was like for the rest of us. However, as a famous poet once said, 'All's well that ends well.'"

"I could have done without some of the stuff between the beginning and the end."

Patty appeared in the doorway. "Sorry to bother you, but Matt's on the phone for you."

Polly Ann listened for a minute before saying, "Kat's here with me. We'll be there as soon as we can." She swung her feet out from under the covers. "Kat, we're summoned. Matt doesn't sound happy. Patty, do you know what's going on?"

"Things went sour after Matt dropped you off," Patty said and told

Polly Ann about Edwards' escape from Freddie's house. "About midnight, I made Matt stop pacing the floor and come to bed. But he tossed and turned half the night, second-guessing himself."

"I saw how fast Edwards got away from them at his house," Polly Ann said. "He was desperate, and I doubt they could have stopped him the second time. Who'd have suspected golf shoes, for pity's sake?

"Give me a couple minutes to get dressed. Oh, hell! I don't have any clothes."

"You've borrowed outfits from me before," Patty assured her. "Go wash your face and I'll bring something suitable."

Polly Ann took one look at Matt. "My friend, you look awful. Have you had any sleep lately?"

"Not much. I've been busy – mostly spinning my wheels."

Katrina got straight to business. "How can we help?"

"Actually, probably you more than Polly Ann. I asked a colleague in Denver with better equipment than ours to do some backwards age progressions on Edwards' official photograph. I suggested making him 10-15 years younger and adding things like a beard, longer hair, a hat. Edwards is in his early forties now, and might have changed a lot over the years. I'd like you to look at the doctored pictures and tell me if any of them appear to be the guy you saw shoot his companion."

Matt spread four 8" by 10" pictures across the desk top. Katrina stood up and leaned over to study them. She straightened up abruptly and turned her head so she was eyeball to eyeball with Matt. She smiled to take the sting out of her words, "Give me some space, man. You're breathing down my neck."

Polly Ann stifled a snort. "Why don't you make yourself useful, Matt? Maybe provide some coffee or pop or even water?"

Matt muttered, "I know when I'm not wanted," but he was grinning. When he returned with a tray of drinks and a plate of crackers and cheese, Katrina had pushed three of the pictures aside and was pointing at the one that showed a younger man with a scruffy beard, wearing a watch cap. "This kind of looks like the guy I saw that day. Will this age regression technology stand up in court?"

"It would if you could make a positive identification, but 'kind of' wouldn't be sufficient. Polly Ann, did you ever see a guy who looks like any of these pictures when you lived in Michigan?"

"Oddly enough, yes. I did. Kat rejected the picture that I recognized." She pulled one photo from the reject pile. "This one. Youngish guy with sort of hippie hair, OSU sweatshirt, and cargo pants. Look at the posture – semi slouch with both hands in his pockets. I've seen Regent Edwards in that same pose at campus meetings."

"Where and when did you see him when he looked like that?" Matt asked, pointing to the picture Polly Ann held.

"A day or two before I went to help out at that kids' camp. I'd gone into the Sav-Rite Drug for some bug spray and calamine lotion and this person was there talking to the pharmacist.

"I wouldn't have remembered that, but I overheard their conversation. The older man said they should be ready to leave by 6:00 a.m. The younger one asked how long it would take to get to Saginaw. Camp Ketchame was – maybe still is – about five miles west of Saginaw, and I remember hoping that they weren't planning to set up anywhere near the kids' camp."

Matt nodded, tight faced. "Thanks. Thank you both. There is no statute of limitations on murder, so Edwards isn't going to get away with that one, if I can help it. More evidence would be helpful. I'll be getting in touch with the Michigan authorities asking for their assistance."

Matt looked at them with a wry grin. "Patty always says I have a tendency to put the cart before the horse. I assumed you'd both be willing to testify. Are you?"

Katrina took her time, coolly picking up her handbag and rising from her chair. Straight-faced, she said, "Presumption can be dangerous, Detective Brophy." She couldn't sustain the attitude. She giggled. "Of course we will. Or at least I will. I shouldn't try to speak for Polly Ann."

Polly Ann shook her head. "Kat, you're bad. Of course I'll testify. After what that bastard has put us through, I want to see him hung out to dry."

"May I take you ladies out for lunch?" Matt asked.

"I'm meeting Chad at the Sidetrack," Katrina said, "but I'm sure he'd enjoy hearing about what we've been up to this morning."

"Do I correctly assume that he knows everything that's been going on since September?"

Polly Ann nodded. "Ever since Kat told me that she'd sent him to case Turner's house, we've kept him up to date on everything. He and Kat spend so much time together, it would have been impossible to keep secrets from him."

Chad stood in the café doorway, waiting for them. Matt shook the young man's hand – the one that wasn't on Katrina's shoulder. "It doesn't take a trained observer like me to see that you two are more than casual acquaintances. How come your friends haven't twigged?"

Kat laughed and removed Chad's hand from her shoulder. "Our real friends have known since last year that Chad and I are steadies. Other people can think what they please. We plan to announce our engagement to our folks at Easter. We're careful in public, although most people are so involved in their own affairs they don't notice what going on in other peoples' lives.

"Having most of those on campus 'know' I'm lesbian is useful: lesbians don't have straight boyfriends, just friends who are boys. That's what people assume when they see Chad and me together. Despite the assumption that all members of LBGT groups are 'other,' many are as heterosexual as Chad and I. I was elected president simply because I'm good at organization and I care deeply about prejudice."

A dimpled blond coed carrying a tray of water and beer stopped at their booth and deposited the beverages on the table. "Hi, Kat. Hi, Chad. Hello, Dr. Passareli and Chief Brophy. Have you had time to decide on the menu?"

Polly Ann opted for the BLT salad with blue cheese and a double order of breadsticks. Matt chose a Reuben sandwich. "Kat, Chad, the usual for you?"

"Yes, thanks Becky." At Matt's raised eyebrow, Kat explained. "French Dip with extra meat. We don't get a lot of really good beef at the dorm."

While they waited for the food, Matt picked up the conversation from where it had left off. "Kat, did either Regent Edwards or Regent Turner suspect that you weren't gay?"

Kat shook her head and Polly Ann laughed hard enough to choke before she said, "No. I think Turner and then Edwards were buzzing around her out of curiosity about lesbians. And maybe they were hoping to discover something salacious about my love life. Of which I have none."

Becky brought their food, two plates balanced on each arm. Chad teased her. "Becky, you've been here long enough to start balancing the basket of breadsticks and bowl of beef juice along with everything else."

She teased right back. "Are you offering to sit there while I practice? Have you already forgotten getting Julie's salad dumped all over your head and shoulders the week I started?" She set down the food. "Enjoy your meal. I'll check back with you later."

They ate in companionable silence. Leaning back, Matt said, "That was wonderful. I'm feeling almost human again."

The conversation moved away from the previous topic to the chances for the university hockey team getting to the playoffs. Becky returned with two bills. "I trust that this was the guys' day to treat?"

"It always is when I come here," Chad grumbled.

"Oh, let me get this," Matt said. "I owe all of you for helping me solve this case. If you can apprehend my fugitive, I'll treat you all to dinner at the Country Club."

Chad didn't argue. "Chief Brophy, you should know by now that whenever one of our elders offers to pay for a meal, we accept."

Katrina checked her watch. "I don't know about you, Detective Brophy, but the three of us have 15 minutes to get back to campus. Thanks for everything."

STRIKE VOTE

59

Monday, February 4

After a rare free weekend – no robberies, no accidents, no kidnappings, not even a lost child or dog – Matt spent Monday reading through the blackmail files Hunter Edwards had taken from Stanley Turner's house. His mood grew darker the more he read.

Turner's entry about Frederick Ferrett noted that Freddie's grandfather's surname was Ferrenzetti, leading him to the unsubstantiated conclusion that Freddie was an illegal alien. The additional note in Edwards' handwriting was another imaginative leap: "Maybe FF's lover is the illegal?"

Wills Gladwin's page referenced William Brasseth, so Matt looked in the file labelled Regents for the data on the bank president, seeking a connection between the two men. A Ridge University Foundation check for $50,050 paper-clipped to brief penciled notes answered that question. The check was made out to Brasseth personally and signed by Wills Gladwin. "Fraud!" was Turner's assumption and Edwards agreed: "Nothing like a long-forgotten useless check to hang someone out to dry. I can use this to twist a couple arms."

Matt could think of a few innocent explanations for the money, but he would have another chat with Gladwin and Brasseth. He strolled into the outer office for a coffee refill and asked Alice to set up an appointment.

He returned to his desk and pulled out the next folder. "Jorge Martin. Hmm. What might he have done to attract attention? Maybe Turner saw him with Glynda."

Matt pulled out Regent Gianetta's file. Turner's note asked, "Planned Parenthood Clinic in Denver? Pregnant? If so, by whom? Scheduling an abortion?" Matt was disgusted but not surprised at Turner's prurient descriptions of her body and what he'd like to do with it. For once, he agreed with Edward's comment on that observation: "What a pig!"

Edwards had been somewhat more imaginative, less nasty. "Maybe secretly married and trying to get pregnant?"

Matt turned back to the notes on Jorge Martin. Turner found him to be too clean, suspected he was gay. Edwards planned to break into Martin's apartment and discover if he lived alone – or even lived there at all. Matt began to laugh. "Oh, boy! You two were so close!"

He rubbed his eyes and decided that he needed a break. "Alice, would you call Jorge Martin and see if he's free for lunch? Tell him I'm buying, and I'll meet him at the Black Steer."

Matt got there first; Martin arrived a few minutes later. "Hi, Chief, what can I do for you?"

"You've already done it – provided me with the first laugh I've had today. Let's order first, so I can tell you about it without being interrupted."

As soon as their waiter brought their steaks, fries, salads, and water, Matt took a long drink, and said, "You do know that Regent Edwards was the man who sent the threatening notes to your search committee?"

"Yeah. When we got your notice to be on the lookout, Adam told me a couple details. I'm eager to hear the rest of the story."

"Well, here's where a nasty story has a humorous bit. Turner was the original blackmailer; Edwards swiped his files and continued what Turner had started. On at least one occasion, Turner apparently followed your wife into Denver and saw her entering the Planned Parenthood Clinic. His assumption was that she was scheduling an abortion.

"Edwards' imagination took him further. He was pursuing the thought that she might be pregnant, might even be secretly married and was trying to get pregnant. He did wonder if you were gay and possibly used your apartment only for an accommodation address, but," Matt had to stop to wipe his eyes, "he never put you and Regent Giannetta together."

Matt stopped laughing and finished his water. "If you two ever wondered if your secret was safe, there's your answer."

By now, Martin was also laughing. "Matt, I owe you. You've made my day."

Back at his office, Matt glared at the two remaining files, Polly Ann's and the one with notes about the other regents.

Polly Ann's was fat enough to need heavy duty rubber bands to hold it together. Newspaper clippings made up most of the bulk. Either Turner or Edwards – maybe both – had filed them in chronological order.

The earliest ones dealt with the death of Clarence Hunter. Turner had given the testimony that led to a coroner's verdict of "accidental death." A fading penciled entry – or maybe partially erased? – at the top of the Ann Arbor News clipping read "He knows I saw him, and he'd better hope that kid is in the wind." Edwards had added, "I'm not so sure. I think she's right here in town and Dr. P. knows who she is."

Matt made a note to himself to ask Polly Ann and Kat if and when Kat's name change became official. Evidently neither Turner nor Edwards had twigged to the linguistic similarity between Tolliver and Tallfeather.

The rest of the clippings featured Polly Ann: a list of Ph.D. recipients from the University of Michigan with her name highlighted; a notice of her hiring by Ridge University and her successive promotions from assistant to full professor; her election to head the campus AAUP; her role on the collective bargaining committee that led to the first faculty union contract.

Each of the more recent ones detailed her numerous publications and service to university and community. None of them contained any personal information.

"Nothing in here tells me why Edwards might want to harm her," Matt said to himself, "only that he suspects she knows about the murder in Michigan and that he believes the witness is here in Ridgeview. But he's apparently unaware that Katrina Tallfeather is the witness."

Matt put away Polly Ann's file and opened the one for the remaining regents.

The folder with Edwards' name on it was empty. Matt figured that either Turner had found his colleague so uninteresting that there was nothing to say or, more likely, Edwards had removed incriminating evidence.

No one, including Turner and Edwards, ever had anything negative to say about Rick Gregory. Turner's notes in Gregory's file brought a smile to Matt's lips. "Other women? No. He hardly even looks at them. If either of my wives had looked like Rick's wife, I'd still be married. Alcoholic? No. Probably pours his champagne at weddings into the potted plants. Cooks the books at work? Why bother? It's his practice and the best CPA in town does his taxes."

Matt wandered into the break room. "Chief," Alice called out, "if you have any more coffee today, you'll start twitching."

He picked up a bottle of water and returned to his desk. He leaned back and closed his eyes. He nodded off, but was too uncomfortable to sleep. And there was still work to finish.

He stood up, stretched, and walked to the window and back before sitting down to drink half the water and read the next file. He'd spent so much time sitting that he could feel his center of gravity shifting downward. He knew a few police chiefs whose nickname behind their backs was "lard ass," and he prided himself on keeping as physically fit as his officers.

As he read through the notes in Joanie Jameson's file, Matt swore aloud. "Those bastards!"

"Something wrong, Chief?"

"Huh? Oh, no. Thanks, Alice. I'm just expressing disgust at the inhumanity of some so-called humans." Turner's notes detailed Mrs. Jameson's collapse when he told her that the medical examiner who performed her husband's autopsy reported excessive alcohol in his system. Edwards' note was, if anything, even nastier: "I'll bet I could have her if I swore to keep her secret."

A copy of the ME's report was attached. No trace of alcohol or drugs. Matt slammed the file shut and threw it onto the pile. It slid off, scattering its contents onto the floor. Matt left it there. He picked up the half empty water bottle and attempted to step around the scattered papers as if the filth might adhere to his shoes.

He slipped, dropping the water bottle, which emptied its contents all over the papers. "Oh, shit! If Alice sees this, she'll have my scalp. Maybe I can ask Freddie to send dry copies. Meanwhile, I'd better clean up my mess." He snatched up the now empty bottle, hurried into the break room, and picked up a sponge. He made sure Alice wasn't

STRIKE VOTE

looking, and mopped up. He spread the damp pages on the floor near the heat register to dry, after rescuing the one page and its attached clipping that he'd yet to review. One corner was soaked, but most of the information had somehow avoided the spill. He set napkins on his desk, three under the wet spots, two on top and gently patted.

Matt had known Burt Lincoln for over a decade – head of a tough trucking union, once accused of embezzling pension funds. Turner's file had the first newspaper article with the accusation, and his notes expressed his glee and having some dirt on the man. Edwards' addition asked only, "So why isn't he in prison?"

Matt knew the rest of the story. Burt had, indeed, used $5,000 of the union's money, but it was to buy meals for those on the picket lines. And he paid it back out of his own pocket. Burt didn't want the full story getting out and embarrassing his workers.

Matt added the note and the clipping to the array on the floor and decided to leave everything to dry overnight. In the morning, he would put the files back in their box, and lock them in the office safe. He stood looking out the office window for a minute.

Alice called out, "Boss, you've been talking to yourself and it's nearly 5:00. Mr. Brasseth and Dr. Gladwin are coming in tomorrow at 10.:30. Why don't you go home and get some rest? Patty called a while ago: she wants you to pick up broccoli and tomatoes on your way home."

"I'll be right behind you, Alice. And I'll lock up."

60

Tuesday, February 5

Alice showed Dr. Gladwin and Mr. Brasseth into Matt's office. "Thank you both for coming," Matt said. "Do sit down. There's coffee, if you wish. I asked you here in the hope that you can help me clear up a mystery."

The two men seated themselves and sat up straight, looking attentive and curious.

"You've no doubt heard or read that Huntington Edwards is a person of interest in our investigation of several local crimes. What you may or may not know is that Edwards took certain files from Stanley Turner's home hours after Turner was murdered. Turner used those files for blackmail. We suspect that Edwards decided to continue that."

Both men appeared puzzled. Finally, Brasseth asked, "What does that have to do with us?"

"Your unsuspecting involvement in all this started with that lost bank deposit envelope."

"I don't understand."

Matt pulled several photographs from a folder and pushed them across the desk. "Our conclusions are tentative, but judging by the photos, what we think happened is this: Turner was at the scene, Mr. Brasseth, when your bank manager was killed in that traffic accident. The passenger door of her car flew open and the envelope fell out. In the ensuing chaos, Turner picked it up. He thought no one saw him. The young man who did – the one on a bicycle in this picture – didn't think anything about it. To his credit, he tried to help the victim.

"You'll recall, Mr. Brasseth, that in the deposit envelope was a check from the Ridge University Foundation for $50,050. Can either of you tell me what that was all about?"

Brasseth shook his head and smiled. "Wills, you tell him."

Gladwin threw up his hands. "Oh, for God's sake! This will take a few minutes. I'll take that coffee now. Bill, you want some? Matt?" His hands were steady as he poured three cups of coffee and passed the cream and sugar to Brasseth.

"You know we're going to start breaking ground for the Ridge U golf course this spring?" He glanced at Matt for assent. "It's been a very long time coming. We hired the best people we could find to design the facility.

"We had a capital campaign going and were getting close to the money we needed, but we were $50,000 short and in danger of losing the architects. I approached Bill and requested a short term loan until we could raise the rest of the funds. He gave me a check from his personal account. A month later, I wrote the check to repay the loan, with interest. I intended to mail it, but Mrs. Wozniak happened to be at the Foundation that day. She came to pick up one of my secretaries for lunch and offered to save me a stamp."

Brasseth nodded and rolled his eyes. "And she was on her way back to work when the accident happened. The check was never found. Wills had it cancelled immediately, of course. As far as we know, there was never an attempt to cash it."

Matt said, "What's that saying, 'A good deed is never left unpunished'? A sad accident with such complicated results."

Matt took the now empty coffeepot to the staff lounge and refilled it. He stopped at Alice's desk to thank her for making a fresh pot and to ask her to make lunch reservations for three at the Country Club.

When they were all reseated, he invited the other two to join him for lunch when they were finished here. Both accepted. "Sounds better than the brown bag lunch in my office," Gladwin said.

"So let's tie this up," Matt said. "Turner obviously never tried to find out the why of that check. He liked intrigue and dirty dealing. We found the check in Edward's files, with a note in Turner's handwriting suggesting a different scenario. You're gonna love this.

"Dr. Gladwin, he imagined that you might have embezzled the money from the Foundation for your own pursuits, that a sudden threat of an audit would expose your crime, and that you pleaded with your good friend the bank president for a temporary loan. When he agreed, he became a co-conspirator."

Brasseth stood up, walked to the door, and turned around. "Well, I'll be gob smacked. So that's where the fraud rumor started. I need another cup of coffee. Actually, I could use a drink."

Gladwin got up to fill their cups and stood waving his in the air before he realized the coffee was spilling onto Matt's carpet. "So he wanted me to become the next president, thinking he could blackmail me into doing anything he asked. That's insane. Well, maybe he is."

Matt nodded his agreement. "Now, as Bill suggested, you both could probably use a drink. How about I drive?"

Over lunch, conversation turned to the so far unsuccessful search for Hunter Edwards. "That reminds me, Matt," Bill said. "I was looking over the list of safety deposit renewal notices. There's one that Stan Turner was renting."

"I'll get a warrant. There may be something in there that would shed a bit more light on this whole mess."

They didn't linger over coffee. Matt phoned Judge Forbisher and they picked up the necessary warrant before going to the bank. Brasseth signed the paperwork releasing the contents of the safety deposit box to the Ridgeview Police Department and put them in a box provided by one of the tellers.

Gladwin's car was still parked at the precinct, so Matt didn't have to detour to campus to drop him off before taking the box of Turner's belongings to his office. "Alice, postpone anything on the calendar for this afternoon, please."

"Actually, you're free all afternoon. To catch up on paperwork, you said."

"It'll keep. I have a more urgent task."

The box was half full. There were a few documents – birth certificate, two marriage licenses, two sets of divorce papers, and a jumble of photographs, mostly innocuous. Matt sorted them as best he could by approximate time frame: Turner's childhood with parents; college parties with friends, none of whom he recognized; the front of Turner's Tours office building; a stack of photos of groups of men in hunting gear, some with dead deer surrounded by grinning human faces; and a small set showing men with fishing rods.

Matt looked more closely at those. Five Polaroid photographs, somewhat faded, but the facial features were recognizable: Turner and a man Matt didn't know in two of them and three with the same person and another man who could have posed for the wanted poster of Hunter Edwards. "Gotcha!" Matt shouted. Alice came running. "Are you okay?"

"More than okay. I've got a critical piece of evidence that will lock Hunter Edwards up for the rest of his life. If we can ever find him."

61
February 4-18

As if in apology for the four day blizzard, Mother Nature produced a spring thaw. Crocuses popped up in sun-kissed lawns. A few shrinking remnants of snowmen lingered in shady areas.

Chairman Brasseth called the February 7th regents' meeting to order. "Today's agenda is short, but important. We have the input from all the groups that interviewed the candidates, including the recommendation of the search committee. We're all here, except, of course, the one member sought all over the country by various law enforcement agencies. By the way, does anyone now doubt that our missing person was the source of the notes telling us to support his preferred candidate?"

Rick Gregory shook his head. Burt Lincoln said, "We should've denied him membership in the first place."

Joanie Jameson looked at the floor. "He always made me feel like a stupid child. I'm not stupid, and I'm not a child." She promptly burst into tears. No one was misguided enough to pat her on the head and say, "There, there." Rick handed her a handkerchief.

Brasseth ignored her. "Are we ready to vote? Every recommendation we received was unanimously in favor of Dr. Angelocci. Do I hear a motion to accept the recommendations?"

Joanie mopped her face and for the first time since joining the board, did not wait for someone else to speak. "I so move."

"Is there a second?"

Burt smiled at Joanie and the others. "I second the motion."

"All in favor say 'Aye.'"

Brasseth pounded the gavel and said, "The Ridge University Board of Regents does hereby declare Anthony Angelocci to be the next president, pending his acceptance of the offer. Meeting adjourned."

STRIKE VOTE

Polly Ann picked up her newspaper from the driveway, saw the headline on the front page, and ran over to the Brophy's house. "Patty, lookee here! They've done it! The Ridge University Board of Regents has unanimously voted to have Tony Angelocci as the next president! We won!"

The news was in every paper and on every TV channel and radio station from Cheyenne, Wyoming to Pueblo, Colorado, all across the state. Hunter Edwards didn't hear for five days, since two of the vehicles he stole had no radios and the flea bag he stayed in had no TV. He finally got the news from a days' old newspaper left in a diner. He threw his cup of coffee at the waitress, who ducked in time and promptly called the police. He ran.

The trail of stolen cars and switched license plates led Colorado law enforcement officers all over Denver and its suburbs. More than one patrol cop made the observation, "That fucking man watches too much TV."

Edwards stole several cars and minivans from suburban driveways and shopping centers when overly trusting residents left them running while they ran inside, "Only for a minute." Some residents were fortunate to find their vehicles intact in impound lots. Those same lots reported numerous missing license plates.

Less fortunate owners received phone calls from local police departments informing them that their precious rides had been found in insalubrious areas, stripped and in some cases, torched.

A fellow police chief from one suburb phoned Matt. "Your fugitive is always minutes or – usually – hours ahead of us. We get the call from an unhappy victim; we charge to the scene; by the time we find his or her vehicle, your guy is driving another one to a motel across town and hiding out for a day or two. Then he ditches that hot car and probably takes a bus to a new neighborhood for his next set of wheels."

Minutes after Matt received that call, Polly Ann was on the phone, anxious to know where Edwards was and what he was up to. "If you and Patty have time for a drink when you get off work, come over. I have questions."

Patty waited on their front walkway as Matt drove up. They walked over to Polly Ann's house, knocked on her front door and walked in a few minutes later, stopping inside the door to return Simba's enthusiastic greeting – weaving around their ankles and purring. He led them to the kitchen where Polly Ann handed them hot rum toddies.

"This is a real treat," Patty said. "Just the thing on a nippy day. Cheers! Can we sit in here? I love the view out your kitchen windows."

Polly Ann let them savor their drinks for a few minutes before asking, "Matt, what's new?"

He grinned. "Well, we've had one missing child who turned up in a neighbor's kitchen sipping cocoa, and . . ."

"Not in Ridgeview, idiot. I want to know what's going on in Denver with what's-his-face."

"We're getting daily reports from Denver and its suburbs about stolen vehicles that follow a unique pattern."

Polly Ann frowned, looking doubtful. "How do they know it's Edwards? He eluded your people and drove away in your patrol car, which he swapped for a car he stole in Longmont. Is that his pattern?"

Matt finished his toddy, took the mug to the sink and rinsed it before returning to his bar stool. "It is and it isn't. He swaps one stolen vehicle for another, but no one has seen him do it. His usual ploy is to stroll through a neighborhood or shopping mall waiting for someone to leave a vehicle unlocked. Some victims were careless enough to leave the keys in the ignition. Not sure it would matter. I'd bet Edwards knows all about hot wiring anything on wheels."

Polly Ann picked up her mug and Patty's to rinse them and put all three in the dishwasher. "Does he leave the most recent theft behind? If not, how does he get around the city?"

"We think he takes city buses. Those drivers deal with so many people every day that they don't notice ordinary looking folks. And Edwards would be careful to look very ordinary."

Polly Ann realized that her next question sounded whiney, but she was frustrated. "Why can't they catch him? It can't be that hard to locate a car that's been gone only a few minutes."

Matt sighed. "It takes even really good cops several hours to interview an owner, fill out the paperwork, and get the word out. That gives

Edwards time to drive to his current hidey hole, set up his clients, do his deals, pick up food, ditch the stolen vehicle and burrow in for a night or two. Do you have any idea how many seedy motels there are in the Denver area? Places that don't ask for identification or license plate numbers?"

Polly Ann loved her car, a now vintage yellow Dodge Dart with over 100,000 miles and only one dent. If it got lost some day, she'd be frantic. "Matt, do the owners of the stolen cars get them back?"

"If they're lucky. I suppose it depends on how much time Edwards has. Mostly, he leaves them in parking lots or structures. A couple were located at the Denver airport in long term parking."

"And if they're not lucky?"

"Bad neighborhoods, vacant lots. With missing tires, radios, tape decks, anything that can be easily removed. Sometimes torched. I doubt Edwards is responsible for that sort of thing. He leaves it up to area vandals."

Polly Ann said peevishly, "I don't understand why he keeps running around Denver. Why doesn't he simply leave Colorado?"

Matt said, "I think he's motivated by revenge. He hasn't given up on trying to silence you. Then he can disappear. But to do that, he needs money. He's not moving around Denver arbitrarily; he's contacting his drug suppliers and customers. He'll be back in Ridgeview when he's ready.

Patty eased herself off her stool. "Polly Ann, we need to go. My pot roast should be about done. Can you and Matt resume this conversation another time?"

"Sure. For now, I have only one more question: Is he really planning to kill me?"

Matt gave her a quick hug as he said, "I hope not, but I fear so."

62

Monday, February 18

Matt had a couple ideas for moving the investigation along. "Ahmed. I have a job for you. You've still got Edwards' computer, I believe. I want you to drop whatever you were doing for a few minutes, and look for draft letters and e-mails to these people." He spelled out the regent's names.

Half an hour later, Ahmed got back to him. "Are you psychic, boss?"

"What'd you find?"

"On the 15th of every month starting in October of last year, I found copies of short letters to every regent, except Gregory and Lincoln, that said essentially, 'I'll keep your secret as long as you support Wills Gladwin.' There's also a slew of e-mails to Turner during the summer, ending mid-September. He thought he'd deleted them, but like so many people, he didn't realize that clicking the delete tab doesn't really get rid of them. You want copies?"

"Yeah, please." *Nothing on Lincoln; Edwards must have done more checking than Turner did,* Matt thought to himself. *Speaking of checking, there is something I can do that I don't have to ask Ahmed to do for me.*

He spent an hour on the phone. He asked the postmaster to compile a list of Ridgeview residents who'd put their mail delivery on hold and for how long. "You could e-mail it to me, John, or if that makes you uncomfortable, I'll send someone around to pick it up." John opted for the latter.

Matt's next call was to the editor of the *Ridgeview Reporter*. "Hiram, would you send me a list of your subscribers who've suspended delivery of the paper between the first of the year and now? I need the stop and restart dates, please."

Minutes after he completed that call, the fax machine hummed. Ahmed had sent several pages of what he found on Edwards' computer.

Matt skimmed the e-mails, noting that they were various ways of saying, "Do as you're told and I won't tell." He took his time with the e-mails to Turner from last summer. Several were forwarded copies of earlier pleas: "Why won't you meet me for lunch or at least coffee?" and "I've promised you again and again that I'll stop dealing as soon as this last score pays off. I can't quit this crappy drugstore job until I can afford to retire."

Slightly earlier notes made Matt pay close attention. Edwards seemed much more concerned about Polly Ann than Turner was. The first one, dated May 17, 2013, read, "That professor bitch gave me a funny look yesterday. Can't you lean on her about the kids at the camp and whether she knew the brat who saw me?"

There was a reply from Turner: "I've told you that she might have taken the kid back to town. For a while I thought they'd come to Colorado together, but I have seen no suspicious contact between Dr. P. and any Indian girls in the area. Do you really want to risk stirring up a hornet's nest? If Dr. P. does know you're a murderer, I'd guess she'll keep quiet to protect the girl."

The few e-mails from Edwards during the summer contained no new information. The final one, sent September 14, 2013, two weeks before Turner's death, read, "I think your pet prof is just biding her time. I'll get her alone where she can't call for help and make her identify the girl. Then they'll both disappear."

Turner's reply may have signed his death warrant: "I've kept quiet about your uncle's death. Leave this alone, or you'll live to regret it. Don't forget that I have a file on you as well as several other people."

Matt carefully re-stacked the evidence, put it in an envelope, and locked it in his office safe. "I wonder how much longer people will continue to believe that deleting an e-mail gets rid of it permanently."

Alice poked her head in the door. "You talking to yourself again, chief?"

"Yeah, I was. Alice, I know we archive important e-mails. How do you make sure the others disappear?"

"I start by emptying the recycle bin. As computers get more sophisticated, it may get harder."

"You'll figure out something, Alice. When George gets back from the post office, he'll be bringing a list of residents who are away for the rest of the month. And the newspaper will be e-mailing a tally of those who've suspended delivery for a few weeks. When you have that information, would you compare the two, and make me a list that includes them all, omitting the duplicates?"

STRIKE VOTE

63

Tuesday, February 19

Matt looked through the list of snowbirds – Ridgeview residents known to be out of town until at least early March. He highlighted half a dozen addresses within a mile radius of Edwards' home.

Charlie, George, and Dana were in the squad room filling out reports and waiting for the next distress call. Matt interrupted them. He handed each of them a list of names and addresses. "I need one of you to check with DMV and find out what vehicles are registered to these addresses. As soon as Edwards approaches Ridgeview, we need to stake out these homes."

Charlie spoke up." You think Edwards might 'borrow' wheels from one of his neighbors?"

"I hope so. I'm betting he's coming back to town, determined to finish what he started with Dr. Passarelli."

Alice poked her head around the door. "You're popular this morning, Chief. Phone call on line 1 from Denver."

"This is Brophy."

"Hi. This is Officer Truscott. I'm working undercover for the Denver PD. I've been on a stakeout watching a drug deal go down. An hour ago I saw a man matching your fugitive's picture driving away from a rent-by-the-hour motel in an old blue VW bug. I followed him as best I could, but you know Denver traffic. It was too risky to get close. That motherfucker is fast! He was in and out of a MacDonald's parking lot in a forest green Cadillac as I turned in.

"The owner was jumping up and down in a tantrum. Turns out he was more upset about losing the brand new parka in the back seat than he was about having his car stolen. Insurance, I would guess.

"One of our people spotted the car speeding toward the I 25 on ramp, but couldn't pursue, again because the traffic was too congested."

"Thanks, Truscott. I think I know where he's headed."

Less than two hours later, the officer phoned. "Chief, a dark blue Dodge Caravan was stolen from the parking lot of the First National Bank in Longmont about an hour ago."

"Was a forest green Caddy left in its place?"

"Yeah. How'd you know?"

"Fortunately, we seem to have friends all over the place."

Then their luck ran out. City cops and highway patrol personnel between Longmont and Ridgeview were on the lookout, but there was no sign of that minivan.

It took a night watchman in the guard house of an impound lot outside Berthoud to fill in the missing hours. He'd seen one of the junkers in the lot inch its way to the nearby road and trundle off northward.

He rousted a pair of homeless men from their improvised camp close to the lot. They admitted to letting another bum join them for stew and a sleeping spot, saying that he'd rolled himself up in a really snazzy looking parka. "We considered relieving him of it until the sonofabitch pulled a gun."

Further conversation revealed that, some hours later, the man had made enough racket to wake them up when he climbed over the fence into the impound lot.

The junker turned up in the early morning hours on the edge of a smoking pit in the Larimer County Landfill. A Ridgeview resident who was dropping recyclables in a bin saw something strange and phoned the precinct. "I don't know if this is anything, but I just saw a guy jump into the back of a lady's pickup. She's driving south toward Ridgeview."

Matt thanked the caller profusely before alerting his officers that Edwards was coming. "Get in position at those snowbirds' homes. I think he's planning to borrow another vehicle."

Then he phoned Polly Ann. "Edwards is moving toward Ridgeview, and I'm still pretty sure his primary target is you. Are you planning to meet Miss Tallfeather someplace for lunch?"

"Yes and no. She's here. We decided not to go out for lunch."

Matt swore. "For pity's sake, Polly Ann, have some sense! Get out of there. Take Simba with you. The first place he'll head for is your house, and I can't guarantee that we can move fast enough to get to him before he gets to you. I won't have you staked out like a sacrificial lamb."

Polly Ann hung up the phone, her eyes almost shooting sparks, her fists clenched. "Men can be so superciliously bossy!"

The phone rang again. Kat raised an eyebrow. "Aren't you going to answer that?"

Polly Ann stalked down the hall, talking over her shoulder. "No, I am not. Call me a sacrificial lamb, will he? We'll see about that."

Kat followed her. "Let me guess. Edwards is either already here in town or he's on his way. Chief Brophy thinks, quite reasonably I believe, that he'll come here, probably to kill you. So he's suggesting you make yourself scarce. What's wrong with that?"

Polly Ann turned around so fast she nearly bumped into Kat, jabbing her in the chest with her finger. "I'll tell you what's wrong with that. Edwards is going to burst in here, discover I'm not here, and go into hiding – again. He'll wait as long as it takes for me to come back here and get complacent. Then he'll strike. And no one – Matt, the whole Ridgeview PD, you, and the entire English department – will be able to stop him."

Kat backed away and glared. "Put your finger down. I hear you. I wish I didn't agree with you, but I do. So we're just supposed to sit here and wait for that yahoo, that scumbag, that . . . that murderer?"

Polly Ann didn't move. This was not the time for a motherly, "There, there, dear, it'll be okay." She settled for saying, "You need to calm down."

"I will when you do."

A plan was forming in Polly Ann's brain that she thought might work. "Nope, Kat, we're not going to just sit here. When he does come, we'll be ready. We should have a few minutes to put on our war paint."

"What are you talking about? Mascara, eye shadow, and lipstick aren't going to stop him from killing us before the cavalry arrives."

"Kat, stop talking and come with me. Trust me, when he comes, we'll be ready for him."

She led the way to the guest room closet, slid open the door, and opened the old trunk. Kat started to laugh. "Seriously, lady, you've kept all of the Halloween and other costumes we wore?"

"Sure. They're precious. And, at the moment, precisely what we need. Here, pile some of this stuff on the bed. I'll know what I want when I see it."

From a bag full of hair pieces, Polly Ann removed a ratty looking grizzled gray wig and set it aside. "That'll do for me. Your hair's fine, Kat. I just need to find the headdress." She set two folded blankets on the floor before pulling out a long, beaded, deerskin skirt. "Now where's that shawl?"

Kat rolled her eyes. "Polly Ann, that thing's awful. Not even a freezing homeless person would wrap that around their shoulders. Are you sure it isn't a floor-mopping rag?"

"It was perfect at the time and it will do nicely for now." Polly Ann had played the part of an old woman in a community theater play. Her single notable line, repeated at least once in each of the three acts was, "My little boy is all grown up." The tremor in her voice became a habit she could recall at a moment's notice. Genuine fear would enhance the vocal shakiness of her coming performance.

From the bottom of the trunk, Polly Ann gingerly lifted out a set of white leather pants and matching long-sleeved shirt. "Here, these are for you. And here's the final crowning touch!" Kat reverently took the wolfheaddress from her and set it on the bed next to the pants and shirt.

Polly Ann glanced at the clock. "We need to hurry, but there's time for makeup." She lifted a small box from the closet shelf, set it on the dresser, and opened it. Kat remembered it from a costume party a few years earlier. "If you'll do your own war paint, I'll turn myself into an ancient crone."

64

Officer Juanita Ortiz peered through the lace curtains of the house next door to Edwards', and punched a number into her phone. "Hi, Alice, it's Juanita. There's a guy sneaking up the driveway here at the Wilson's house, heading for the garage. I can't see his face – he's wearing a ski mask. But it could be our man."

Within minutes, Matt and a half dozen of his people surrounded the suspect as Matt yelled, "Turn around, hands in the air. And take off that mask."

A young face, eyes like saucers, mouth open stared at them. Matt wasn't the only one who swore. "Who the hell are you? And what are you doing here?"

"I'm Norman. Norman Wilson... My folks live here... They're in Arizona... Dad said I could borrow the car."

Matt briefly explained what was going on and apologized for the confusion. He returned to his squad car, telling the other officers, "Get over to Dr. Passarelli's place and start praying we're not too late. Thank God I left Charlie on lookout from my garage. He can handle things until we get there. Sirens off, people. Bloody woman, why didn't she listen?"

On the other side of town, two blocks from Polly Ann's house, Officer Dana Jonsgaard was bundled up and shoveling snow two doors down from the Rosenberg's house. Doing her best to look like an ordinary homeowner, she watched as a man enveloped in a hooded parka moved carefully up the icy driveway and punched in a code for the garage door opener. Not too surprisingly, it worked; the door screeched and squealed its way up. She muttered, "Will people ever learn to change the code as soon as they sign the purchase papers for their new home?"

The man backed out minutes later in the Rosenberg's silver Taurus. Jonsgaard alerted Matt, who immediately phoned Polly Ann, thankful that this time, she answered. He told her, "He's getting close. Expect him any minute. We'll be there in a jiffy. Nothing bad is going to happen."

Polly Ann's voice was a bit shaky as she declared, "We're ready."

Matt fumbled the phone and had to punch in the numbers twice, but Charlie's voice on the other end reassured him. "I'm here, Chief, and ready to move."

Minutes later, Edwards burst through Polly Ann's front door, holding the gun with both shaky hands. He stared at the apparition in front of him, a stooped crone with straggly, stringy gray hair, dressed in a muumuu of what had to be deerskin. Moccasins covered the feet that shuffled toward him. The gun wobbled. "Who the hell are you?"

Polly Ann raised her rheumy eyes to his face. He wasn't to know what contact lenses and a smear of Vaseline could do. Polly Ann spoke her carefully rehearsed lines. "My granddaughter may be an orphan, but she has family. Star Wolf, come!"

Edwards' eyes darted from the ancient shaman to the enormous warrior in full war paint, cloaked in skins, holding a feathered spear, and crowned with a wolf's head, bared teeth and all. Edwards' voice shook, "Where's Dr. Passarelli?"

The creature's voice demanded, "Drop your weapon and raise your hands." He was given no opportunity to refuse. The spear poked him in the chest. He yelped and dropped the gun. Fortunately, the safety was still on. Behind him, the old crone said, "Get down on the floor and put your hands on your head."

Nervously eyeing the spear still pointed at his midsection, Edwards did as he was told. To ensure that he stayed put, Katrina planted a moccasin covered foot in the middle of his back. Simba, who had wisely stayed out of the way until the threat was contained, paced out of the hallway, glanced at the man on the floor, and reached the front door just as Charlie opened it, gun at the ready.

He looked at the scene in front of him and took a minute before holstering the gun. Polly Ann thought he sounded a bit annoyed. "Here I was all set to rescue you ladies, but I guess you didn't need much help. I could handcuff him for you, if you like."

Charlie snapped the handcuffs onto Edwards' wrist, perhaps a bit tighter than necessary. He pulled the prisoner to his feet and shoved him out onto the icy front porch as a squad car pulled up to the curb. Matt and Adam got out of the vehicle and hurried up to the house. "Adam, you and Charlie can take care of Mr. Edwards. I need to make sure Polly Ann's all right."

The two officers marched Edwards to the waiting police car. Adam opened the back door; Charlie put a gloved hand on the prisoner's head to assist him into the seat. The gesture may have been more push than protection. Adam said, "I wouldn't bother with the seatbelt if I were you, Charlie. He might try to bite you or something, and it's only a few blocks to the station."

"Gotta obey the law, partner. You hold his head while I buckle him in." Charlie wrinkled his nose. "You might want to open a front window, Adam. This guy smells pretty ripe." He turned to Matt, who was standing in the doorway of Polly Ann's house. "You coming with us, chief?"

"You two go ahead and book him. I'll be along in a few minutes. I'll follow you in my wife's car." He turned away and closed the door before going in search of Polly Ann and Kat. Kat had removed the wolf headdress, but otherwise the two women were still the stuff of nightmares.

Matt tried to say something. The tension of the last hour gave way to visible shaking and finally, helpless laughter. Polly Ann tried to appear offended, but couldn't keep it up. She giggled. Kat gave a war whoop that degenerated into howls of laughter, which set Matt and Polly Ann off even harder.

When Matt finally got control of himself enough to scold Polly Ann for being a bloody-minded, stubborn ass who could have gotten herself and Kat killed, he pulled his camera from a pocket. "Katrina, would you put the wolf back on your head, please? Now, both of you, snarl." He clicked the shutter several times before Polly Ann succeeded in squirming out of Kat's hold.

"Would you two stay here until I come back?" Matt asked. "I'll be as quick as I can." Matt hurried to his own home next door and let his wife know that he was borrowing her car. "Patty, we got him. And Polly Ann is fine. I'll tell you the whole story when I get back – probably within an hour."

65

When Matt got to the station, Edwards had already been taken to the conference room, which doubled when necessary as an interrogation room. Charlie said, "We gave him some coffee. You want me to get a mug for you?"

"Thanks, Charlie, I'll get it myself. Is a tape recorder already set up in there?" Charlie nodded and followed Matt into the break room where both men took companionable sips from their mugs before Matt moved toward the room at the back of the building.

Edwards looked as if he'd been on a week long bender: grizzled stubble covered his chin; his clothes looked like they'd been slept in – which they probably had; his normally well-coifed hair resembled a small haystack; and his blood-shot eyes attested to lack of sleep.

Matt sat down and set his coffee on the table before turning on the tape recorder. He started to recite the Miranda warning, waiting expectantly for Edwards to demand a lawyer. Edwards said nothing.

After uttering the final words, ". . . may be held against you in a court of law," Edwards muttered a snarky, "I understand. Just get on with it. I didn't do anything wrong."

"For starters, you are being charged with numerous blackmail attempts. We have sworn testimony from several people and documentary evidence as well – written threats." Matt waited for a response.

Edwards thrust out his chin. "They'll change their stories as soon as they remember that I know all their dirty little secrets. And I know that nothing that comes out of a computer printer can be traced to a specific machine."

Matt asked, "How do you know the notes were computer printed?" While Edwards was still stammering, Matt spoke again. "We've seen all the supposed dirt you and Turner had on people. None of it is backed up by facts. Maybe I'll tell you about it sometime. Apart from attempted blackmail, you're also charged with two counts of kidnapping and numerous auto thefts."

"They never saw me." Edwards' face lost whatever color it had, but he tried to correct his statement. "I mean, no one can prove any of that 'cuz I didn't do it and no one can prove that I did."

Matt made a few notes before he continued. "Some of that will come up at trial, but the actual charge will be first degree murder."

"Of who?"

"That's an odd question to ask, unless you may be guilty of more than one murder. Colorado can't try you for a crime committed in another state – Michigan will have to wait its turn. Before that, you will stand trial for the murder of Stanley Turner." Casually, Matt asked, "Just out of curiosity, why did you kill Turner?"

"I didn't."

"Sure, you did. You swallowed your twitch-alleviating pills, filled a vial with mead, pocketed a syringe, and went off to the reception with murder in mind."

"It wasn't like that. I'd never kill anybody. He was just supposed to get sick enough to get scared. It was an accident."

"You claim you would never kill anyone. Aren't you forgetting your uncle?"

Edwards backed away, muttering, "That was an accident. Stanley testified to that at the inquest.. You can't prove otherwise."

"Oh, we can do that. You and Turner were on the right track. There was and still is a link between Polly Ann Passarelli and the Native American child who witnessed your uncle's murder. Dr. Passarelli rescued that child and they ran, hoping you couldn't follow them. Accidentally, or maybe not, you and Turner did just that. But you weren't able to identify the witness; you needed Dr. Passarelli to do it for you. We've sent the information to the Michigan authorities."

"Passarelli again! I should've taken care of that bitch when I had the chance." Edwards collapsed back onto his seat.

Matt leaned forward. "So, why'd you kill Turner?"

Deflated, Edwards didn't argue. "I told him I'd make sure he got the presidency if he'd just let me make a final score."

"Drugs."

"Yeah. Then I'd stop dealing if he'd continue keeping quiet about my uncle. But he said it was time for him to speak up."

"About your uncle. Whom you shot in the back because he was going to cut you out of his behind-the-counter drug business. Why did Turner lie for you about that?"

"I never did know if he saw what actually happened. I thought he backed me up, not because he cared about the truth, but because he owed Uncle Clarence a lot of money and was happy that now he wouldn't have to repay it. This summer, I realized he thought he had something to hold over my head. I wanted to scare him into keeping his mouth shut."

Matt changed the subject. "I don't get what you thought blackmailing Gladwin would do for you."

"Not just Gladwin – both him and Brasseth! People who will launder money once will do it again, given the right incentive. See, I'm using the pharmacy for hiding a few hundred a month from my other business dealings . . ."

"Peddling drugs."

"Well, yeah. But I needed a way to handle thousands. I had proof that money getting passed between the Ridge University Foundation and the First Ridgeview Bank left no trail. Having Gladwin running the university would give him access to all the budgets. Anonymous donations could be made to the foundation and then get dispersed to impressive sounding charities. Charities that I control. You wouldn't believe the overhead costs of some legitimate outfits."

"Actually, you didn't have proof of anything," Matt said. "The foundation records show the deposit of a $50,000 loan from William Brasseth, a voided check for $50,050 made out to William Brasseth – the one that went missing from the accident scene, and another cleared check to William Brasseth for $50,050, the repayment of the loan he made personally to the foundation. Your blackmail scheme wouldn't have worked. No fraud was committed."

Edwards' response to that news included several words and phrases that Matt had rarely heard in his long career of apprehending crooks.

He turned off the tape recorder, picked up his notes, and left, telling

Adam and Charlie that the prisoner was ready to be escorted to a cell. "Would one of you guys follow me home and bring me back? I have to return Patty's car."

He retrieved his coat from his office, slamming the door on his way out. He put the tape recorder and notes on Alice's desk and said, "Please make a few copies of this. I'll warn you, Edwards' language is enough to make a muleskinner blush."

Charlie said, "Me and Adam can hold the fort and guard the prisoner tonight and one of us will pick you up in the morning."

Matt left his wife's car in the driveway and walked over to Polly Ann's house. She and Katrina had removed their costumes and make-up. Their broad grins were still in place.

"Do join us, Matt. Kat and I waited for you, but it's time to celebrate with a stiff drink. What's your pleasure?"

"Bourbon and branch, please. A light one. I have to be sober enough to tell all this to Patty and the kids and show them the pictures."

"Oh, no, you don't."

"Polly Ann, I can't begin to describe you two to Patty. I need the photographs. I promise I won't show them to anyone who doesn't need to see them."

Kat reached into the cupboards for glasses and bottles. She poured a generous shot of brandy and a shot of white crème de menthe into one glass, two shots of bourbon into another, and popped open a can of beer before adding water and ice cubes to the two glasses.

"What gave you the brilliant idea of slowing Edwards down by disguising yourselves?" Matt asked.

Polly Ann grinned. "Our costumes were awesome, weren't they? I think I told you about killing time in that basement by putting together a reading list for a SF/fantasy lit course. Well, several of Robert Heinlein's novels use aging as a plot device. So I got thinking about a disguise that would confuse him long enough for you and your folks to rescue us.

"When Kat asked how I could turn her into someone else, it dawned on me that Edwards had been looking over his shoulder all these years for the witness to his long ago murder. I hoped a hostile Indian in full battle mode would get his attention. I don't remember when or where I acquired that wolf headdress, but it was the perfect final touch."

The photos got out, of course. Matt showed them first to Patty, who agreed that she would have dropped a gun if she were holding one, and would probably have fainted. The kids, Kate and Dan, were suitably impressed. "That's really Polly Ann? And Katrina? Wow! So, Dad, will we see Chief Star Wolf and whatever Polly Ann is supposed to be at Halloween?"

"You'll have to ask them yourselves."

After two days in the Ridgeview lockup, Edwards was transferred to the county jail. His lawyer's request for bail was denied by Judge Forbisher, who agreed with Margery Chamberlain, the D.A., that the man was a flight risk, a danger to others, and with known ties to drug dealers.

Chamberlain asked Matt for copies of Edwards' confession and his evidence about the death of Clarence Hunter. "I checked with the Michigan authorities," she said. "The case was closed years ago, as you know, after the death was ruled accidental, but they're willing and eager to reopen it with new evidence. Would Miss Tallfeather agree to appear as a witness for them?"

66

February 20-22

Matt spent most of the next few days on the inevitable paperwork. By 4:00 on Friday, his eyes itched. Alice told him to go home. He followed her advice, and the sight of Polly Ann shaking snow off the tree in her front yard cheered him up. "Hey, Polly Ann, come on over and have a drink with Patty and me."

"Thanks, Matt. I'll be over in a minute." Polly Ann hurried into her house to pick up a gift wrapped package before heading next door. "Happy birthday, Patty. Here's a little something I think you'll like."

Polly Ann heard the distinct pop of a champagne cork, followed by Matt's voice from the kitchen. "I'll bring a tray into the living room for the celebration."

Matt raised his glass and smiled at his wife. "Happy birthday, sweetheart." Polly Ann raised her glass for the toast and took a sip.

"This is delightful. It sure beats the stuff Edwards provided for me while I stewed in that basement." She shivered. When would she stop remembering?

Matt said, "I wasn't planning to let that man intrude on our party, but I do have another question, Polly Ann: why did he keep you prisoner and what did he plan to do with you?"

Polly Ann thought for a minute. "You know, I had a lot of time to ask myself that question. He believed I was in touch with the witness to his long-ago murder and desperately wanted the name before the story came out. He may have thought that killing the witness would solve the problem. Anything I had to say would be mere hearsay.

"The only personal thing I can think of goes back two or three years. When I heard via the campus grapevine that a local pharmacist was being considered for the Board, I got on the internet and tried to look up Huntington Edwards III. One site gave the information that showed up in the vita he sent to Human Resources. However, two others had no information prior to his taking a job at a drug store in

Grand Junction about eight years ago. He moved up here three or four years later.

"About then Kat moved into a dorm at UC for her freshman year. Regent Turner, who supported Edwards' bid to be considered for board membership, hadn't shown any particular interest in me, but when Edwards came to town, I was relieved to have Kat miles away. We felt safer spending time together in Boulder than we ever did here. And she was finally able to have an active social life. I got to meet several boyfriends."

Matt leaned forward. "What did you do with the information about Edwards?"

Polly Ann licked her lips. Suddenly her mouth felt very dry. "I spent a day trying to decide if sending a letter to the entire Board was the best approach. I was having coffee in the faculty lounge when I saw Robert Jameson – you remember him? Board chairman at the time? – sitting alone, so I asked if I could join him. He and my older brother were roommates at college years before, and when I came to Colorado, he took me under his wing, treated me like a younger sister. He was great.

"Anyway, I told him what I had learned, and he agreed with me that the Board should investigate further."

"Wasn't Jameson killed in a hit and run accident?"

Polly Ann fished a Kleenex out of her pocket and dabbed her eyes. "Yes. Less than a week after our chat, he was riding his bike near the football stadium and a speeding car hit him."

Polly Ann excused herself to go wash her hands – and the tear streaks on her face. She returned to say, "I suppose the regents meant well when they appointed Joanie to take her husband's place, but it undermined her already fragile self-esteem. Turner and Edwards always treated her like a not very bright child, even in public."

Matt stood up and carried the champagne glasses to the kitchen. He brought back cups of coffee. "Such a sad story. However, that doesn't answer my original question: why does Edwards hate you?"

Polly Ann poured a dollop of cream and a spoonful of sugar into her coffee and stirred. No one commented on the fact that she always took her coffee black. Finally, she replied. "I think Robert told him what I said. Being such a nice guy, he'd have given Edwards the opportunity to explain before informing the other regents.

"If that's what happened, Edwards might have talked Robert out of any suspicions, but assumed I was less apt to accept any story he could come up with. I think he tried to bad mouth me to several administrators and the other regents. Fortunately, the regents have no say about faculty promotions.

"And there you have the whole story. And I have to get home. Kat's coming over."

Matt walked her to the door. When he rejoined Patty, she asked, "Are you thinking what I'm thinking? That Edwards was driving the car that killed Robert Jameson?"

"Jameson's death shortly after Polly Ann told him her suspicions about Edwards is too much of a coincidence. However, unless Edwards admits it, we haven't a hope in hell of proving it after all this time."

67

March to August

Dr. Anthony Angelocci was formally offered the presidency of Ridge University on March 7. He immediately accepted. He and the Board of Regents agreed on an official start date of July 1, the beginning of the new fiscal year.

The posting for the about-to-be-vacant position of Vice President for Academic Affairs appeared in mid-March. Freddie Ferrett chaired the search committee. Six applicants were interviewed; one candidate was unanimously recommended; and the Board accepted the recommendations at their mid-June meeting.

Easter Sunday dawned fair and, considering it was the last day of March, warm. By noon, the temperature was predicted to be in the high sixties. Patty, Katrina, and Polly Ann admired each other's Easter bonnets, flower bedecked and elegant additions to their colorful new outfits. Kat muttered, "If jeans and a clean shirt are acceptable for other Sundays, why do we have to get so gussied up for Easter? I feel like a court jester."

"More like a fashion model," Patty observed. Chad and Matt squirmed a bit in their suits and ties, but Matt answered Kat's question. "All the CEOs come dressed to the nines, and we don't want to look like slobs."

"CEOs?"

"Those who come to church on Christmas and Easter Only."

After the service, Katrina and Chad lingered in the sanctuary, where Chad formally proposed, slid the ring on Kat's finger, and they received the blessing.

They gathered for a celebration at the Moot House. The food was excellent, although no one would later remember what they ate. The wine and conversation flowed freely.

STRIKE VOTE

As they exited the restaurant, a limousine cruised up in front. Charlie was at the wheel. Matt laughed at the reactions of the others. "We've all had enough champagne to qualify us for driving under the influence, so Charlie offered to take us all home so he wouldn't have to arrest anyone."

The spring term ended in early June. Kat received her master's degree. Work on her doctorate would begin in the fall. Polly Ann opted not to teach either of the summer sessions. Instead, she took Kat on a glorious Alaskan cruise for two weeks in July, feeling that a complete getaway from the events of the past year would be good for them both.

Matt felt the same way. He took Patty and the kids to Disneyland for a carefree week. The grownups had at least as much fun as Dan and Kate.

Shortly after they all were home again, Polly Ann called to Matt over the back fence. "Did you have a splendiferous time?"

"We did. How about you?"

"It was fantastic. We'll have to get together soon to share pictures. What was really great was having no TV, newspapers, or e-mail. I didn't even have to try not to think about the trial. Is it scheduled yet?"

"It is. Due to start August 12th. As Katrina probably told you, Edwards' trial in Michigan is scheduled for the week of the 5th. If it takes longer than three or four days, Colorado will reschedule.

"So we can forget about that for at least a little while longer. The week Patty and I and the kids were away, we, too, avoided any home town news. And the guys and gals at the precinct honored my request not to contact me except in dire emergency. The rest of the time, we dealt with the usual vehicle accidents, muggings, holdups, missing children and adults, and two cats stuck in trees. And preparing for the trial."

68
August 12

The courtroom was full, but not overcrowded. Few of the townspeople came. They tut-tutted about the latest scandal at the university, but most of them had better things to do than listen to lawyers.

The remaining five regents, accompanied by the spouses of those who had spouses, were asked to empty handbags and pockets on a table where Officer Thomas Bentley checked for banned items. Joanie Jameson was glad she cleaned out her purse recently, leaving only pristine tissues, a lipstick and comb, her reading glasses in their case, and a favorite fat paperback – Diana Gabaldon's *Outlander*.

The group was ushered to the first row of spectators, behind the half wall that separated them from the prosecution and defense tables. Joanie made sure she was close to the aisle. She told Burt, "I'm so nervous, I may have to get to a rest room in a hurry."

The regents held their heads high to proclaim their lack of support for their disgraced former member. Chairman Brasseth had sent a stiff note to Edwards shortly after his arrest, suggesting that a resignation would be preferable to the messiness that being fired would produce.

Most of the vice presidents found other, more pressing business to attend to. President Anthony Angelocci was in Denver, awaiting the birth of his third grandchild.

Freddie and other witnesses stayed away until told they would be called to the stand the next day. Several hoped they would not be called at all.

Edwards strode into the courtroom, flanked by two armed Ridgeview PD officers, Lt. Devers and Sgt. Johnsgaard. The scruffy, smelly creature that Charlie and Adam had taken into custody months earlier had been transformed into his dapper, former regent self. He wore a charcoal gray suit with a tasteful pinstripe, set off by a lemon yellow tie flecked with navy polka dots.

He barely glanced at his lawyer as his eyes slowly traversed the area. He smiled slightly at the few people who met his gaze. Finally he sat down at the defense table.

In her opening argument, the DA, Margery Chamberlain, carefully outlined the prosecution's case, explaining that the Colorado court was not charging the defendant with a 15-year old murder in Michigan, only as the recent one here at home. She made eye contact with each of the jurors before saying, "I'm sure you've all recently read or heard that Mr. Edwards was found guilty of that murder in a Michigan court last week after a closed case was reopened on the basis of new evidence. Michigan agreed to extradite him to Colorado for this trial." She smiled. "We'll decide later where he should begin to serve time.

"Because there is a link between the two deaths, we will call a witness to the Michigan one. That testimony will provide a motive for the murder of Stanley Turner, which we are here to adjudicate. However, we have no jurisdiction over a prior murder case in a different state."

There was no mention of illegal taps on Frederick Ferrett's telephones. At Matt's request, Chamberlain had casually made inquiries. Evidence indicated that Edwards was technologically inept, ignorant even of how to save messages left on his answering machine.

Throughout much of the trial, Edwards toyed with the polka-dotted tie, loosening and tightening the knot, stroking the fabric. Observers noted that his hands shook constantly.

The prosecution's first witness was the medical examiner, who described how Turner had died. Matt followed him, explaining his officers' discovery at Edwards' home of bottles of mead and syringes. He went on to tell about the discovery of the e-mails between Turner and Edwards, which Chamberlain placed into evidence.

Chamberlain asked, "Did Mr. Edwards confess to the murder of Stanley Turner?"

"Yes, at the precinct shortly after his apprehension."

Judge Forbisher directed the bailiff to have the taped confession played for the benefit of the jury.

In cross examination, the defense attorney, an eminent trial lawyer named Giles Polanski, dropped what he thought was a bombshell, revealing that Edwards suffered from Parkinson's disease and that it was getting more severe, suggesting that a medical condition excused much, if not all, of his behavior.

The DA's next witness was Edwards' personal doctor, who explained that his patient suffered from a thyroid imbalance that, yes, did cause a form of palsy in the hands, but was not serious and was successfully treated with medication. "No, sir, Mr. Edwards does not show symptoms of Parkinson's disease."

Matt's testimony covered the kidnapping of Ivan Ellis, the threat letters to members of the search committee and the Board of Regents, the phone calls to Ferrett and Ellis, and the kidnapping of Dr. Passarelli. The DA presented as evidence excerpts from a journal found at Edwards' home, handwritten notes on clippings in Edwards' file, e-mail messages between Edwards and various recipients, and a copy of one of the threatening notes.

On cross examination, Giles Polanski asked Matt, "Did you find Mr. Ellis, the first kidnap victim?"

"Yes."

"How?"

"We dialed the number of Mr. Ellis' cell phone as we stopped at each of several motels. At our last stop, we heard a ring tone coming from a dumpster at the motel where Mr. Ellis was being held. We then were able to locate and free Mr. Ellis."

"That sounds like something one might see on television."

Matt did not reply.

Polanski continued. "You mentioned threatening notes. These were the notes received by some members of the search committee and two or three regents?"

"Yes. I believe Ms. Chamberlain presented a sample as Exhibit C or D. All members of the committee and the board received the notes and told me about them. A few people destroyed theirs."

"Can you prove they came from my client?"

"Yes. The text was found on the computer in his home."

Polanski argued, "Which does not prove he actually sent them."

Matt glanced at the jury box. No one appeared to be convinced. Polanski moved on to his next questions, trying to downplay the seriousness of Polly Ann's kidnapping.

"Had she been mistreated?"

"I'd call being chloroformed, kidnapped, and locked in a basement for two and a half days mistreatment."

"Had she been injured, deprived of food, water, a bed, a toilet, a source of heat?"

Matt held onto his temper – barely. "You think victims should be beaten up, raped, and left outside?"

Polanski wisely ignored that question and continued his own. "You claim that Mr. Edwards assaulted an officer and left his home. He insists that the incident with the officer was an accident, that he simply left in a hurry because he had an appointment in Denver. Do you dispute that?"

Matt detailed the two abortive attempts to arrest Edwards and referred to the testimony of the many Denver police officers who had followed his trail. He finished with the events leading up to the arrest at Dr. Passarelli's home.

Many of the spectators had seen the pictures of Polly Ann and Katrina in their disguises, and those who knew who they were shared that information with others. A wave of subdued laughter came from the gallery. The judge called for order, but he couldn't stifle a smile.

Polanski declined further cross examination.

69

Then it was Polly Ann's turn. The DA led her through the chronology of events from her rescue of twelve-year-old Katrina to the confrontation at her home leading to the finally successful capture of Hunter Edwards.

After the lunch break, Polanski took over. "Dr. Passarelli, you said that you didn't actually witness the death of Clarence Hunter. Is that correct?"

"Yes."

"But you believed the tale of a panicky, lost, twelve-year-old child?"

"Yes."

"Believed her to the extent that you essentially kidnapped her and eventually brought her to Colorado where, when Mr. Edwards happened to move here as well, years later, you feared for her safety and avoided being seen with her in public?"

"Yes."

"And you are convinced that Mr. Edwards was determined to kill the witness to his supposed murder in Michigan and that you were taken so that he could persuade you to give him the name of that witness?"

"Yes."

"Would you care to elaborate on your responses?" Mr. Polanski sounded annoyed.

"No. I think you have done that admirably."

Polanski gave up. "No more questions." He didn't inquire about Edwards' keeping her prisoner for several days; Matt had already drawn a clear picture for the jury of what those days – and nights - were like. Nor did he ask anything about Edwards' invasion of her home and his subsequent capture. He, too, had seen the pictures of Polly Ann and Kat as well as the TV cameraman's shot of Edwards being led in handcuffs from Polly Ann's home.

The DA suggested that the recent guilty verdict from Michigan precluded the necessity of reviewing the evidence that led to that verdict, but Polanski insisted.

Chamberlain presented the pictures of Edwards as a younger man in hunting camouflage, his official university publicity picture, and the computer regressions of the latter, showing the match with the former. Then she called Katrina to the stand.

Katrina led the jury back to the Michigan woods and put each of them into the mind of a child witnessing a murder. "I wanted to turn my head away to avoid watching a man pee, but before I could, I saw one of his hunting buddies raise his rifle and fire. The man's back looked like he'd been shot by a red paintball, but I knew it wasn't any paintball. I ran."

The expressions on the faces of the jury convinced Polanski that he was not going to shake this witness and that any attempt to argue that her testimony was based on the faulty memories of a lost, confused, panicky twelve-year-old would only damage his client's case further. Edwards had the best lawyer his drug money could buy, but even a great lawyer can only do so much.

Chamberlain summed up the prosecution's case, summarizing Katrina's testimony about the Michigan murder, reminding the jury of the incriminating evidence of the e-mails exchanged between Edwards and Turner, and reviewing Edwards' confession.

70

In his summation, ignoring the evidence of the e-mail from Stanley Turner to Hunter Edwards threatening to reveal the truth, the defense attorney argued that a long-ago death in Michigan had nothing to do with the subsequent violent death of Stanley Turner. "Mr. Edwards' Michigan attorney has appealed the guilty verdict, so my client is for now innocent of that death." Polanski also tried to paint a picture of a young man who'd never intended to hurt anyone led astray by evil companions. One juror rolled his eyes.

Judge Forbisher recessed the court, pending a verdict from the jury. They were ready the next morning.

The judge turned to the jury as he asked, "Have you reached a verdict?"

The jury foreman, Walter Beagen, manager of a local UPS business, nodded and said, "We have, Your Honor. We find the accused, Huntington Edwards III, aka Theodore Hunter, guilty of murder in the first degree."

The courtroom, which had been silent, as if all those present were holding their collective breath, began to buzz. Reporters, seated in the back rows to facilitate quick exits, scurried to the recently opened doors. Other spectators stood around talking or moved up the aisles toward the exits.

In addition to Lt. Devers, standing guard immediately behind Edwards and his defense team, Matt had stationed an officer at each of the exit doors, another at the door leading to the judge's chambers, and fourth behind the jury box where a hallway led to a lounge area and a back exit from the building. A van waited there for the return trip to the state prison.

The defense attorney saw his client begin to move, but he was too late to prevent what happened next. As he said later, "Like greased lightning he was – slouching in his chair one minute and then . . ."

Edwards had taken advantage of the commotion following the verdict to surge to his feet, swivel, grab the gun from Lt. Devers' holster, and fire into the air. That brought back the silence, broken by Edwards ordering, "Everybody stay put. I'm walking out that door. I don't want anyone playing hero. I will shoot to kill next time."

Every eye was on him as his gun hand and his eyes swept the room. He took one step and then another into the aisle. Before he reached the first row of spectators, Joanie Jameson leaned over and moaned.

"Stay where you are, Joanie," Edwards said, not unkindly. "Your tummy upset can wait a minute."

Joanie locked eyes with him as she slowly stood up. Her next move took him – and everyone else – by surprise. She swung her right hand, which firmly clutched the strap of her heavy leather handbag, and caught the left side of his face and neck with the full weight of the bag.

Burt Lincoln, who had surged to his feet as Joanie moved, reached his long arms around her to grab the gun as Edwards went down. He handed it, grip first, to the red-faced police lieutenant.

By the time Edwards was revived, he was handcuffed and in leg irons. The prison guards half walked, half carried him out of the courtroom and into the waiting van.

Chief Brophy shook Lincoln's hand and smiled at Mrs. Jameson. "You two prevented an ugly situation from getting worse. Had you practiced that move?"

Joanie's eyes went blank and her body seemed to wilt. Burt caught her and gently lowered her to the floor. Polly Ann hurried over to help. She rubbed Joanie's hands. Finally, the woman returned the pressure and her eyes fluttered open.

"Is he dead? Did I kill him?"

"No," Polly Ann told her, "but you knocked him out and bloodied his nose."

"Damn! I wanted him dead."

People were still pushing and shoving to get out of the courtroom. Matt stood in the aisle, slowing them down and forcing them to move to the other side, away from the two women.

"Mr. Lincoln, as soon as the traffic clears, would you help Dr. Passarelli take Mrs. Jameson to the judge's chambers? I'll meet you there as soon as I can."

When he was finally able to leave the courtroom, Matt found Polly Ann, Mrs. Jameson, Mr. Lincoln, and Judge Forbisher waiting for him. The judge said, "Welcome to my man cave, Matt. Would you care for coffee?"

"Thanks, sir, but not right now. I have a few questions for Mrs. Jameson."

The lady was looking quite pleased with herself. "Sure, Chief Brophy. What do you want to know?"

"Were you seriously trying to kill Mr. Edwards?" She opened her mouth, but before she could speak, Matt stopped her. "No, don't answer that. Pretend I never asked. Let me start over. Were you annoyed with Mr. Edwards for some reason?"

Joanie looked at him, clear-eyed and resolute. And suddenly sad. "You know that my husband was out riding his bicycle when a speeding car hit him – and kept going. Robert was still alive – barely – when I got to the hospital. He uttered a name: Edwards. I thought he was trying to tell me that our friend Hunter would look after me.

"But reading the papers, hearing the news these past few weeks, and now listening to all these witnesses, I've finally realized how blind I've been. Hunter Edwards is pure evil. With his last breath, my beloved husband was warning me, was giving me the name of his killer."

Polly Ann reached out a hand. Joanie grasped it, as if it was a lifeline. "Polly Ann, when I saw that man marching toward the exit, looking straight at you, waving the gun, I had to stop him. You were a row or two behind me and I feared for your life."

"Bless you, Joanie. This time, he might have succeeded in pulling the trigger."

Matt straightened his shoulders and looked at the judge. "Sir, I don't believe Mrs. Jameson has broken any laws here today."

"Seems to me she prevented a threat from turning really ugly. Mr. Lincoln, you'll see that Mrs. Jameson gets home safely?"

Patty Brophy was waiting outside the judge's chambers, "Is everyone all right, Matt? You've been in there quite a while."

Matt put an arm around his wife's shoulders. "Everything's fine, dear. Let's go home. Polly Ann, you need a ride?"

"No, thanks. Chad and Kat went to get my car."

Matt raised his eyebrows. "You let someone else do the driving?"

Polly Ann smiled. "Yes, Matt. Over the past months, I've begun to realize that I don't have to run the world all by myself. When I am forced to keep my nose out of things, other people manage just fine."

Epilogue

Then it was September and time for the annual reception for new hires and old retirees. Tony Angelocci got a thunderous welcome when he entered the ballroom. The applause for Cecilia Cantrell, was almost as loud. She had applied for Tony's vacated vice presidency as soon as it was posted, and was the unanimous choice of the members of the search committee and the Ridge University Board of Regents.

For Polly Ann, the best part of the annual reception was eavesdropping on conversations as she circulated.

Jim Beagen, taking with a small group of other department heads, was asking, "With four vacancies on the board, who wants the job?"

Marsha Ellsworth, from the math department said, "I heard about several: the director of Mercy Hospital, the manager of that putt-putt golf course, a divorce lawyer, a bankruptcy lawyer, and the owner of that Edgewood Appliance Company. Oh, and a shopping center developer who moved here a few months ago."

Polly Ann and her friends edged a bit closer to the bar, still several yards away, catching a lot of chatter about former regents, including the recent news about Glynda Gianetta and her campus cop husband. "Dija hear? She's expecting."

"I heard it was gonna be twins."

The raspy voice of the football coach joined in. "And don't forget Joanie Jameson. I guess it's Joanie Lincoln now. She's filed a wrongful death suit against Hunter Edwards for the murder of her first husband. And the odds are on her winning."

"Speaking of Edwards, where's he now?"

"I thought everybody knew —he's in that high security prison here in Colorado. Michigan was more than happy to let Colorado impose a life sentence without parole for Turner's death. The guilty verdict on the murder in their state is still on his record, and they reserve the right to sentence him in Michigan at a later date."

STRIKE VOTE

The next group wasn't interested in what might or might not be going on with the regents. Jean Hubbard from the French department asked, "Did you hear that Dr. Passarelli doesn't want to continue as AAUP president? Without a presidential search or a reason to call a faculty strike, it wouldn't be much fun. . . Oh, hi, Polly Ann. Have you decided?"

Polly Ann laughed. "Jean, do you really think that search committees and faculty strikes are fun? No, I haven't decided, but if the regents seriously consider asking that shopping center developer to join them, I will mount a faculty protest. Ridge University is not WalMart."

When Polly Ann reached the bar, she heard guests request beer or mixed drinks, and she watched as the three bartenders shook and stirred and poured under the eagle eye of Hal Bennetolli.

An unfamiliar – probably new – faculty member behind her asked her companion, "Did you see the ambulance parked by the back door. I guess they're prepared in case something happens."

Polly Ann turned to reply to the woman's question. "There's always an ambulance standing by for university events. It's a sensible precaution. They rarely are needed."

Taking their drinks to a quiet table, Polly Ann, Anne McGregor, and Patty Brophy made themselves comfortable. Anne whispered to Polly Ann, "You done good this year, girl. What do you suppose the coming year will bring?"

"Well, my not quite namesake would probably say it's going to be a wonderful year. And for once, you can call me Pollyanna."

Judie Freeland

STRIKE VOTE

Made in the USA
Columbia, SC
27 February 2021